SEDUCING
GOD

Magnum Opus
Publishing

SEDUCING GOD

A Love Story

by

Joy English

ABOUT THE AUTHOR

Joy English was born and raised in Chicago and later attended Florida A&M University's School of Business and Industry.

She currently lives in Ohio with her husband and two Rottweilers.

Seducing God is a work of fiction. Names, characters, places, and incidents are the product of the author's imagination or are used fictitiously. Any resemblance to actual events, locales, or persons, living or dead, is entirely coincidental.

Library of Congress Catalog Card Number: 98-88565

ISBN 0-9668122-0-4

First Edition

For my high school teacher, Ms. Shirley Durr,
who wished me myself

For my grammar school teacher, Ms. Beverly Roberts,
who helped compose my first Haiku:

In gazing skyward
Toward God's deep blue creation
Clouds drift like angels

Acknowledgments

Thank You, God, my Savior and Comforter, for choosing me to write this book. This calling I pursue with great zeal.

To my husband Christopher, the one who carries Christ, through you I've learned the meaning of love.

Endless gratitude to my sister Amber, for her thorough editing, yet most importantly for being my best friend.

Great appreciation to Dee for making it her mission to ensure this book was the best it could be, and Carol for reading with eagle eyes.

For my mother Thelma, there are no words that could ever describe our connection to one another. Thank you for sparking my love of words by reading to me and surrounding me with books. I love you for your intelligence, sense of humor and gracious nature.

To my father Ambrose, thanks for setting the can-do example of a self-starter that taught me I could accomplish anything. I'll always love you.

Great blessings to GrandRuby for always having a newspaper in front of your nose and Daddy Elmer, for your desire to learn and help others.

Thanks to Nickie, Keith, Jennifer, Ron, Julie, Chi-Chi, Kimuel, Christine, and Ed for always inquiring about the book.

To my fellow writers of songs and books, including The Artist, Sting, Erica Jong, Deepak Chopra, Marianne Williamson, Terry McMillan, Sarah Ban Breathnach, John Berendt and others, your words have inspired me as well as millions, serving to strengthen the human connection on a deeper level.

DESTINATIONS

BOOK I

THE ABUSER

Chapter 1

Chicago, Illinois

Her many sins have been forgiven–for she loved much. But he who has been forgiven little loves little.

Luke 7:47

I can see through your bullshit. Can you see through mine? Turning the cubic crystal Delta faucet handle midway between the hot and cold temperatures, I first place my palm under the stream of water and watch the blood bead beneath the surface of my skin. It would be a painful thing to burn my clitoris.

Methodically, I scoot my hips under the powerful flow and slide the travel-sized Pantene shampoo bottle inside of me. My legs extend upward in a convoluted gynecologic pose, the cold tile of the wall sensating parts of my feet and calves. Twisting and pushing the container into my canal in varied directions, my thoughts shift from work to Def Comedy Jam. *Stir it like coffee*, Bernie Mac said, *stir it like motherfucking coffee.*

Finding the best rhythm, I pause intermittently to delay my excitement and press my nipples with my index fingers and thumbs. If only I had three hands. Will this be a let down like the many times I've rushed it in the past?

Sliding back from the flow, I marvel at my breasts, wishing they were as buoyant on land as they appear in the rising water. I resume, shoving my hand under the current for a scoop of water, and splash it onto my face. My face has to be wet; it just doesn't feel right dry. I lick the water from my palm.

As the pleasurable feeling rises within, I ruminate on a button a girl in college wore to class one afternoon. *Happiness is coming*, read the double entendre. Did it mean happiness is forthcoming or happiness is having an orgasm? Was ambiguity the whole point?

The fact that it simultaneously inferred that rapture, like Jesus, one day would return and speak so blatantly about sexual release intrigued me then and now. Knowing her, it was probably the latter explanation. But then again, it all depends on your perspective, doesn't it?

With a few more thrusts I switch to my ION oil-free anti-frizz anhydrous hair glosser bottle, a bit longer and thicker. Using the index and middle finger of my left hand, I spread open my major and minor lips for a more direct contact with my nerve endings. Bearing down, the edge of the cylinder stimulates my G-spot and brings me to the brink of climax. This will be a good one, I predict, allowing the arousal to rise into wracks of gratifying contractions that I desire every person to experience.

Collapsing my face against the plastic tub as the remnants of ecstasy shake my body, I long for my writing to be this true. Yet this feeling surpasses all words, thoughts and explanations. This is real.

There is a noise at the door. The knob is twisting. I jolt from my euphoric state and grab the nearby bottle of bubble bath, squeezing the creamy liquid under the running water. As the white foam gradually forms, I recline onto the cold tub with a Cheshire cat's grin.

"What are you doing in here with the door locked?" AC says as he bursts inside, still clinging to the opened wire hanger used to jimmy the lock.

"Taking a bath," I say sarcastically.

"Yeah, and what else?"

"Nothing."

I swear the man has a sixth sense about anything sexual happening away from his presence, like a bear sniffing out human food from miles away upwind. Extra sensual perception.

"Put that hanger down," I groan. "You look like you're about to perform an illegal abortion."

"Do I need to?" he jokes, his red eyes and freshly shaved bald head adding to his devilish appearance. AC's face is that of a carved African mask, its prominent features defying normality, his broad nose, deep-set eyes and staunchly cut jawline demanding recognition.

"Not in this lifetime," I say, scooping large handfuls of foam and covering my torso.

"I just wanted to know if you wanted to smoke one."

"*Roll it up, my nigga', roll it up,*" I chant, as he stares at me with the same furrowed brows he always uses when I sing any weird songs I'd learned down south.

"Okay, Paris."

"No, you're supposed to say *I'm with it.* Get with the program."

"Whatever. We didn't have that bama shit at U of C."

With that, he leaves and returns promptly to perform the ritual. First, he places a towel under the door and sits on the closed toilet lid with an upside-down shoebox top containing the marijuana, scissors and rolling papers. Sometimes it's an old album cover. Any smooth surface will suffice.

Engaging the same concentration and countenance used when he paints, AC cuts the weed into small pieces and employs a credit card to roll the seeds to one end. Next, he expertly glues two sheets together and sprinkles an even amount of the greenery within the folded bottom, like a chef disbursing the perfect amount of oregano to his simmering sauce.

Finally, after fellating the small white tube with a singular pull from his wide pursed lips, he lights the open end and sucks. Waving the flame until it's reduced to a bright orange glow, AC takes another deep hit then positions himself next to the vent in the ceiling.

"Come up here," he grunts with the cadence of a dying man, trying not to exhale prematurely.

I cluck my tongue against my teeth, annoyed at having to depart the warmth of my bath, but I comply, exiting dripping wet. The burning joint beckons me more than the water compels me to stay. Two quick pulls and it's back to him.

We repeat the rotation until the cigarette is a nub, and I refuse it. No roach burns for these fingers, which will be visible to many as I sign my book. I sink back into the comfort of the liquid as AC pops the lit remnant into his mouth and swallows.

"So, tomorrow's the big day," I hint, succumbing to the calming effect of the drug overtaking my body.

"What?" he asks, stupefied.

"I'm giving my two-week notice."

"Oh yeah...So, you're really gonna do it, huh?"

"Of course I'm doing it. You think I've been bullshitting all this time?"

He looks down and frowns. "Why can't you just take a leave of absence?"

"Because, I told you the only way to get a lump-sum distribution is if I quit. Or if I'm disabled or dead."

"That can be arranged," he grins, his playful sneer revealing crooked, ashen teeth.

"Ha, ha. I just wonder what my boss is gonna say. I can't wait."

AC stands, kicks the fraying blue towel from the door and leaves without a word. I know he's mad, yet I don't follow him or call out. Instead, I recline farther in the tub and close my eyes. He's not going to blow my high or goad me into another fight with him over leaving my job. I'm doing it, and that's that.

Shoot, if he's so concerned about losing my income, he should find a damn job. It's been long enough—two whole years since he graduated from the University of Chicago with a Fine Arts degree, and he still hasn't found employment 'worthy' of him. He got mad when my grandmother asked, "They still hiring at McDonald's, ain't they?"

I've done everything to help, from sneaking to type his résumé at work to actually lugging his paintings to galleries around town. But AC thinks my urgings were for naught and wants to give up and brood because they didn't fall at his feet and make him the next Patrick Nagal. He blames it all on White people, or his mother, for not buying him the right equipment, or his dad, for not sending him to art school when he was young. It's everyone else's fault.

I bought into his griping at first, spending most of my paychecks at Utrecht on Michigan Avenue, buying him supplies I thought would cheer him up and inspire greatness. When this too wasn't enough, I received an epiphany while reading *The Artist's Way* that I might as well stop living vicariously through others and focus on my writing. Obviously, the art thing wasn't going to happen without his own determination firing the cause, and his lethargy hasn't changed in seven years.

I never would have guessed that icy December day we met at the Art Institute, his eyes ablaze studying a sculpture as research for a school assignment, that the fire inside was really fueled by a cocaine buzz. Catching my attention in his quirky torn jeans, a dusty old wool blazer and wild naps of hair, my lanky awkwardness and red nose attracted him. We discussed the panorama of art and life, exploring the downtown streets until by happenstance we arrived under the awning of his Printer's Row loft apartment building.

AC prepared steak smothered in wild mushroom sauce, and as the aroma permeated the open space, I marveled over his paintings mounted on the exposed brick walls. Mainly exotic depictions of nude women, the surrealistic self-portraits were the ones that caught my eye, their dark haunting mood reminiscent of the Mexican artist Frida Kahlo. Instead of giving me pause and insight into a disturbed psyche, the tortured faceless subject intrigued me, and as his living, breathing counterpart handed me lunch on a magenta plastic plate, I fell in love.

After devouring the meal, smoking a joint and fighting the urge to touch, we had raunchy sex on his weight bench, me indulging in the artsy newness of it all. I flew back to the canopied roads and rolling hills of Tallahassee to start the spring semester of my junior year, unable to forget the offbeat stranger I'd left behind.

We kept in contact every subsequent day, proving there was more depth to the coupling than the physical level and created a mounting phone bill that forced me to pick up a weekend job. Any time I could gather enough money, I made the long trip to Chicago to see him, not even telling my parents I was in town, and he would do the same, sometimes driving solo sixteen hours non-stop to visit me.

Waving my hands at my sides in the water, I smirk, treasuring the undeniable connection that has kept us together through five years of marriage and seven years of knowing one another. Yet the idiosyncrasies I once found fascinating now irk me, and he seems to worship my body more than my being. I wonder now if he'd even travel across the street, let alone the country, for me. The seven-year itch has spread to a rash that has festered.

Emerging from the tub, I rub CK One oil down the length of my long body, inspecting my widening hips and broad rounded shoulders in the vast mirror. I still got it. Even though my breasts sag and the fat of my thighs fights to plump over the lean definition of the muscle, the inherent sensuality of the shape that speaks pure eroticism and attracts many remains.

Barely dry from a few swipes of the towel, I think of my books. I have to check them. Drops of moisture cling to the red polyester robe I slide on as I walk to the second bedroom of our River Plaza condo, silently thanking God for blessing me with the space to house them.

The down payment of our place was a gift from AC's mom at his college graduation, so overwhelmed was she that he actually obtained a degree after seven years of being a permanent fixture on the campus. Never mind that I'm the one now stuck with paying the high mortgage, a struggle even with her $1,000 monthly wire to our joint checking account, compensation for both her parental guilt and AC's lack of responsibility. Not to look a gift-horse in the mouth, but I'd rather the funds come from his hard work. He should also pay his own child support to the mother of his son Tyson, instead of AC's mom picking up that bill too.

There they are. My books. I behold their literary glory and stand before the altar of brown boxes of mostly unopened copies, crammed into the painting studio-cum-writing room. I move AC's pigments farther away, for fear they will damage my work, my livelihood. Two thousand self-published copies of my masterpiece, *The Sex Files by Paris Gibbins*, a sexual memoir of sorts, detailing the sordid exploits of my wanton past. After laboring two years to complete the opus, I decided to skip the rejections of a plethora of publishers and got the trade paperback printed myself. I couldn't be more proud.

Gingerly removing a copy from atop the stack, I fondle the black and red cover, fanning the pages but not looking at the blur of words, for fear of catching a typo this late in the game. Oh well, I resign and begin to read my memories, errors can always be corrected on the second print run. Because this book will go back to press again and again–the book tour will ensure that fact.

"How many are you taking with us?" AC's voice booms, abruptly present in the room.

I jump and shut the book. "Damn, are you just gonna keep sneaking up on me all night? You know I'm high."

AC emits an odd giggle. "Sorry."

"I guess as many as we have room for. If I need more, I can have my mother ship 'em to me."

He has stopped listening and a predictable glare overtakes him as he spirits the book away from my grasp. I know what he wants. *I know what boys like, I know what guys want...*

AC never stands this nigh unless for sex. My suspicions are confirmed as he pulls my robe down, making me as aware of my stark nakedness in the brightly-lit room with the shades open as Eve after munching the apple. He makes a small attempt at passion by placing his cracked lips upon my delicate bust. Formalities. For he knows I loathe kissing just as I understand his indifference to head. We cut to the chase.

I try hard to hide the fact that I don't desire him, and not due to prior satiation, but because I haven't wanted AC in a long time. Yet I deny him so many times that he has taken to calling me frigid and that, I abhor. At least the weed will get me through.

AC yanks his T-shirt over his head and his shorts down his hairy legs, exposing a high rounded behind and matching belly that betrays a lack of exercise. His body appears more worn and haggard than its 33 years. Not that my 26-year-old physique is going to put Tyra Banks out of business, but at least I still go to the East Bank Club and use my membership, unlike him.

Forcing my eyes away from the flab, I focus on the scars. Aged mutilations of the flesh which make my heart sink every time I witness them for the little boy who endured the pain. The least I can do is provide some semblance of love to heal the man that now wears them like battle wounds.

However, AC doesn't understand the language of tenderness, he only knows pure, raw, unemotional sex. Physical gratification. Sex for the sake of sex. He leads me to the window and my throat closes. I turn to face the glass as he positions himself behind me, pressing my chest against the chilled pane. A pang of excitement wells within as I tilt my hips upward for him to enter. I am afraid yet thrilled. He begins plodding away as I stare downward at the thousand points of light illuminating the nighttime sky, wondering which is the bulb of a video camera recording the sordid scene. The amazing scenario plays before my mind's eye, a nude copulating couple shattering the high-rise window and plunging to their deaths on a buttress of the Wrigley Building.

I pray for him to come early, but as usual, he is still pumping away after what feels like an hour later, and I can't take the raw friction any more.

"Come on!" I whine, turning around to grimace at him.

"Okay, okay," he moans, willing himself to release.

As soon as he does, I pull myself off of him and return to the bathroom, pushing up the crystal faucet handle for another bath.

📖

I wait outside of 171 N. Clark Street, pondering the slope of the State of Illinois building's circular roof across the street and anxiously looking down the block toward Lake Street for my best friend, the wild-child Dana. She is always late, I think, peering back into the starkly white marble lobby for signs of my boss, until I catch myself. It doesn't matter. He can time me for lunch all he wants now, what's he going to do, fire me?

Soon, Dana's familiar stride comes into view, approaching in a fierce lime-green wool suit with an ankle length slim skirt and a jacket that camouflages her greatest nemesis–a flat ass. An average-looking man turns to admire her perfect size-six frame but she rolls her eyes, dismissing him.

"Hey," I laugh, as we come within earshot. "Do you want to walk?"

"All the way to the Water Tower?" she frowns, twisting her pug nose. "Not with these heels on." She lifts one of her matching shoes in the air, the bumps formed by her toes rising into the pointed tip.

"But it's such a beautiful day."

"Uhn, it might rain," she says, shifting the umbrella from her right hand to smooth down her sleek ebony bob in the wind. Heaven forbid if Dana got her hair wet.

"Okay, let's just go to the Merchandise Mart then. We can eat there and spend more time shopping."

"Cool beans."

We trek down Lake Street to Wacker Drive and turn left, as various brothers turn to admire me and comment on my short Calvin Klein skirt slit up both sides. Striding along the river, I take a deep breath of the gamy current, its dirt green water melting away the last chunks of winter ice.

"So, I gave my notice today," I say, watching for her reaction.

"What did he say?"

"He counteroffered."

"To what?"

"Well, I lied and told him I had a better offer with another company downtown. So he asked me how much they were giving me but I wouldn't tell him."

"Did you take it?"

I tilt my head down to her. "Hell, no."

"Shoot, I would have. You could've got more money and still took some time off."

"It's not worth it. You don't understand. There are much more important things at stake here than money. I'm trying to make this writing thing a career."

Dana huffs. "Yeah, you wish."

I ignore her snide comment and remain unprovoked. Little does she know, it was her declarations that I would never finish the book that spurred me forward.

"I'm serious. They only respect you when you leave. Then they realize you're a human being with value. Besides, what's it going to matter 100 years from now that I was a 401(k) Plan Administrator? It won't. I want to go down in history for something meaningful."

"Like *The Sex Files*?"

"It's a start," I declare. And what have you done? I want to ask, but decide to remain quiet.

I should have just shopped alone today, like I prefer, but I wanted to be nice and invite her along to thank her for agreeing to come with me and AC to the first two cities of the promotional tour. Already, she is beginning to get on my nerves with her disparaging insults, something she has done since the first day I met her our sophomore year of high school.

In fact, I think back, that is exactly how we met that day in art class in the southeast wing of Kenwood Academy. I confronted Dana, a boldly unusual move for me, after someone told me she called me a slut. She lied and denied the whole thing, yet somehow, in a strange fateful way, we became best friends ever since.

"Are you getting your hair done?" Dana asks as we round the corner onto the Wells' Street overpass, walking with trepidation over the center where the bridge opens.

My hand flies instinctively to my short light-brown hair, brushed back tightly into a ponytail holder, as a city bus whizzes by and causes the concrete to bounce beneath our feet.

"I don't know, I want to...it's just...I'm gonna be working out a lot and swimming, and I don't want to get it cut so short that I can't brush it back anymore. I don't want to deal with the maintenance."

"You need to do something, all those people will be seeing you." Dana scrutinizes the back of my wide round head and grimaces.

"Yeah," I say, briefly wondering if it's too late to cancel her plane tickets and hotel reservations.

Dana is right, my hair is a mess, but she doesn't have to be so rude as to point it out. I feel like asking when she'll get her brain done, but figure that comment might send us into another nail-scratching fight like we had in our youth. I had become fed up once with her nagging and attacked her other Achilles' heel–her deeply rich cinnamon brown skin. To me it's gorgeous, radiant and flawless, yet Dana always believed she was too dark and coveted my café au lait complexion as the sole reason for my attractiveness.

With her, outward appearance is the end-all be-all, because it's the only gift she thinks she has to work with. That's why she cringes every time a stunning woman walks in the room. Why do I still hang out with her? Is it loyalty, or the fact that I've isolated my other friends and she's the only one left? Or is it, as I suspect deep down but dare admit, that I long to be close to Eric, her fine-ass boyfriend. Not that I've seen him very often in the two years they've dated, as Dana's crazed jealousy has ensured, but at least through her we still have a connection.

"What?" she interjects, as if to read my carnal thoughts.

"Spring has sprung," I say, lifting my face toward the sky and inhaling the cool spring air.

Roaming clusters of dark gray clouds threaten to overtake the blue sky, but the sun holds steadfast in the background, fighting to warm us. I am that ray of light, breaking through the gloom. The hopefulness of the new season pays homage to my new path in life, and I am recharged.

"Yep, another summer," Dana heaves.

I ascend the few stairs to the shopping mall and pull the door open for her to enter, following right behind into the nearby Limited Express.

"I need to find something to wear to the publication party Friday night, and then just normal casual clothes for the rest of the trip."

"I need a lot of stuff, but I'm broke as a joke," Dana snickers, fondling a red short sleeved shirt folded on the display in the front of the store.

"You and Eric *are* coming, Friday night, right?"

"Yeah, we'll be there, just not until later on. He's taking me out to dinner first."

I pause and stare at her. "You better not fake. This is really important."

"I'll be there!" she smiles.

Inspecting a beige mini-skirt, I try to sound as casual as possible. "So, did you ask him if he wanted to come with us? I can pay for his airfare. The more hands to carry books the better."

Dana immediately shakes her head before I even finish the last sentence. "No, he said doesn't want to go. I asked him, but he said he needs to stay here to watch his car washes, and make sure the guys don't fuck up. He's afraid they might steal from him. Plus, I'll only be gone for a week."

"Oh well," I shrug, hoping I don't look too disappointed.

Dana sounds just like a child making up a story as they go along. I know her too well. Who would turn down a free trip to Boston and Miami for a week? She hadn't even mentioned it to him, knowing good and well she'd never want me that close to her man for a week. Too afraid of tit for tat, literally. It's probably hard enough for her bring him to the party.

"Oohh!" I blurt out, lunging toward a black Lycra dress with flat, bra-like straps. "I'm getting this."

"Can you fit it?" Dana asks in her condescending tone.

I'll show her, I scoff, checking the label. "Hey, it's a size ten. I'm trying it on."

Heading straight for the dressing room with Dana in tow, a salesperson lets me inside. I quickly strip off my blouse, skirt and bra, sliding the tight dress over the length of my torso.

"Let me see!" Dana yells through the door.

I open it with flourish, and model the fitted dress, ribbed with criss-cross pieces of fabric that hug every curve of my amazon frame.

"You can't wear that, it's too tight."

"No it's not, it's perfect," I taunt, turning my ample backside to face her as I fondle the material, watching Dana's contorted expression through the mirror. "AC will *love* my ass in this."

"He always wants you wearing that freaky stuff. It'll be too cold to wear that anyway."

"Na ahn, I can wear my black crocheted sweater over it. Plus, look, I don't even have to wear a bra."

"You need one."

"No I don't, see."

I thrust my boobs together higher in the top, showing off a mound of cleavage. Dana's mouth is agape as I shut the door in her face. I can barely contain my laughter as I admire myself once more before disrobing.

I can tease any man better than her, and she knows it. If Dana thinks I'm gonna spend a whole week watching her flaunt herself in front of a drooling AC then refuse to sleep with him again, she has another thing coming. I'm tired of that little game. Dana's relished the fact that there is one guy who wants her more than he wants me, and that man is my husband.

AC has wanted her ever since he laid eyes on her one spring break when I came home from college, only months after I'd met him that passionate afternoon. Especially after I revealed to him that Dana and I had engaged in a ménage à trois in high school with another guy, and had experienced a few lesbian episodes, he was gung ho to get the two of us in bed.

Dana was alone, and having finally broken up with her long-time abusive beau, Derrick, she was at a real low point in her life. Maybe that's why she played the innocent flirt to the hilt the night AC and I picked her up at her far south-side apartment and drove to the China Club to party. She wore a semi-translucent white blouse, sans bra, that glowed inside the bar, flaunting the fact that unlike me, she had a perfectly perky bosom.

AC was smitten, and regaled her with his intellect and Jell-O shots the entire night. Never one to hold her liquor, by the fourth shot, Dana was having the tattoo guy place a temporary sticker deep in her cleavage. She turned toward the wall and AC as she unbuttoned her shirt and exposed herself.

"Let's go to the Point!" AC exclaimed, grabbing her hand and dragging her out of the club, taking an exaggerated interest in the rose on her breast during the walk back to his black Mazda RX-7.

I walked behind, not jealous, but aroused at what would transpire that evening. Stopping at the corner store to buy a pint of Bacardi, AC drove with maniacal urgency through the curves of Lake Shore Drive to 55th street.

After leaving the car, we sauntered through the tunnel, where AC succumbed to his lust and pushed her against the graffiti-strewn wall, carnivorously sucking her nipples. She grabbed my hair and drew me to her small lips, her ecstatic moans vibrating against my tongue.

"Hey man," a voice echoed down the tunnel. "Let me get some of that!"

"Let's go down on the rocks," I said, afraid.

That night, with jagged rocks beneath us and the constant sound of waves lapping against the shore, Dana leaned against my body as AC forced himself inside of her, and I wondered how differently her pussy felt than mine. I eagerly tasted her skin as he forced my head against the stone while pounding inside of her.

We would repeat the scenario as the sun rose through the sheer curtains and silhouetted plants in Dana's apartment that morning, and several subsequent times when I made the trip home.

But then, as suddenly as it started, it ended, at least with the three of us. I suspect that AC and Dana shared other episodes while I was back at school, him sucking up her sensuality and her his mother's money. But I was no angel after I returned to FAMU, so I never mentioned it. Besides, I was the one he asked to marry, presenting me with a teeny diamond as soon as I graduated and returned home.

Dana and I still hung out, sometimes with AC and other times without, but not as frequently as before. The minute she met Eric, everything changed. She fell so hard for that man, with his golden skin and naturally straight black hair, that she reinvented herself to become the perfect woman for him.

Dana stopped smoking cigarettes and weed, didn't curse, and began to dress more conservatively. The biggest change, however, was her newfound spirituality. She was now 'saved.' Every chance she got while in his presence, she would quote from the Bible as if it were her native tongue. I secretly believed she woke up every morning and memorized a passage, waiting all day to spring it on him.

All the racy stuff from her past, including me and AC, disappeared, and was replaced by a spotless history that only included a few serious boyfriends. It was an unwritten rule not to speak of our sexual liaisons in Eric's company, which wasn't a problem, since the instances were so few and far between.

One of the last times I saw him was when she brought him over to our condo for a party to watch the fireworks last Fourth of July. As I showed them around the apartment, Eric lingered over a portrait AC had painted of my ass, with my legs parted invitingly to all comers who beheld the image. Dana quickly escorted him out of the room and out of our lives.

Or so she thought. As if fate was defying Dana's obstinacy, I ran into him alone one day under the elevated train tracks on Wabash, and we talked for more than an hour, each not wanting to leave. Our eyes said everything our voices could not, and afterwards, neither of us told Dana we had seen the other. It was our little secret.

But he was always present in her conversation. Dana would lament to me frequently of how she wished he would spend more time with her, and how disappointed she was that he hadn't asked her to move in with him or proposed marriage. With a sympathetic sigh, I secretly rejoiced, wondering arrogantly if he wasn't in fact waiting for me.

"What are you getting?" I ask, slinging the black dress over my shoulder while picking out stockings.

"Nothing," Dana groans with a worrisome look. She so easily wears her heart on her sleeve.

"Dana, you better be there."

"I will, stop buggin' me! I'll be there."

I glare at her questioningly. And you better have that sexy man on your arm, I think, as I step forward to the counter. This will be my only chance to corner him and find out if Dana actually invited him to Boston and Miami with us. If she hasn't, I will and pray he'll take me up on the offer. Afterall, if I have to spend the first two cities watching Dana tease AC, I'm gonna die.

📖

When I was a child, I would stare in the mirror for such a long time that the individual thinking my thoughts and the image before me seemed to be two distinct entities. Years later, I read in *Simple Abundance* that psychologists call this phenomenon the 'displacement of self,' which happens mostly to those who are abused.

I'm experiencing the emotion now as I stare in our wide vanity mirror, applying coats of Prescriptives liquid foundation and translucent powder #4 with the precision of a surgeon. I use every beauty trick I know, placing concealer not only under my eyes but also down the bridge of my shiny nose to provide definition. Foundation down the center of my breasts to enhance cleavage, and under my arms to provide a flawless sheen. Tonight, I must look irresistible.

But I'm not satisfied, so I apply more crimson lipstick, the kind that stays all night, regardless of what I eat or drink, who I kiss...

I can't make myself beautiful enough. Removing my new bow, I slick my hair down once again with more gel until it lays flat on my head. After decorating my eyes with subtle, blended shades of shadow, liner and mascara, I inspect myself. Another spritz of Eternity, the stuff my sister Terra claims attracts men like the Superbowl.

Once again, I just don't seem finished. Something is missing, and the longer I stare in this mirror the uglier I seem. I have to just walk away. But I can't.

AC walks in, dressed in olive-colored ripped combat pants and a Metallica T-shirt.

"Who are you getting all pretty for?"

"I'm not pretty."

"Yeah right, you know you are."

Lighting the miniature heart-shaped candle, I set it atop its holder and allow it to float onto the surface of the pool, sending it farther to the center with ripples from my ruby fingernails.

"Why are you putting candles in there? Don't you know the chlorine could catch afire?" AC asks, hovering over me to steal a light for his Kool cigarette.

"I'll take that chance. Why don't you go light the hurricane candles and place them on the patio?"

"Okay. I'll put them on the edge so if a big gust of wind comes, it'll land on somebody's head and kill them," he laughs with exaggerated malice, grabbing his red Marine jacket from his pre-college days off the nearby chair.

I don't care, just get the fuck away from me. Semper Fi my ass. The military turns out more lunatics than jails.

It isn't even the major indignities I've suffered at his hands that turned my love sour, I think, watching him yank open the sliding glass door. Not the time he threw the base of the cordless phone into my thigh, barely missing my kneecap, and producing a huge purplish bruise. Nor the time he shoved me from his slowly moving car onto gravel that sliced my palms. Neither is it the many other times he disrespected me, either throwing my clothes into the street in a fit of fury or screaming as many derogatory female insults as came to his mind, inches from my face, like a drill sergeant breaking the spirit of a new recruit.

Those occurrences, though dramatic, were few and far between, memorable yet rare and outdated enough for AC to argue he had turned over a new leaf. But his illogical reasoning didn't matter, because the traumatic events, ironically, didn't diminish my affection.

It is his constant nagging and non-stop berating that erodes my passion. Not unlike Dana, AC finds ways daily to tell me how stupid, clumsy and dippy I am. Never mind all my accomplishments, in his eyes, I just can't do anything right. The only compliments he does pay me are based on my body. But those misdirected words can't possibly rebuild a soul that has been chipped away by a barrage of insults like a chisel carving away at stone.

"What are you guys doing?" Susan asks, snapping me out of my philosophizing.

Her shoulder-length bleach blonde hair highlights her wide smile as she picks up a candle. It is the clubhouse of her 77 W. Huron Street apartment building that we're decorating, the location I chose to hold my book party ever since I saw the pool, party room and top story patio with a wondrous vista of the city.

"We just got started," I say. "AC's out there."

"Come on out, I've got one to smoke."

"Cool."

I follow her into the crisp night air, watching AC's face beam with admiration as she approaches him with a tight hug. Susan's naturally slim, lofty, Polish traits have always enamored him, and she loves his free, artsy nature.

"So what time does it start?"

"I guess people will begin showing up in about an hour, I hope."

She sets the joint aglow with a tall flame from her silver lighter, drawing smoke through thin peach lips, causing her boyishly flat chest to rise against her knit sweater.

"Who's all coming?"

"Well, I invited a bunch of reviewers and stuff but I bet mostly my friends will come looking for free liquor and food."

AC inhales the smoke and chokes out his response. "Yeah, a bunch of moochers."

His hypocrisy makes me grin, and as he hands me the joint, I stop to dig in my purse.

Susan looks to me with wide-eyed glossy stupor. "What are you looking for?"

"My Visine."

"It's a party, who cares if your eyes are red? People will be drinking."

AC shakes his head. "Yeah, it's not like they're work people. You're an artist now."

"I know, but old habits die hard, I guess. I just don't want to get a review saying I was blowed or something." I hastily tilt back my head and press two drops in each eye, blinking away the excess.

They both chuckle as I take the cigarette and inhale my two puffs, my stomach quivering as I look over the edge of the rail and across the downtown skyline. I don't admit that it's really Eric's reaction that concerns me, being so accustomed to the virginal Dana, I don't want to scare him away or give him any reason to say no tonight.

Adorning the room after getting high becomes an easy, creative adventure. I tape cherry-colored crepe paper over the fluorescent lights and replace white bulbs in the lamps with red ones. My books are positioned on the display table neatly over a scarlet velvet cloth. The sweet aroma of vanilla and lavender scented candles waft through the air, creating the atmosphere of a lady's boudoir.

Next, I place Maxwell's *Urban Hang Suite*, *The Velvet Rope* by Janet, Me'shell Ndegeocello's *peace beyond passion*, Michael Frank's *The Art of Tea* and of course, The Artist's second disc from *Emancipation* into AC's five-disc CD player and set it to shuffle.

21

After about an hour, just as I had suspected, my friends began to filter in, congratulating me for finishing the book and begging for free copies. I only oblige a few of them, while continually checking the door for signs of Dana and Eric.

When a couple of the local reviewers I invited arrive, I delight them with witty small talk, pleased that someone legit actually came. The hour grows later, with still no sign of Eric, and I become more upset with Dana by the minute. I can't believe my best friend would stand me up so rudely at such a monumental event in my life. I always knew she was jealous, but this is the final straw. Tomorrow morning I'll make up an excuse and cancel her plane tickets and hotel reservations, no matter how much it costs. I am so sick of her bull–

Mid-thought, I see Eric. I notice him before I recognize Dana, looking dapper in his linen banded-collar shirt and beige gabardine pants that neatly drape his lean legs. I force myself not to be as bold as the champagne in my stomach commands, and instead I stroll over to them easily with a confident smile.

Eric extends his arms to me, embracing my waist and kissing my cheek. My heart flip-flops.

"Long time no see," he beams, displaying a perfect row of teeth, framed by vampire-length incisors.

"I know," I say, releasing him, catching Dana looking as if she swallowed her tongue.

"It looks like hell in here," she says, turning her nose up to the decor.

"Nice to see you, too, girl. Let me get you guys a drink."

"You know I don't drink," Dana says wistfully, placing her arm in the cradle of Eric's.

"Yeah, right," I say with as much sarcasm as possible. "Eric, do you want a beer?"

"I'll take a Bud."

"Okay." I dart off to the small bar area, feeling his stare sear my backside, and request a beer from the bartender. Walking back, I see Dana lean over and whisper close to Eric's ear in a secretive stance. I can almost hear her cajoling, Let's not stay too long, honey. You know I don't like to party.

"Thanks," he says, his fingers inadvertently touching mine as I give him the cold bottle, his magnetism charging my bones.

"Hello dear," AC says behind me. "Hey Dana."

"Hello."

"How you doing man?" Eric asks, extending his free hand, as AC returns his greeting with a forceful shake.

"Well, we better go mingle," Dana says, ushering Eric to the other side of the room. When he picks up a book and turns it over to the back cover, she takes it from his hands and sets it down, pulling him onto the dancefloor to slow drag.

Shit! Of all the times AC can't stand being within two feet of me, why now? I plan fast, returning to the bar for another glass of champagne, steeling my nerves to approach Eric later.

Circling the room all evening, I ensure everyone has enough to drink and eat, specifically plying Eric with beer to weaken his defenses and Dana with water so she will be forced to leave his side at some point during the night to visit the restroom. The fourth time I approach them, Dana stretches and yawns.

"Oh well, we better get out of here," she says, nudging Eric with her elbow.

"No, you guys can't leave yet, you still have to try the dessert. It's Tiramisu."

"I don't like that."

"What is it?" Eric asks, staring up to me.

"It's like lady fingers soaked in espresso–"

"He won't like it, he's such a picky eater," Dana interrupts.

"Oh well, I tried. You guys be safe on the way home," I pout and remain there, not wanting to move.

As soon as I force myself to walk away toward AC and Susan, I see Dana in my peripheral vision entering the ladies room while Eric walks to the closet to retrieve their coats. This is my last shot; I trot across the room to his side.

"Did you get a chance to see the view from the patio?" I ask, panting.

"No," he smiles.

"Come on, you gotta see it before you leave."

I dash ahead, sliding open the pool room and patio door, leaving both ajar for him to follow. If Dana should exit prematurely, it would appear as if he's following me of his own volition.

Positioning myself in the farthest corner from the view of the party, I point out the Merchandise Mart and other buildings I can recognize.

"This is beautiful," he says softly, staring directly into my eyes and not at the city, his plump succulent lips causing my walls to involuntarily pulse.

"I know, I'm going to miss Chicago while we're gone."

"Yeah, but it won't be that long."

Out of the corner of my eye, I see Dana in the party room approaching AC and Susan, and they in turn point toward the patio. I know it's now or never.

"Well," I lean forward, "I'm so sad you can't come with us to Boston and Miami. I offered to buy your plane tickets but Dana told me you just couldn't break away."

A look of sheer surprise crosses his face. "She told you that?"

"Yeah," I say, watching Dana run into the pool area, followed by AC. "I wish you could. I mean, Dana's hotel room is already paid for, so that would be no extra expense. Plus, I really need you. The more help the better. Don't you wanna come?"

Dana and AC step onto the patio and seize Eric's attention. As soon as she sees us, pure anger crosses her face.

"Yeah, I'll come," he says with quiet urgency.

"Great! I'll get the tickets and everything."

I grin widely as they rush up to us.

"What are you so happy about?" AC asks.

"Guess what? Eric agreed to go with us to Boston and Miami!"

Simultaneously, AC and Dana's mouths drop open. I continue, looking directly at Dana. "So I guess those car washes won't hold him back after all!"

"Let's go," she huffs, accidentally kicking over a candle and bursting the glass.

Chapter 2

Boston, Massachusetts

Do not be yoked together with unbelievers. For what do righteousness and wickedness have in common? Or what fellowship can light have with darkness?

2 Corinthians 6:14

Ain't this about a bitch? My life is shit. I cannot believe this mother-fucking pretty-boy wannabe is actually sitting on this plane. I should bust him in his mouth right now for throwing a monkey wrench in my whole damn game plan. Three days ago, everything was straight, I was all set to kick it with Dana, poised to catch that tiger by the tail again after four years, and now it's all shot to hell.

Instead, Dana's in front of me now, cradled innocently in Eric's arms like Mother-fucking Theresa, and Paris is beside me acting like the whole thing was out of her control. Claiming he put her on the spot and invited himself on *our* dime. Yeah, right. She constantly bitches about not having enough money when I need something, but after one conversation with this faggot she charges two plane tickets on her credit card lickety split. Fuck that, I'm not dumb. I know Paris goes gaga over those tall light-skinned boys, but she's got another thing coming if she thinks this is gonna be some swinging swapping trip because I'm not about to watch another man fuck my wife. She can hang that up right now.

I smirk as Paris twitches nervously in her seat when the large jet begins to rapidly descend toward the earth. She leans her big-ass head in front of the glass, blocking the view of Boston Harbor, then sits back and slides the window shade down.

"Why're you acting so geeked out?" I ask, reaching over her, reopening the shade.

"It looks like we're going to land on the water!" she says, pure fear in her eyes.

"If we do I want to see it. Just like that flight, I think it was a USAir plane that took off from here and went right back into the harbor." I lift my hand upward then slam it back down to my lap for effect. "I can't remember how many people died on that one. The water was freezing, just like now."

Paris inhales sharply and grabs both armrests as the landing gear drops with a loud rattle from the belly of the plane. I turn my head and giggle, yet the tickle in my stomach reminds me at the last minute to take my ulcer medicine. Removing the ever-present brown bottle from my jacket, I swallow a pill dry, tasting the bitter coating slide down my throat. I don't want to chance waiting for water and forget to take it like I've done before, then wake up with churning stomach pains in the middle of the night.

"Okay," Paris says after we disembark and collect our bags and my gun, unloaded in its locked black case, from the luggage carousel, "we can take a bus over there to the Airport Dock."

"What dock?" Eric asks, unable to block the smile that automatically springs to his lips every time he looks at her. Cockblocker.

"There's a boat that'll take us right to the Boston Harbor Hotel. It should only take like ten minutes."

I walk ahead of them and light a Kool as soon as we hit the outdoors. The nicotine fills my lungs, and I suck the numbing menthol urgently after the long flight, as if I'm a newborn baby taking its first breath.

"It's gonna be cold on there," Dana whines. "It's freezing here."

"I know," Paris says, clasping her jacket closed with gargantuan hands, newly decorated with the fuchsia-colored acrylic nails Dana convinced her to get.

"Just wait till we start moving," Eric says.

"Aw, quit bitchin' Dana, it feels good out here." I lean my face up to the grayness and howl a puff of smoke into the frosty air. Dana cuddles again under Eric's arm as we load onto the navy and white boat's canopied deck.

After slicing over the choppy surf for awhile, the crowded skyline looms larger and we reach the arched passageway nestled among a group of red-bricked buildings.

"It's so pretty," Paris says, gazing wide-eyed for agreement.

"It's alright," I say.

"Which building is it?" Dana asks.

"I think that one, behind there." Paris points to a multi-storied building. "And we both have harbor views from our rooms."

"Good," Eric winks.

Yeah, good for you, I think. "What are y'all doing tonight?"

Dana cuts in and stretches her thin, hairy forearms forward. "I'm so tired, we'll probably just go to our room and go to bed."

"I know," Paris agrees. "AC and I have to get up early tomorrow anyway for my radio interview, but we can go out after that. Make sure you guys listen."

"What station is it?" Eric asks, leaning past Dana's protective grip with great interest.

"Jammin' 94.5."

After checking into our 16th-floor room, I roll a joint and smoke it alone, sending the signal that I'm not yet ready to forgive Paris for bringing the asshole with us. Exiting the bathroom, I open the mini-bar and remove a Coke along with several little bottles of Jack Daniel's.

"You're gonna drink that now? You know we have to be up by eight, right?"

I twist the tops with a crack and pour them into the glass. "I know."

📖

The next morning, blinding rays of sun illuminate the room in a pinkish glow, disturbing my deep slumber. Paris is rustling about, making an inordinate amount of noise.

"Get up sleepy head, we can't be late."

I blink at her while she buttons up a low-cut Gap sweater.

"For what?" I mumble, feigning deep sleep.

"The interview!"

"I'm not going."

"What?" she says, her voice rising an octave.

"I don't feel like it, I'm just gon' stay here."

"No, but you said you'd go with me."

"I can listen from here." I roll over and pound the inverted pack of Kool's against my palm.

"I told you not to drink that stuff. You're just being lazy."

"Whatever." I reach for the remote control and turn on the television.

"But I want you to come with me," she squeals louder. "It's all the way in some suburb."

"All the more reason for me to stay here."

Paris stands with indecision, hands on hips, looking as though she might cry or scream any minute. She then walks over to the table, grabs her black Coach purse and leaves, slamming the solid door with a loud thump. I snicker, somewhat disappointed that she didn't resort to begging so I could refuse her more coldly. At least I don't have go out in that hawk right now, like she does. That's what she gets for bringing Eric and expecting me to just accept it and do what she wants. I'm not going for the oke-doke. I ain't the one.

Falling back asleep, I reawaken at the exact time for Paris' spot.

"Shit," I curse, frantically flipping the dial on the small clock radio until the announcer's voice is clear.

"...and your local weather...'" he continues, and I wonder if I've missed the whole thing. After several more commercials and a song, he finally introduces her.

"Today in the studio we have Paris Gibbins, welcome."

"Thank you for having me," she says in her deeply familiar drone.

"Paris is the author of the book *The Sex Files*, a rather erotic book of tales about–shall we say–experiences of the sexual sort."

They both laugh a nervous giggle. I try to imagine for a split second what this guy looks like.

"You know, I opened this book to the first chapter called *All the Guys I've Loved Before*, and I was shocked to see a letter to your father."

"Yes," Paris laughs, "but let me explain before anyone gets the wrong idea. When I began writing I realized that every girl's love life in a way begins with her dad, because normally he is the first male she comes in contact with. So, I thought it was appropriate to write that letter as an opening for the chapter."

"It's a really powerful letter. Why don't you read it to our listeners?"

Oh, boy. Not this shit again. Here we go.

"Dear Daddy," Paris sighs, "I've been writing you this letter in my head for a long time now but always delayed putting it on paper due to fear or procrastination. Well, God has blessed you with 75 years on this Earth and I must face your mortality and realize the sooner I write this the better.

"You are, to me, the ultimate mystery man. Even though we've spent 20 years in the same household, the few things I know about you could fill a ring box. I know you were raised in Knoxville, Tennessee by a Black father and a mother who was also Black yet mixed with Swedish, giving you your green eyes, fair skin and curly hair.

"Your college career was cut short by a call to the military, hence your passion for World War II memorabilia to this day. You were married to a beautiful woman named Heidi for ten years whom you divorced under unknown circumstances before marrying Mommy.

"I know your Dad died when you were only 21-years-old; I'm not sure when your mother passed away. You have a penchant for Budweiser and Agatha Christie novels, and are well read, intelligent and an excellent mathematician.

"However, the stuff I don't know about you could fill a coliseum. There are so many unasked therefore unanswered questions. For example, how did your Dad's death affect you at such a young age? What were your parents like? Were they nice to you? How did they handle a semi-interracial marriage back in those days?

"What happened with your first wife? Did you and she have any children? Where are all the details? Where are all those stories that parents tell about their own childhood that bore their kids to death?

"The tales of Mommy's early days in Wetumpka, Alabama are endless. Since an early age, she's entertained Terra and I with stories of her parents' underage liaisons in the back woods and even their parents' lives. The genealogy of my maternal side is well defined. But with you, I feel as though half of my history is gone. I am incomplete.

"Perhaps these aren't the important questions, but maybe I just don't know what to ask. To let Mommy tell it, you are the worst husband in the world. In some respects that may be true, but that isn't the purpose of this letter. This is not a blame game. My only goal is to express my view of our relationship in order to gain some closure.

"Do you really love me and Terra? I know you do, I've just never heard you say it. Maybe once, recently, while handing the phone back to Mommy after she forced you to say hello, I thought I heard you say 'Love you.' Terra said if that were true, you must be dying.

"Due to your aloofness and absence from home to go to work or visit the taverns, I never learned how to connect with a male figure. Growing up, I assumed the only way to get a man's affection or attention was to give him my body, and I did that many times. Suffered fools gladly at the expense of confidence and self-esteem while becoming the quintessential textbook case of codependency. I was a country love song gone wrong. Seeking out love in all the wrong places while all I really wanted was my Daddy.

"The critical fact is that you stayed with us. Although I know you could have deserted the family many times, like my friends' fathers have done, you never did, and for that, I thank you. While it pains me that you and Mommy both sacrificed your own happiness not to abandon your flesh and blood, I am so grateful that you honored your obligations despite the unhappiness of infidelities and alcoholism.

"You're a changed man. You have found the Lord, and hopefully, peace. I guess the true intent of this message is to let you know how pleased I am that you are my father and I love you wholeheartedly."

"Wow," the announcer says after a brief pregnant pause, deeply touched. "That's amazing. What did he say when he read it?"

"Not much," Paris answers.

Lot of good that letter did her, she should have never written it.

"That's too bad. Well anyway, you'll be appearing at the WordsWorth bookstore in Cambridge tomorrow, right?"

"Yes, thank you. And I have a reading at Sever Hall at 5:30 p.m."

"Please, all you listeners, stop by and see her."

Make me barf. If I have to listen to that Daddy letter one more time, I swear I'll burn every copy of that book. Poor Paris, always bitchin' about how hard it was to have a father who was emotionally unavailable. Give me a break. Compared to my childhood she grew up in friggin' Disneyland.

Her parents never even laid a hand on her, and at least they stayed together. My parents couldn't make it past my seventh birthday before getting divorced. My ol' girl got fed up with my dad beating on her so she decided to screw another man while my father was working late nights to put food on our table. But that ended quickly the day he came home early and caught them; her coward-ass boyfriend ran out the back door. My dad snatched Gloria from that bed and lit into her while I cried in the doorway for him to stop. He didn't hear me. Dad was so enraged that he forced her out the front door, butt naked, running down the street screaming like a maniac.

It was a surrealistic movie scene. I waited for days on that ratty living room sofa, rolling up the dusty beige shade to watch for Gloria to come home, expecting her to steal me away to the museum or Grant Park like we used to do. Only this time at the end of our excursion I knew we would actually board that Greyhound to Los Angeles instead of standing listlessly by as the bus pulled away, her squeezing my hand tightly and wiping away her tears. I got ready because I knew she wouldn't dare leave without me. Gathering my things into a miniature suitcase, I shoved it under my bed in preparation just like Gloria taught me.

The bitch never came. When the days melded into months I thought my heart might crack waiting for my best friend to come home. My father certainly had never been an ally of mine, and since she left he seemed to grow crazier and meaner by the day. His drinking increased, and during fits of rage he would punish me for reminding him of Gloria. Don't let that song with her name in it come on the radio, it would send him into a frenzy. Soon after, the beatings began. First, just mild spankings like any child would receive, but the longer her absence, the more tortuous the whippings became. Eventually, after a couple of years and as I grew taller, they turned into outright punches.

Then, one dazzling spring afternoon, as abruptly as she disappeared, she returned. Slim and polished, Gloria was a little heavier but still fine as wine. But she wasn't alone. Her new husband joined her as she argued with my dad about taking me away to Tacoma, Washington, where she now resided. There was stilted conversation, money exchanged hands, and before I knew it, I was on the plane with Gloria and my new step-dad flying west.

I was still pissed, but I forgave her. At least she came back, even though it took a few years. Their crib in Tacoma was huge, an elaborate art deco spread bought with the proceeds from her own interior design firm. I began to adjust. Even though her new husband was corny, I did have fun shooting a few hoops with him in the driveway and listening to his stale jokes. I breathed a sigh of contentment and the knots in my gut subsided.

"So, AC, do you like it here?" she asked one day after we had eaten dinner.

"It's okay," I said with a nonchalance that threatened to betray my bliss.

"Good, I'm glad. Because I want you to come back on holidays or your summer break if you want to..."

My abdomen caved in as I comprehended the fact that I hadn't actually escaped the madman afterall.

"...any time you want to, really. Just call me." Her voice trailed into a whisper as she cast her eyes from my gaze.

My own mother didn't want me. I couldn't speak. Her knit navy blue and white designer sweater ruffled slightly as her husband leaned down to kiss her on the cheek. She was sending me back to the lunatic. Surely she could see the fear in my eyes. She had to know how much I wanted to be with her. I was only ten years old.

I glanced down at her belly as she smoothed the fabric over a visibly formed round pouch. Our eyes met then quickly darted away. Then, I knew. It all became clear. She was starting a new family, and I wasn't part of it. I was being erased like an error made while typing. I felt utterly unloved. Neither my father nor mother wanted me because I reminded them both of horrible pasts. I was a mistake.

"Besides, I'm sure you don't want to leave your friends and...your father."

"Yeah," I said.

Returning alone on that flight to Chicago, I was loaded down with new clothes and money, but the aching in my stomach reappeared.

Things only went downhill from there. It was as if Gloria's presence and obvious success at both business and love touched a raw nerve in my father and he went off the deep end. One silent night he entered my room for what I assumed was his usual badgering about my failing to take out the garbage or wash the dishes. Instead, he sat on the bed next to me, pulling down the covers and my pajama pants.

"This is all bitches are good for," he growled in a foreboding tone.

I froze as he took my penis in his mouth and began licking and tugging at the flaccid flesh. The alcohol on his tongue burned me, and I cried for him to stop. Miraculously, he obliged. Standing, he left the room without another word. We never spoke of the incident, and although he never abused me again sexually, the beatings continued throughout my first three years of high school. Once, he attacked me as soon as I came home late one day, in front of my two friends.

After that, I spoke to no one at my private Catholic high school, for fear that my friends had told the whole class what happened. I couldn't relate to anyone there anyway, with their normal, Jack and Jill lives. I began to sit out of mass, thus becoming the target of even more torture from the nuns and one particularly vicious priest.

I only visited my mother a few more times, the obvious misfit in an otherwise normal family.

They say be careful what you wish for, you just might get it. Somehow that rang true when I came home one day after school, loosened the dark blue tie of my required uniform, and collapsed on the couch, only to get up again when I saw an object on the floor. It was my father, dead from a self-inflicted gunshot wound to the temple.

I placed my dinner of Doritos and Dr. Pepper on the table and walked over to his motionless body, intrigued by the mixture of blood, brain matter and fluid that had leaked onto our cherry wood floor. It was over. The death I'd hoped for had finally occurred, but I didn't feel as happy as I thought I would. It felt so incomplete. There seemed to be so much more suffering he should have endured, so many apologies he never offered. It was too late; his essence was seeping through the floor-boards into the wet dark cement basement.

Gloria arrived later that evening, and by the weekend she had already had my father cremated without a funeral, and me declared an emancipated minor so that I could live in my own apartment in Chicago. There was no need to pretend, she didn't want a screwed up, pierced-eared freak near her young children.

Newfound friends thought it was cool that I lived on my own at sixteen, but they didn't know the price of that freedom. They couldn't understand the pain I held inside that caused me on occasion to bang my head into the wall and scream. I always thought I would kill my father, but now that he was gone, I hated him more.

I despised Gloria too, for leaving me in the first place. For cheating on my father. For everything. Therefore, when I graduated high school I joined the Marines without telling her, hoping to disappear without a trace. I made it through basic training at Parris Island with those damned sand fleas, and even suffered having one removed that had crawled up my urethra out in the field.

But it didn't last. I had been such a pushover, holding in so much anger every time someone hurt me, I was bound to explode. Which is exactly what I did to this White boy from Kentucky who wouldn't leave me alone. It was the smallest infraction, he might have messed with my bunk or flicked my dog tags, I don't even remember, but I know I flew into a blind rage that caused me to choke him until he turned purple. It took two friends to pull me off of him as he fainted to the ground. He survived, but I was dishonorably discharged, and forced to move back to Chicago and tell my mother where I'd been. She rented me a loft and paid to enroll me in U of C, but I still hated her.

Even after hearing all this and worse, Paris still tells me to forgive, that it's only hurting me not to. As if it were that easy. I will hate both my parents until the day I die.

📖

"Let's all go to Sugarbaby's tonight!" Paris says excitedly, throwing her purse onto the dresser and pulling off her jacket as soon as she enters the hotel room.

"Where?" I say, preparing another joint, glad that she's not mad at me.

"It's some martini bar the people at the radio station told me about; it's supposed to be good."

"Sounds straight." I lick the joint and present it to her, but she begins undressing.

"Not now, I gotta go work out."

"You just got back."

"I know," she says, pulling a tight jog bra over her tits. "But I want to now before I lose the momentum. You should come with me. They have a nice pool and everything."

My chest heaves with exhaustion as I contemplate leaving the room. I want to get out, but not for physical exercise. "That's okay, you go on. It'll be waiting for you when you come back."

Paris pulls a T-shirt over her biker shorts, puts on her gym shoes and leaves in a hurry.

📖

"So, did you all listen to the interview?" Paris asks anxiously later that night as the four of us squeeze into a circular booth at the somewhat empty bar.

Eric has already ensured his seat next to Paris in the middle while Dana and I sit at the outer ends, with Dana practically in Eric's lap.

"Yeah, we heard it," he grins. "It was a good interview, talking about your father and stuff."

"I know. I liked the part about him finding God. That was so touching," Dana places her hand on her chest as if caught by emotion.

"Here we go. Now I gotta hear this God shit all over again," I say, extracting a Kool from my pack.

Dana gasps. "Don't say that!"

Paris steals a glance at Eric.

"Why not Goddamit?" I chuckle with delight.

"*In spite of all this, they kept on sinning; in spite of His wonders, they did not believe,*" Dana says, fingering her Peter-Pan collar.

"Come on now, you ain't the only one who knows the Bible. You forget I had twelve years of that Catholic school crap. *You hypocrite, first take the plank out of your own eye, and then you will see clearly to remove the speck from your brother's eye.*"

"*I will put an end to the arrogance of the haughty and will humble the pride of the ruthless,*" she seethes as the waitress approaches.

"*Wives, submit to your husbands as to the Lord,*" I say, wagging my finger near her nose.

"And husbands, be Christ-like, or something like that," Paris teases, glancing over the extensive menu. "Man, look at all these different martinis."

"I don't know which one to get," Eric mumbles.

"Do not get drunk on wine, which leads to debauchery," Dana continues, as the dark-haired server looks unsure of whether to interject. *"Instead, be filled with the Spirit."*

"I don't drink hard liquor," Eric says to no one in particular. "May I just have a Bud?"

"No," Paris stops him from handing back the menu, "you can't come to the best martini bar in the country and order beer. At least try one."

"Okay..." he hesitates.

"You don't have to drink that stuff if you don't want to. It's no good for you," Dana says. "I'll take a Sprite, please."

I let out a loud sigh and roll my eyes at Dana.

"Okay," the waitress says, taking her menu.

"The chocolate one," Paris decides.

"I'll take the Atomic." I deepen my voice for effect.

"I guess I'll have the Black Martini," Eric says.

"Once you go Black..." I laugh, watching Dana crinkle her nose at his choice.

"So, can y'all stop with the Bible battle long enough to talk about the rest of the interview?" Paris asks.

"Dana started it."

"No she didn't, you did. You Anti-Christ. That's what AC really stands for."

I laugh with pride at the nickname Paris gives me. Anything is better than the real Christian name by mother came up with–Anslam Christopher. "I thought you knew."

"Do you believe in God Eric?" Paris asks, startling him.

"Definitely," he says quickly. "I grew up going to Sunday school. But I don't know all the verses like Dana."

"Me neither. I may not know all of the Bible, but I know I feel close to God."

"Well," Dana says, "if you don't know His Word, you can't be all that close."

"Shoot, AC knows His word, but that hasn't helped him."

"Because I know it's all bullshit," I say, fed up with Dana's little holier-than-thou act. She looks at me with outright disdain, fronting like I never fucked her tawdry ass. Any other time she would be giving me that lusty glance that Paris is now giving Eric.

"Just stop it, AC. I don't want you corrupting us."

Please, I think, but am not yet drunk enough to say, I will bust you out right here and now. Instead, I pause and think of the perfect passage.

"So now I will expose her lewdness before the eyes of her lovers; no one will take her out of my hands."

The waitress returns with our round of drinks, just in time to provide Dana with a convenient distraction to my retort.

Paris raises her glass. "A toast to a prosperous book tour and appreciation for good friends who support me and will help me carry all those books in the cold tomorrow."

The group groans as everyone sips their drinks.

"Ew, this is awful," Eric grunts, twisting his face in disgust.

"I told you those martinis are too strong," Dana says.

"How would you know?" I wink. She rolls her eyes to the ceiling. Cunt.

I tip my glass into my mouth and allow the powerful liquid to flow down my relaxed throat, devouring the entire drink before slamming the empty glass to the table.

"Oh God," Paris says, turning her attention from my antics and sipping her chocolate concoction. "Mine's good, do you want to taste?"

Eric blushes and takes a sip of her drink. "That tastes better than mine."

"You should get one of these," she declares, taking the V-shaped glass back from him.

"I don't know, I think I better stick to beer."

Paris giggles like a schoolgirl and sighs. "So, your parents are from Chicago, too, right?"

"Yeah," he responds, tapping his fingers against the vinyl seat behind Dana's head. "They live on 80th and Jeffrey."

"Oh man, my parents live at 93rd and Paxton. That's not that far away."

"That is close. I didn't know you used to live there. Dana never told me."

"Yeah, I'm surprised I haven't seen you around there."

Eric begins to grin again. "I know, I come home almost every weekend to help my parents cut the grass and do stuff around the house. Plus, my brother comes home with my niece and my baby sister visits too and we all meet there."

"Oh, that's sweet."

"I got a picture of them, everybody except my father, he doesn't like taking pictures," he says, tilting his face close to her chest as he retrieves his wallet from his back pocket.

Paris flips through the pictures. "They're so pretty, is that your mother?"

"Yep," he answers, taking the billfold back, brushing her fingers in the process. "I love my Mommy." He kisses the photograph before closing the wallet and putting it away.

A regular fucking Brady Bunch. Hell, Paris and Eric already look like they could be brother and sister, just like that guy David she was fucking around with down at FAMU.

I can't believe Paris is literally flirting with Eric, right in front of me and Dana, like we can't tell. As they continue their engrossing conversation above the din of the swing music in the background, I notice her body language lean toward him, even when she turns to speak to me.

Paris does look sexy, as always, but especially tonight. Wearing the form-fitting black bodysuit that I picked out, which contours her abundant breasts and reveals a tiny hint of cleavage, any man would find her irresistible. Below, she dons an ankle-length cherry wrap skirt that falls open every now and then as she crosses and uncrosses her legs. At one point, I catch a glimpse of bare skin above her thigh-high lace topped stockings.

I'm sure Eric can see; I haven't caught him looking, but I know he has. Afterall, he is a man. When did she buy those? She's never worn them for me. Paris secretly shops and hides clothes from me, knowing I'll get mad at how much money she spends. I'll bet you she'll be playing those bad boys for me tonight.

"Heathen," Dana says, as I flag down the waitress to request another martini.

"Please," I respond, "don't start again."

Paris laughs. "You can save your breath with AC. He is a bona fide atheist. Him and his college friends could have written that article that said God was dead."

Dana and Eric stare blankly at Paris as I order my drink.

"Well it's true. There is no God. Everything is based on scientific creation, from the forming of the world to dying."

"How could you say that?" Dana asks. "Don't you believe in heaven and hell?"

"Hell no," I chuckle. "That's all fantasy talk to give weak people something to believe in. All you hypocrites go to church and pretend to be so holy but then act just like me when you get out. I just don't front."

"Yeah," Eric agrees. "We found out the pastor at our church was having sex with some of the young girls when I was growing up. I never really went back after that."

"You see," I say, wondering if he wasn't cool afterall.

"That's blasphemy," Dana squeals. "The Bible is our instruction on how to live a good life."

Paris jumps in. "I'll tell you what's blasphemy. Janeane Garofalo, and I love her, said the Bible is like some novel they wrote hundreds of years ago that we're taking as fact. She said hundreds of years from now, civilization will find *The Bridges of Madison County* and begin worshipping it."

"That's not true," Dana declares.

"I know," Paris says. "It's just that AC has a lot of anger inside. I keep telling him my favorite saying is that hate does more damage to the object in which it is stored–"

"–than the object on which it is poured." I complete the sentence, huffing disapproval. "I heard it a billion times. Don't try to psychoanalyze me just because you're blind."

"Whatever," Paris says, "I may not know what really happened but I do know that I believe in God. I know there is some greater power than–"

I jump up from the table, gulp down the rest of my fresh drink and head outside. Stopping at the sidewalk in front of the bar, I pause to steady myself against a parking meter. The alcohol is taking effect, and it feels good to be out in the open, away from the religious zealots inside. But I know Paris will exit any minute, asking what's wrong and begging me to come back in the bar.

Extracting my small circular steel pipe stuffed with weed, painted to look like a cigarette to allow for discreet smoking in public, I light it and pace the curb. Bozos. I've had just about all the God talk I can take for one night without going off. I don't want to hear anymore. What has God ever done for me? Where was Jesus those nights my father beat me? How could God give me a mother who didn't want me?

"Nigger!" the voice yells, snapping me back to the present moment. A sleek burgundy pickup truck careens by, its teenage occupants staring at me instead of the road as they pass. Their insult lingers in the air like the pungent pollution trailing from their exhaust pipe.

I stand frozen in time, unable to conceive of the fact that I have, for the first time, been called a nigger to my face, boldly and loudly. As they speed up and fishtail around the corner, I drop my pipe and lighter to the ground, yanking my 380 semi-automatic from the leather fanny pack around my waist. Pointing the gun square against the bed of the vehicle, I rest my index finger against the trigger. It is too late. The culprits are gone.

"I got your nigger," I say to the wind, cautiously bending down to pick up my belongings, while keeping my eyes fixed on the street.

I realize Paris still hasn't followed me outside, so I charge back into the bar. The first thing I notice when I reach our booth is that Paris has not shifted from her position next to Eric even though the space is available in my empty seat. I stand there, glancing at the white tablecloth that now covers both of their legs.

"What's wrong with you?" Paris asks, tearing herself away from their gleeful conversation.

"I just nearly got jacked."

"What?" Dana asks loudly.

"Let's go," I say to Paris, looking down.

"What happened?"

"I'm ready to go now," I demand, turning and walking away.

This time Paris joins me soon after I get back outside, but with Dana and Eric in tow. I wish I had my car here, then I could just threaten to strand her ass like I do in Chicago, and I wouldn't have to bring anyone with us that I didn't want to come. Instead, we all pile into a cab, the three of them gabbing all the way back to the hotel, not once asking me if I was okay.

"So you were all up in Eric's face tonight," I say as soon as we are alone in our hotel room.

"What are you talking about?" Paris says, unwrapping her skirt to reveal her bodysuit and stockings.

"You were cheezin' and staring so bad, I thought you were gonna jump his bones."

"No I wasn't. I was just talking to both of them, having a good time."

"Yeah right, having a good time ogling him. Dana could tell, too, that's why she was looking all funny."

"No she wasn't."

"I saw her and you. Don't try to tell me I didn't see what I just saw. I'm not crazy."

Paris slips off her hose, avoiding my stare. "I didn't say you were crazy. You were so busy running around outside and sucking down those martinis I don't see how you saw anything."

"Whatever, I'll just leave it alone, but I know what I saw."

I decide not to press the issue since Paris obviously isn't admitting anything. Plus, she looks so good standing there in just her bodysuit, its long French cut exposing the front of her thighs all the way up to her waist; I'd rather fuck than fight.

After partially disrobing and sliding beneath the cool sheets with her, I remove myself from my underwear and rub it against her butt cheeks.

"I want some ass," I whisper.

She exhales with obvious trepidation, but then finally says, "Okay."

I leap out of bed and retrieve the Vaseline from my wet pack. Slathering her and myself with the gooey jelly, I press myself into her anus with steady force.

"Go slowly," she says, reaching back to control my movement.

I oblige, taking each thrust more deliberately than usual, until I finally press part of the head inside.

"Ow! Stop, it hurts!" she screams.

"Okay, okay," I say, halting my motion as she pulls herself off of me.

"Here, let me just try again, I'll go slowly."

"No, it hurts too much."

"Alright," I sigh, disappointed. "Let's just do it the regular way."

"I don't want to."

"What? Come on! I'm all ready. Let's just do it," I yell, the martinis fueling my anger.

"No," she says with her back still to me, "I don't want to. I'm tired."

I hold myself in my hand, staring at the back of her head and thinking how easy it would be to punch her off the bed. I bet she wouldn't be too tired for Eric right now. Instead, I get out of bed and go to the bathroom to jack off.

"Frigid bitch," I say, slamming the door behind me.

📖

The next afternoon the four of us take the clean T train to the Brattle Square exit and walk right into the WordsWorth bookstore for Paris to do a short book signing before her reading. I haven't spoken to her all night and morning, so she seems overjoyed to talk with an occasional person milling about her table. Dana convinces Eric to leave and hang around Harvard Square and get lunch, promising to meet us at the reading.

Not wanting to be with any of them, I walk around the Cambridge area until the meeting time as well. The gothic structures remind me of the University of Chicago's historic buildings, the wealth of knowledge palpable through each edifice.

I grow nostalgic for my college days, when I could just get high, paint and party all day with my friends, not having to worry about finding a job and making a living. Passionate days filled with having sex with Paris when she was in town, Dana anytime I wanted to, and any of the females on campus who wanted to hang out at the loft.

Smiling in remembrance as I smoke a jism in a corner of the campus, I glance at my watch and realize I need to find Room 113 in a hurry. By the time I enter the three story brown-bricked building with rounded sides, I am late, but Paris has not yet begun reading to the scant crowd of mostly students.

I take a seat in the front row next to Dana with Eric on her opposite side.

"My sister was my first lover," Paris begins, her pretty round face lit eerily by vanilla candles. The gathering turns silent as she smiles with wicked glee before continuing.

"Under the shadows of our slanted bedroom walls, we practiced Freudian inspired acts of curious sexuality, exploring the unknown. Long after our mother had yelled for us to sleep, we remained awake, talking, probing, lusting. I looked to her to provide answers to the many inquiries that swirled through my young brain: Why did my nipples sometimes change in shape and form? How could you have sex with a boy and not get pregnant? Comrades in a tumultuous household, she tried to shield me from the violent cries of our parent's discord. As we aged, she lost interest in the sensual experimentation just as she stopped wanting to play with dolls–always prior to my desire to cease.

"Our closeness was apparent, even though my mother preferred my sister to me. My father was indifferent, but with our mom, it was obvious who was her favorite. When I pointed this out, my mother promptly denied it, giving me the patented answer that she loved us equally. Yet my heart told me differently. I attempted to gain her favor by placing a dollar bill inside of a hand-made card and presenting it to her. In my innocence, I tried anything for love.

"Never mind that my sister, Terra, was running amok with out-landish behavior, which evolved into amusing anecdotes my mother relayed to relatives with a tone of pride. I, the good child who never caused a fuss or talked back, still couldn't measure up. My older sister caused the most strife but was still the shining star. I was the peacemaker, trying to compensate for her actions by being the perfect child. In the end, it didn't matter.

"My mother admitted years later that Terra was in fact her fa-vorite, and excused it away by the fact that she was the first born, as if that alone should justify the bias. It's funny how our negatively perceived childhood attributes can turn in our favor. I used to hate my lanky, gangly nature, but now it is sleek and refined, a stature many women desire. In the same respect, I've turned my people-pleasing tactics into a great sense of fairness and compassion for others, especially underdogs.

"Honestly, some undesirable characteristics have remained. I'm still too much of a pushover and I also have an unconscious need to compete with other females, physically, intellectually and mainly for male attention. That little girl inside of me is still trying to be the favored one."

Applause erupts in the tiny room as people stand and walk up to Paris. When she begins signing more copies of her book, Dana shouts to her through the crowd.

"We're going back to the hotel," she says, clamping down on Eric's hand.

Paris looks up from her book. "Just wait for me, I won't be that long. We can go get something to eat."

"That's okay," Dana says, steering Eric to the door. "I'll call you tomorrow."

"Okay, thanks guys."

"You're welcome," Eric grins, practically tripping out the door from Dana's grasp.

I wait another hour while Paris talks, signs books and answers questions. By the time we make it back to our room, I am exhausted, but ready to make up, seeing how well everyone responded to her reading.

"Do you wanna smoke one?" I offer.

"Sure," she says, following me into the bathroom.

This time, when we rejoin in bed, Paris obliges my lust and allows me to fuck her, normally. With her eyes closed and moaning, I get the urge to start talking to her.

"Do you like my dick inside you?"

"Yes," she murmurs.

"Does it feel good?" I increase the depth of thrusting and tempo.

"Mmnn."

"Do you think about Eric being inside you?"

She continues to grind beneath me, then finally says in a hushed tone, "Yes."

"Do you want him inside you now?" I ask, sex seemingly her truth serum.

"Yes," she wails.

Paris grabs me tighter and we thrust against one another, elevating the pace until she shrieks and I explode in a shiver of convulsions. It is the best sex we've had in a long time, and not once does she ask me to stop.

Chapter 3
Miami and The Florida Keys

If I dwell in the remotest part of the sea, Even there Your hand will lead me.

Psalm 139:9 - 10

consider myself a commodity," I say, moving my head from side to side for emphasis.

"So you can be bought and sold on the open market?" Paris looks up from her copy of freshly printed laser pages with a shit-eating grin.

"In a way, yeah. It's gonna cost my future husband a certain amount of money to take care of me and keep me happy."

She shakes her head and laughs. "You know Dana, if you put half as much energy into your own career as you do Eric's, you would be totally successful right now."

"Right, like you? You work your ass off to finish college, write a book and you can barely pay the rent with AC's broke ass."

"Well that will all change soon," she says, looking back down at the papers. "Come on, what kind of massage do you want? I need to call now to see what they have available."

I stare at the sunny shoreline directly outside of Eden Roc, the ritzy Resort & Spa Paris changed our reservations to at the last minute.

"I don't know. Maybe we should just go catch up with AC and Eric; the spa probably can't fit us in with this short a notice."

"Oh, please. Can't you leave that man alone for one minute? Besides, they need time to do some male bonding."

Can't you leave him alone? I want to ask, but instead roll my eyes skyward. "I know what kind of bonding AC has in mind."

"They'll be fine. Besides, we deserve some pampering. We've been working hard all year and this is our vacation."

"What put you on this self-improvement kick all of a sudden? Working out all the time..."

"Well, we all can't be a skinny Minny like you. You started it with these nails, now I want the whole shebang. Plus, I bought a new bikini and I need to get my shit together. I haven't been in a swimming suit for a whole year. Now come on, I think I want the Deep Tissue and the Lavender Aromatherapy Kur. We can even get them done on the beach–"

I place my palm close to her face before she can go any further. "Hold the phone. I am not about to be out in that sun. It's bad enough we'll be out there when we go to the Keys."

"Fine, I'll just call and see what they have available."

📖

As the short, stocky masseuse takes my head into the crook of her arm and slides her thumb down a muscle in my neck, I can't stop wondering what Eric is doing. It's just my luck he's at a bar meeting some Spanish hussy.

Unable to relax, I glance around the room for a clock, but don't see one. Hopefully the fifty minutes will go quickly. Although her firm touch feels good as it forces painful knots out of my neck, I'm ready to go.

At least he's not with Paris right now. My mother always tells me to keep my enemies close, and that's what I try to do. Especially Paris. She's been the horniest horn-dog around Eric I've ever seen. I still can't believe she went behind my back and asked him to come along. I know that's why she changed the reservations at the last minute to this hotel, partially because she feels guilty towards me and partially to primp herself to look even better for him.

This mess will be all over in a few days, though, and Eric and I will be back on that plane to Chicago. Going back to that flunky job is even better than this. I've worked too hard over the past two years to keep her public pussy away from his sight. It's worked so far, and except for this little faux pas, they would have never seen each other again.

I'm guessing it's just a matter of time before he marries me. Not that he's asked or put a ring on my finger yet, but all things in due time. I have a plan. Since I refuse to take the pill because I don't want to gain the weight, and we don't always use a jimmy hat, a little bun should be in the oven soon. Eric thinks I'd never have an abortion and I know he's too decent a guy to have a child out of wedlock, so we'll get married in a hurry. Then I'll be set. It's cheaper to keep me.

It'll be perfect. He'll sell his condo and buy me a phat crib in Olympia Fields, then I'll quit my job to raise our kids. Because he owns several self-service car washes, he'll be able to spend a lot of time at home. I'm ready. At 29-years-old, I want to start having kids before it is too late. Eric says he's not ready yet, but I know it's because he's still a few years younger than me and scared. Men always need that extra push to make things a reality. They always think they need to hold out until they're an old geezer for the perfect woman to come along. Who else is going to come along? Nobody, if I can help it.

It's way too late for me to start over and go through the whole nine yards of dating and finding out if the man is financially secure enough to marry. Eric is the one. Besides, I love him.

📖

"Rain and sun," Paris observes, this time from the balcony of my oceanfront room, eyeing the magenta coastal landscape.

Droplets of water land on the fine black hair of my forearm. "The devil's beating his wife."

"An always intriguing anomaly."

"Yeah," I agree, not letting on that I don't know what the word *anomaly* means. "I'm going inside before I get my hair wet, they already messed it up enough at the spa."

Sucking on the bottled water we bought after our treatments 'cause the masseuse warned us of dehydration, we duck into the cool air of the suite. I can breathe freely again, away from the thick suffocating air of the outdoors that makes me feel like I'm trapped in a steam room.

Paris sits down on the other side of the bed next to me and groans. Why doesn't she stop faking the funk and just go back to her room? I know she's just waiting for Eric too, right in his bed.

Besides, she pisses me off, using big words all on purpose to test my knowledge. I'm not dumb. Always flaunting her college degree and her grade-school doubles before me like her wide ass. Truth be told, she's probably still mad at me all these years later for not going with her to FAMU like she begged me our senior year of high school. I just didn't want to. I was all wrapped up in Derrick, thinking he was the shit, but he turned out to be a big loser. And I regret not going to school with her, I really do, but I would never let her know that. I could have met a real rich husband down there. A college boy.

That's the reason why I didn't tell her I'm dropping out of DePaul University. I've actually already dropped out, withdrawing from two classes last semester and never registering for the new term. It's just too hard trying to get a degree part time and work. Plus, my heart's not in it. School's never been my thing. Eric doesn't know yet either.

"I am worn out from that massage," I hint, leaning back on the frosty comforter cover.

"Me too, I feel so drained," Paris says, fluffing Eric's pillow and propping it under her chin as she flips on the television.

It takes everything I have not to snatch the pillow from her cheek and order her out of the room.

She is all lustrous skin and raw sex, I think, reflecting on what a nemesis and friend she has been since high school. For me, Paris represents everything I never was, and it drives me insane. Yet and still, I remain her friend. A daily reminder of my inadequacies. Even my few superior qualities pale in comparison to her natural God-given beauty.

Paris' imperfections don't matter, men love her and that makes my gut ache with envy. She's a silky blonde tress dancing in the summer breeze. She's naturally thick, glossy black waves of hair. She's a pair of aqua-blue eyes so transparent their complex inner texture is displayed. She's the cashmere sweater I longed for as a young girl with my mother outside of the Marshall Fields store window, too poor to even enter.

She's a popular cheerleader, the epicenter of the 'in' crowd. A perfectly taut, cellulite-free ass. Flawless creamy peach skin. Paris is a set of shapely calves without stiletto heels. She's a symmetrical alabaster smile with pouty berry-stained lips. She's 18 years old.

She's the funniest joke, the wittiest retort and the most engaging conversation. She's lust and temptation.

Paris is a degree from Harvard, a burgundy drop-top Jaguar, a mansion atop a high hill overlooking plush green acres of land and anything else I can think of that I could never have or be.

How could Eric resist her? I couldn't. How can I compete? I can't.

I've always been second fiddle once a man sees her. I become invisible, like the dust mites you know surround you at all times, but don't acknowledge. My only two upperhand qualities, the ability to sing and my firm round boobs, aren't enough to swing the magnet of attraction away from her.

I'm the bronze medal. The leftover meal. With all the know-how my mother taught me about looking like a lady, I'm what men settle for. I'm the last child left standing in the sports line-up after the cream of the crop has been selected.

And the worst part about it is, Paris doesn't even have to try. She brushes her hair back in that tired ponytail while I get mine done religiously. I kill myself to stay trim, while she pigs out and exercises only sometimes, yet men swoon over her voluptuousness.

I guess the real terror is that she knows she's sexy and doesn't hide it. She flaunts herself in front of men, knowing what they like. She's been the albatross around my neck for years. Why do I torture myself?

"Mmn," Paris moans suddenly, awaking herself with a start. "I'd better go back to my room."

"Okay," I say, not pretending I want her to stay.

She stretches and compels herself off the bed while glancing at the clock. "I can go nap before we go out tonight."

"I don't know, it might storm pretty bad."

"Nah...look, it already stopped."

I glance out to the clearing sky, which is renewed with rays of light. "I want to, but I'm not sure Eric will be up to it, after hanging out with *your* husband all day."

"I'm sure AC will want to go, and so do I, so Eric will be outnumbered. Besides, tonight's the only night we get to really party in Miami, and we've got to check out some of these clubs here."

"Okay, just call me later on then."

"Okay," she says, finally leaving the room.

As soon as I hear the heavy slam of the door, I roll over on the bed and feel along the wall behind the nightstand. When I touch the plastic clip of the cord penetrating the socket, I unplug it. I figure if Eric comes in and tries to make a call and discovers the phone dead, I'll play dumb.

Next, I spring into action. Brushing my hair into a circular cone around my skull, I tie on my silk scarf and jump in the shower, using the fragrant Mariel body shampoo that Eric bought my last birthday. I save it to use only those times he comes over, and even though I've had it for months, I haven't run out yet.

After shaving all the vital areas, I lotion myself down and slip into the lengthy white nightgown that clings to my narrow frame, camouflaging my curveless, straight up and down hips. I brush out my hair until I'm satisfied with its shape, and apply light makeup.

Sliding back into bed, I wait for him. Watching television to pass the time, my eyes begin to close involuntarily, no matter how much I fight to keep them open.

After some time, a noise at the door wakes me up, and I get out of bed to greet him.

"Hey there," he says, smiling awkwardly.

"Hi," I force a smile.

Even though I'm pissed and want to ask him exactly where he's been the last few hours, I don't say anything. My mother always taught me not to be a nagging, questioning wife, bugging a man about his whereabouts as soon as he came home. That will make him want to leave, she says.

As I kiss him, I taste the bitter flavor of beer on his tongue.

"So, how'd you like the spa?" he spits out the words, careful in their pronunciation.

"It was really nice, I could get used to that. Did you have fun?"

"Yeah, it's a wild place. AC had me out there bar hopping. He didn't even want to come back till I told him I was leaving."

"I told you," I say, touching his arm, "he's out of control with that drinking. You can't believe anything he says."

"He is crazy."

Studying his mood, I usher him to the bed, and try to determine if AC has told him anything in their drunken camaraderie that I need to defend. How could I be so stupid and sleep with him? That's the kind of crazy shit that happens when I get drunk–I lose control. I hate getting that way, just like my mother when she drove drunk onto the exit ramp of the Dan Ryan expressway.

I can't worry, though. If AC did spill the beans to Eric, I would deny every word. There's no way Eric could handle knowing about my relationship with AC and Paris; it would be just too much of a shock. And men don't want that in a woman, another valuable lesson I learned from my mom. They want a virgin who knows how to fuck, and that is exactly what I am for Eric.

"You look all pretty."

"I dressed up for you," I whisper. "I've been waiting all night."

Leaning forward, I kiss him again, this time more urgently. Within seconds, his excitement presses against me and I lift his T-shirt over his head, helping him remove his shorts and underwear. From my vantagepoint, I can see the excited smile on his face as my mouth nears his crotch, so I quickly spring up towards his face again.

Of all the things I will do for this man, that is the one thing I won't do. It's a disgusting act, but I tell Eric I don't like giving head because I've never done it before and it's sinful. The times other men have forced my head down there, it didn't do anything for me so I chose not to do it anymore. So what if Eric still likes to eat me out, that's on him.

That's the one thing my mother and I disagree about, giving head. She says I'm crazy not to do it, that you can't keep a man without doing it, but I figure since she hasn't been able to keep one yet I'm not so sure she's the expert in that field. Besides, they pee out of that thing!

"Yeah," he squeals, entering me, and I do my best to do all the work, turning and twisting myself on top of him until he releases inside my womb.

I roll off and lie on my back, stretching my legs in the air to allow the semen to sit in a pool around my cervix, a technique I read about that supposedly increases the chance of pregnancy.

"Why do you always do that?" he laughs, his arm around my belly.

"I'm increasing the circulation in my legs. I don't want to get varicose veins."

"Of course not."

He kisses my cheek and rolls over, and within minutes his light breathing turns to a heavy snore. Drawing my knees to my waist, I stare at the ceiling, praying that Paris and AC don't just pop by when they can't get in touch with us on the phone. Luckily, they don't, and when I twist over into the fetal position and finally fall asleep, it's with the reassurance that Eric is all mine for the night.

📖

I even manage to keep him to myself most of the next day, promising Paris and AC through a slightly cracked door while Eric showered that we will meet them tonight at Bob's Books in South Beach for her scheduled reading.

I'm almost home free, just the reading tonight and then a trip to the Keys tomorrow and Friday back to Miami, where Eric and I will board a plane back to our normal lives.

In fact, maybe I could finagle a way to get out of going to the Keys. Even though I want to see them, my fear of Eric witnessing Paris in a bikini is stronger. Likewise, I don't want to mess up my hair snorkeling, and who cares about seeing Hemingway's house in Key West?

📖

Opening the vast bookstore's rainbow-stickered door that night, we are late, due to my reluctant stroll. But Paris is consumed, in the middle of a heated argument with a store employee.

"I'm sorry, I'm sorry," sputters the petite, Cuban man with skin as dark as tarnished silver. "We just don't have any record of you."

"But how could that be? I spoke with a Manny French and set up the reading for tonight. I sent him review copies, everything. Where is he?" Paris looks around the small store with desperation.

"He is no longer employed here–"

"Great!" she slaps her palms down hard against her bare legs, causing the pop to reverberate throughout the store. "Well, can't you set something up impromptu? I've got all my stuff."

"I'm sorry, we can't. We have other authors scheduled. We haven't advertised, made up any flyers..."

"But," Paris halts, her voice breaking, "we flew all the way down here."

"I'm sorry," the man repeats, walking away.

"Y'all need to get your shit together," AC calls after him, adopting the pace of a protective spouse.

"No, let's just go." Tears of defeat stream down her face.

"What are you crying for? This ain't worth it."

I am sickeningly satisfied watching something finally go wrong for Paris, and glad that our time together will be cut even shorter.

"Don't worry about it, girl," I console, "you have all those other cities to go to."

Eric stands back, with a look of sympathy that appears as though he might reach out and rub her back at any second. I grab his hand and follow Paris and AC onto the noisy street. They walk ahead in mumbled conversation for a few blocks, her tears and rapid breath abating.

"I know!" she stops abruptly and twists her torso to us. "I could have my reading on the beach!"

"What?" I ask.

"Yeah, right now."

"Nah..." AC shakes his head.

"Why not?" Eric says, loud enough to drown out my protests.

I look at him with amazement, but he is staring at Paris.

"I know, why not? I've read all about different sorts of unorthodox ways of promoting in that book *Publish Your Own Novel*."

"But right on the beach?" I yell to be heard. "What if somebody tries to steal the books?"

"Shoot to kill," AC says, patting his fanny pack.

"I don't think so." I pause, hoping everyone will let go of this stupid idea. Instead, it gains momentum.

"And these hurricane candles will stay lit outside, and I have everything we need to set up. We can all sit on the sand–"

I interrupt. "I am not sitting on no sand."

"Oh, Dana, come on. Here." She removes her linen jacket, revealing a clinging peach tank top that is engulfed by her wide shoulders and breasts. "You can sit on this."

"No, that's okay. I don't want to get it dirty." I push it away, but instead of putting it back on, she slings it over her arm and picks up her materials she had set down. "Let's go," she grins and weaves between the stalled traffic toward the beach.

Eric and AC follow like bloodhounds on a scent trail, leaving me running to catch up. Soon Paris finds what she deems the perfect location amidst a backdrop of pussy willow and sets up her display.

"This is perfect," she smiles. "It's a busy night, a good spot, people will at least stop by for curiosity's sake."

Before starting, AC lights the end of his fake cigarette weed pipe, the same one he used to take from my hands and blow me a gun from a joint instead, just to be close to my lips again. He passes it to Paris and she takes a quick puff, looking around nervously before exhaling it towards the ocean.

"You all are going to get us arrested out here," Eric says.

"No we won't," Paris smiles at him with intoxicating eyes that defy my presence. "Live a little."

"Not with that," he says.

"That's right," I agree, snuggling closer to him.

Paris lets out an intentionally loud hiss and takes her position on the burgundy tablecloth that serves as a blanket, copies of *The Sex Files* and flames surrounding her.

"Well, I guess I'll just start now." Paris extends her never-ending legs to the side and slouches forward as she flips through the book, stops, and then looks to Eric with her head cocked.

"This is from the chapter entitled *Fantasia*," she begins, with a raspy tone I've never heard from her before.

"The sun beats down mercilessly on my already bronzed flesh, broadly exposed in the skimpy red swimsuit that narrowly criss-crosses my breasts. I spread the thick musk oil down my abdomen and underneath the V-shaped bottom onto my bare pubic mound."

I cough quietly and try to recall this passage.

"Suddenly," she continues, "I become aware of a figure standing over me.

" 'You need help with that?' the shadowed silhouette asks.

"Leaning up to get a view of his face, I recognize the familiarity of my old friend's broad, even smile and lean body. His stomach muscles ripple like freshly poured golden honey.

58

" 'Kevin, what are you doing here?' I stretch to embrace him, his smooth bare chest rubbing against the oil on mine."

Eric shifts a bit away from me as Paris resumes, this time reading directly to him.

" 'I came for a swim.' he answers, pulling a chaise lounger closer to me and sitting on it.

" 'So, do you need help?' he repeats.

" 'Yes, actually. Would you do my back?' I hand him the bottle of oil and turn over, revealing the thong-like back of the suit that disappears between the mounds of my ass.

" 'My pleasure,' Kevin says, pouring the thick liquid onto his large palms then placing them onto the small of my back. I arch my spine and tilt my hips upward at his touch.

" 'Oohh, that's hot,' I moan.

" 'I'm sorry,' he says sweetly, removing his hands.

" 'No, it's just been baking in the sun–it feels good.'

"He pours the liquid onto my calves, firmly massaging the tight muscles. Stroking more oil onto my hamstrings, he spreads my legs open as his caress travels up my thighs."

I cut a glance down at Eric's shorts to determine if he is aroused, but I can't tell. His eyes are locked on Paris as she pauses to take a sip of bottled water and lick her lips. The flickering flames dance across her cleavage as people stop to listen, and AC focuses on a long-haired Latina girl in the crowd.

"Anointing my butt, Kevin catches the solution which streaks between my legs, his massive hands fondling my protruding lips from the Lycra. I turn onto my back as he instinctively slides the thin straps of material from my breasts and exposes my hardened nipples to the warmth of the sun. Encircling them with a flow of oil, he squeezes each simultaneously, then forcefully sucks one through his teeth and pinches the other. I moan loudly with pleasure, uncaring as to who might over-hear or watch.

"Positioning himself over me while nibbling my tits, he uses his free hand to fondle my swollen labia. The taut crotch grinds against my clitoris as he slips his long middle finger into my wetness."

More people begin to crowd around, but Paris continues to read as if Eric is the only one sitting on the windy beach. I am seething, willing myself to remain perched under his arm, confused as to why I don't remember this entry even though I scoured her entire book.

"I grab his hand, forcing his index finger into me as well. Tightening my walls around his digits, I groan as he places his swollen pouty mouth onto mine. He kisses me deeply, and I return the lust, sucking each lip as he battles to force his tongue inside. Kevin pushes a third finger deeper into me, the knuckles of his fingers pressing into the skin surrounding my opening.

"Suddenly, he breaks away and stands, his erection bulging over the top of his swim trunks. Surveying my semi-nakedness proudly, he slides his shorts down and over his ankles. His large penis falls forward, fully erect, hanging perpendicular to his body.

"Briefly he holds it in his hand, teasing me by stroking its length. Kneeling onto the lounger between my straddled legs, he pushes my suit to one side and gently enters my throbbing hole. I release a quiet scream and he a satisfying groan. His immense manhood fits very tightly, even with me dripping wet. Rhythmically, we move in sync, each thrust creating contractions of pleasure.

"He reaches underneath my arms and lifts me onto his brawny lap without removing himself from me. My body lunges upward as he presses into my cervix. The curve of his penis exacts thrilling pressure onto my G-spot and I find myself succumbing to the mounting orgasm that wells within. At the peak of my coming, he pounds more furiously into me, contorting his face in climatic ecstasy as his warm potion explodes into me.

"Reclining together on the chaise, still connected, we kiss. In silence, we reflect on the sparkling blue water of the nearby pool."

Paris closes the book and looks down. The small gathering stands still, they, like I, unsure of what they have heard and how to react. Eric draws his firmly planted arm from the sand, causing me to topple a little at the loss of support, and claps. Others join in until the thundering noise of applause drowns out the waves undulating against the shore in the background.

"Thank you," Paris blushes, seemingly embarrassed and exhilarated all at once. "Please, feel free to browse the book, don't feel obligated to buy anything."

Eric stands with me and joins the crowd surrounding her.

"I never did get my copy of the book," he says to Paris.

"Well, yours is on the house of course," she smiles, then turns her attention to other interested buyers.

I grab his arm. "Eric, can we go back to the hotel? I think I'm coming down with something."

"Alright," he responds, unable to hide the disappointment in his face.

"May I see your copy?" I ask, holding my stomach as we walk back to the hotel, feigning sickness the entire way.

"Do you want me to get you something?"

"No thanks," I say, flipping to the chapter Paris has just read from, frantically searching for the passage. I turn through the entire chapter again, making sure I haven't accidentally missed the pages. Just as I suspected, that risqué fantasy isn't even in the book; Paris concocted the entire thing just to read to Eric.

Slamming the book closed, I place it hard back in Eric's outstretched hand.

"What's wrong?" he asks.

"I think I'm going to throw up."

We speed up the pace until we reach our room, and I immediately run in the bathroom and turn on the water. Standing over the sink I compel myself to regurgitate, worshipping a familiar throne, heaving my stomach against my rib cage and easily choking up its contents. I truly am nauseated over the way Eric reacted to Paris' reading. And pissed at that bitch for reading it directly to him.

I decide right then and there as I loudly convulse into the sink that we will not spend another moment with them, and I'll use this fake sickness to skip the Keys tomorrow.

"Are you okay?" he says, entering the bathroom and rubbing my back.

I splash hot water onto my face and in my mouth. "No. I don't think I'll be able to make it to the Keys tomorrow."

"That's alright, you need the rest."

When the phone rings early the next morning, Eric picks it up immediately.

"Hello? Hey," he croons, his voice dropping an octave. "Yeah, Dana was sick. She came home and threw up...must've been something she ate."

"I'm still sick," I say sleepily. "I think I have the flu."

"She might have the 24-hour stomach flu or something. So," he turns to me, "I guess the Keys are out?"

I nod yes and close my eyes, silently cursing myself for plugging the phone back in its socket.

"Mmnn," Eric pauses. "Yeah, well I guess. Well, I could still go–"

My eyes pop open and I lunge straight up, grabbing his arm while shaking my head fervently.

"–wait hold on," he says, not placing his hand over the receiver. "What?"

"I want you to stay with me," I whine. "What if I need something?"

"I'll leave plenty of money. You can order all the room service you want. Plus, you'll probably just sleep all day."

"No I won't. I can go out."

"No, honey," he touches my face, "you're too sick. I'll go with them and give you a chance to rest. I can even get a separate car and drive back tonight instead of staying in Key West. I just want to go snorkeling."

"That's okay, I can go. I just won't swim."

Eric puts the phone back to his ear. "She's going to go...Yeah, she says she's okay now. Okay, see you later, bye."

Within an hour, the four of us are cruising down Interstate 1 in a rented red Mustang convertible to Key Largo. The road gives way to a lonely stretch of elevated bridge populated with gulls swooping overhead and the pungent smell of the salty ocean underneath. The songstress on the radio chants, *Who do you love? Are you sure?*

"You feel better now?" Paris asks from the front seat, her arm perched behind AC, who is driving.

"Yeah," I say stoically, "the sun will do me good."

As the bridge ends we continue past several of the red and white 'diver down' flags adorning dive shops.

"Let's go to one that has the reef dive at Christ of the Deep Statue," Paris tells AC.

"What?" Eric asks, leaning forward, brushing against the golden hair of her arm.

"You'll see, it's a beautiful statue of Jesus with his arms reaching up to you from underwater."

AC reluctantly turns into a shop with a Christ of the Deep Statue excursion sign out front, sucking his teeth as he puts the car in park. "I don't want to see a Jesus statue. This is lame."

"Come on," Paris says, "you know you love diving anywhere."

We enter the shop and get information on the next reef dive. Eric and Paris pay snorkeling fees and select their gear while AC provides the divemaster with his certification card and selects more extensive gear.

"You don't know what you're missing," Paris says to me as I walk over to her and Eric, smoothing my hand across his straight black hair.

"You all can have it," I say, rolling my eyes as AC approaches Paris with his equipment, like a child waiting for his mother to buy him a new toy. What a wuss, always broke.

"Man this pressure gauge sucks!" he complains, trying to divert attention from the financial transactions. "I knew I should have brought my own."

"I'm sure it'll be fine."

"If not, I'll be dead."

Everyone carries their equipment along a short pier and onto a small speedboat with our dive master. He starts the engine and expertly steers the craft through an area of boats onto the open ocean. The vessel smoothly slices through the small waves as the driver shouts instructions in case an emergency occurs.

Paris, of course, is the first one to undress, removing her T-shirt to reveal a triangular white bikini top. Next she slides her shorts over her butt and down her legs, and the matching string bottom gleams in the sun.

"Damn baby," AC says, placing his hand on her back. "When'd you get this one?"

"Recently," she says coyly.

"Well, you look hot."

Two can play this game, I think, removing my mid-riff ruffled shirt and blue jean shorts. Even though AC turns to look at me, I can tell Eric is staring at Paris' body, his eyes hidden behind Ray Bans. Isn't that ironic, my conservative two-piece, chosen with his requirements in mind, now makes me feel fully clothed next to the skimpy suit at which he now gawks. Men.

Soonthereafter the boat stops in a crowded area and our divemaster points to the designated diving area. "The diver should go in first," he instructs.

AC prepares and tests his gear, then jumps into the water. As Paris slips the life vest over her head and fastens it, Eric removes his black jogging shorts to expose bright yellow Speedo briefs. I see Paris do a double take.

"Be careful, don't swim too far" I say, grabbing his shirt and kissing him.

"Okay," he says, rushing to put on his vest.

"See you down there." Paris splashes into the water.

I watch him jump in after her and the two float away with their faces in the water, and I begin to wish I'd gotten equipment to go with them.

AC immediately swims under the water while Eric and Paris stay close together. From my vantagepoint, it looks like they could be holding hands, but I can't be sure. Paris pulls the tube from her mouth and speaks to him and they both laugh.

I want to know what they are saying, but the gentle tide sweeps them farther away. Squinting my eyes, I see Paris disappear under the water and then resurface after a few seconds. What is she doing? Is she touching him? I know she's not going down on him in front of me! I wouldn't put it past her.

"I need your life jacket!" I scream suddenly to the boat's driver, snapping him to alertness.

"Why?"

"I've got to get in the water, now."

"I'm sorry, I can't give you mine. It's against the safety re–"

"I have to," I say, grabbing my beach tote onto my lap and extracting my silver perfume purse spray. "My boyfriend forgot his medicine."

"What?" he says again, befuddled, staring at the cylinder wrapped around my hand.

"He forgot it, and if he doesn't have it right now, anything could happen. Especially in the water."

"Well, I could drive over to them and get him back in the boat."

I stand and wait for him to remove the jacket. "No, just give me yours, I'll jump in and be right back."

I literally snatch the vest from him and put it on, snapping each of the four locks closed. Jumping in, I grimace at the saltiness of the water I lick from my face and the thought of what my hair will look like later. But now, it doesn't matter, because I have to get closer to Eric and Paris, who has just disappeared below the water again.

Eric whips his neck around as I doggie paddle up to him. "What are you doing here? Where did you get that vest?"

"The driver gave it to me. I changed my mind and wanted to go swimming."

Paris surfaces after quite a while longer, lunging out of the water and gasping for air. "I touched him!" she coughs.

"Who?" I ask, noticing she doesn't have her vest on.

"Christ! What are you doing here?" she asks.

I ignore her question. "Where's your vest?"

"Eric has it. I had to take it off to get down there to touch Jesus. It was slimy," she frowns, wiping her fingers together in the seawater.

Eric holds the vest open for her like a coat, and as her torso lifts above the water while she slinks into it, I notice her suit is now transparent and the darkness of her hardened nipples shows easily through the fabric. He remains behind her as she buttons the hooks.

"They have pretty fish down here," Paris says, sticking her face in the water and floating away from us.

"Here you go, look." Eric places his mask and tube over my face.

I look under the water, not at the fish, but the definite outline of a fading erection in Eric's yellow briefs.

On the boat ride back to shore, AC speaks excitedly about the variety of fish and brain coral he witnessed. Paris stretches her lengthy body across one side of the boat and pours tanning oil down her cleavage and across her stomach. She stares at the bright sun while stroking it slowly across her torso.

"Did you have fun?" I say, hugging Eric.

He doesn't respond; instead he is mesmerized by the view.

📖

We arrive at the Centre Court Historic Inn and Cottages in Key West just as the sun is setting, and check into our individual cottages surrounding the pool. Before disappearing into the room, Paris calls out to us. "Well, I guess we missed going to Mallory Square to watch the sunset, but we can still go out drinking."

"Cool," Eric calls out, before I can say anything.

A while later, Paris shows up at our door alone, wearing a short black miniskirt and a beige rounded collar T-shirt.

"Where's AC?" I ask.

"We had a fight. He's not going," she says, not offering more.

Eric is jubilant as the three of us trot a mile to the heart of Duval Street, walking past barely clothed patrons and begging panhandlers. As we stride past one, he makes up an impromptu rap about us.

"Now this curious threesome, out for a night of fun, with a leader made of honey, just has to give me some money..."

Paris stops and smiles, realizing he's rapping about her. She digs into her purse for a few dollars and hands it to him.

We land at Captain Tony's, a rowdy bar with a crowd of women in tank tops and cut-off shorts.

"Margaritas for everyone!" Paris shouts as we sit down.

"I can't," I say. "I don't like those."

"Yes you do," Eric says. "I'll go get some."

He makes his way through the crowd to the bar for the drinks. Momentarily, he is back, balancing three large glasses in his hands and grinning.

"What's so funny?" I ask, taking one of the glasses from him.

"Oh, nothing."

"Thank you," Paris drawls.

Settling into the atmosphere of the packed bar, we read off the names of the states on the varied license plates hanging on the wall. Dusty bras and panties in all shapes and sizes hang from the wall.

I sip my drink, while Paris sucks hers down in gulps.

"Drink up," Eric says, placing his arm around me and motioning to my full glass.

"It tastes funny."

"Mine tastes a little weird, too. Maybe it's the salt or something. But it's still good!"

Towards the front, an arm wrestling contest between two women begins. "Hey, Dana. Let's arm wrestle," Paris yells.

"I'm not going up there."

"Okay," she leans across the table, "let's do it right here."

"I don't want to."

"Come on," she grabs my frail arm.

I put forth little effort as Eric steadies the tops of our hands with his and lets go. She slams my slender arm down to the table.

"No fair," she slurs, "you didn't even try."

"You know you're stronger than me anyway. That's a man's sport."

"You can't be that strong," Eric says. "I'll wrestle you."

My eyes nearly pop out of my head as I watch Paris eagerly switch into an empty chair close to Eric and grab his hand. They lock their hands and wait.

"Dana," Paris says, with a glimmer of erotic longing, "you've got to put your hand on top to start us."

I place my hand on top of theirs, wanting to dig my nails into her flesh. I let go.

She and Eric begin to struggle and stare at each other while grunting. It seems like they stay that way an eternity, Paris hunching closer until her knees straddle his and their legs touch under the table. At last, Eric forces her hand down onto the table.

"You beat me," she pants, and they continue to hold hands for a few seconds, laughing.

"Of course," Eric says, picking up his drink with his free hand and taking a swig. I stare at their interlocked hands until they finally let go, but under the table I see their legs are still intertwined.

Eric orders more margaritas from the passing waitress.

"Why don't you leave your bra here on the wall?" I say suddenly, knowing her droopy titties won't look flattering in the top she's wearing.

Eric nearly spits out his drink. Paris is silent for a few seconds, but then stands up. "I like this bra too much, but I can leave my panties here."

My mouth drops ajar as she reaches under her skirt and pulls beige underwear down her unbent legs, providing a full view of her breasts within a push-up bra as she leans down an extra-long time.

"Thongs." She snaps the minuscule panties in front of us and sits down.

Shocked, I ask dumbly, "Don't those hurt?"

"There is pleasure in pain," she coos, handing her panties to Eric. "Will you put them up there for me?"

"Sure," he says, finding a spot to place the underwear.

"Aren't you going to take off something?" Paris glares with an evil smile.

"No." As soon as Eric sits back down, I say firmly, "I'm ready to go."

"Come on, it's so early."

Shit, he really wants to stay. I don't want to argue with him, especially in front of Paris, so I decide to let it go for the moment. I take a drink and listen to a group of drunken people next to us break out in song. The chorus starts with a line *'I ate the last mango in Paris'* that is repeated over and over again.

"Paris," Eric says tipsily, "they're saying your name."

"They're eating a mango in me," she laughs, and I can hardly believe my ears.

That's it. I gulp down the second drink the waitress has placed before me and stand. This time Eric and I are leaving and I'm not taking no for an answer. As I bolt up, dizziness overcomes me and I feel the alcohol I've consumed come rushing into my mouth.

"What's wrong?" Eric says, standing.

I can only place my hand over my mouth and run off in the direction of the ladies room. With Eric following, I push my way past all the drunken patrons and head directly into the bathroom, exploding my stomach contents in the sink.

Sums of liquor burn my throat as I hold my head and allow cool water to run over my hands. It reminds me of the day in fourth grade Dwight Albritton teased me so bad for not having a father that I couldn't stop crying. The tears flowed effortlessly ever since. It's like that with my vomiting, once I start the wheels in motion they don't stop.

I decide to not move for a while, a good idea because soon I throw up again, this time only the yolk-colored bile that is the last of my stomach's contents.

Finally, when I am sure nothing else is inside me, I rinse my mouth out thoroughly and leave the ladies room. Eric isn't, however, standing right outside the door like I expect so I push through the crowd to the area in which we were sitting. A different group is now there.

"Oh no," I say out loud, exiting the bar and searching for his face in a panic. While I was puking my guts out, Paris has actually cajoled Eric away. I walk blindly through the maze of people, unsure of where I am going.

As I approach Sloppy Joe's, my mind reels with visions of their bodies pressed hungrily against each other, him sucking her flesh and plunging his dick into her pantieless pussy in some corner of the island.

"No," I say again, out loud, as I turn in a complete circle outside of the bar. Eric and Paris are suddenly in front of me.

"Are you okay?" Eric says with a strange look on his face.

"Where were you? Why are you all the way over here?" I whimper, my eyes watering.

"Paris got sick too," he says, pointing to her as she clutches her stomach and leans over, not looking at me.

"So why didn't she come in the bathroom?"

"I don't know," she says, leaning up. "I just ran outside." Her lipstick is gone from her mouth.

"We better get you two back to the hotel," Eric says, walking in that direction.

As we all walk in silence, Paris keeps grabbing her stomach and stopping, but she never throws up, only dry heaves.

The next morning, I arise early with the others to tour Ernest Hemingway's house, a landmark Paris just has to see before we head back to Miami. After her being so sick last night, I thought she would have canceled the sightseeing but she didn't. In fact, she bounces excitedly around the home, carefully avoiding the plenitude of six-toed cats underfoot while I walk sluggishly behind.

"Are you sure you don't want to go sit down somewhere?" Eric inquires.

"No, I'm okay," I lie, knowing I look like death warmed over. The truth is I'm not letting Eric out of my sight for one second until we are well on our way back to Chicago.

"Did you know Hemingway would get up early, come into this room and write until he used up about eight pencils?" Paris says brightly to AC.

"Oh," is his only response.

I gather that he is still mad, for some unbeknownst reason. If only he knew about last night.

"So, Paris, do you feel better?" I hint.

"Yeah," she says, "after I threw up, I felt fine."

"That's what you get for drinking so much," AC smirks.

So, I guess he does know something, but that still doesn't prove anything to me. Eric swears nothing happened, and all of me wants to believe him. Whether it did or not, I am sure of two things: Paris is no longer my friend, and after we leave Miami, she will never lay eyes on my man again.

On the drive back to Miami, I nap in the car and am dazed when I awake at the airport. Walking inside the terminal, I look up at the screen to read our gate number.

"Okay," I say sleepily, "I guess we'll go to our gate now." I hug Paris lightly and give AC a short squeeze.

Eric reaches out and embraces Paris, and like the arm wrestling, holds her a little too long.

"Well, I have a surprise for you two," she says, pausing. "You're going with us! I got you guys tickets to New Orleans and Colorado!"

Chapter 4

New Orleans, Louisiana

The serpent beguiled me, and I did eat.

Genesis 3:13

Rows of tombs jut above the ground and soon, a circular basin appears through the hazy fog of the gulf city. The aerial view is entrancing, but mainly, I am fed up with Dana's yapping, which has been going non-stop since our non-stop flight from Miami.

"And why do we all have to stay in the same hotel room? She couldn't find another room in the whole town?"

"She told you that the hotel is real nice; people book it months in advance. Stars stay there. Plus, she said it's a two-bedroom town house with two bathrooms. It's not like we're staying in the same room."

Dana twists her face with contempt, an expression I think makes her look ugly. "I don't have any clothes to wear, and I can't believe she had the nerve to call my boss and request more time off. What if I wanted to use the rest of my vacation days later?"

"Come on, we haven't been nowhere since Disney World over a year ago. At least now we'll get to go to New Orleans and Colorado, free of charge. How can you beat that?"

Her eyes narrow, burrowing into mine. "Why are you sticking up for her? You like her don't you? Something happened last night, didn't it?"

"No!" I yell in a quiet, defiant whisper. "I already told you nothing happened and I wish you would stop asking me! She got sick. Now she's trying to be nice to you, and she's spent all this money on you and look how you're treating her. I wish I had a best friend to take me on vacation. And instead of saying thank you, you roll your eyes at her. That's just plain rude."

I turn my head away, but soon, I feel Dana's petite hand on my leg.

"You're right, I'm sorry. I know better than that; I'm a Christian. I just get so crazy, because I love you so much."

"Me too." I pat her hand, content with the silence.

She bought it. Thank God. Dana wouldn't be this quiet if she had privy to my memory of last night, with me and Paris groping and pulling at each other's clothes and kissing hungrily in intoxicated passion. I pressed her against the brick wall of the bar while fondling her plush body, pausing only to check for Dana's presence, then licking her face to savor the taste of her once again. She reminds me of a porn star I've seen in Heather Hunter's films, a beautiful Black co-star who always wears her hair brushed back. Paris is my living fantasy.

It was that comehither smell of Mariel on her neck, oddly familiar on Paris as opposed to Dana, tempting yet guilt producing while I tasted sensuality, drank pleasure, then pushed her away.

"What have I done?" I said, stepping back, too late to reverse the damage, suddenly sober. My fingertips flew to my head, as if to press the answer into my temple. None came, so I took her irresistible body into my arms and devoured her until the next time she forced me back.

"Here she comes!"

I stopped, sighting Dana just beyond the crowd, walking aimlessly.

Paris composed herself. "I'll say I was sick," she slurred, doubling over.

My girlfriend spotted us. Take One, I was on my mark, and there began the charade.

📖

"Nawlan's," AC repeats in a southern drawl, from the airport to the Maison de Ville, a romantic eighteenth-century mansion in the French Quarter. Entering the black wrought iron gates, we stroll through a steamy garden filled with lush tropical plants.

I am stimulated by the exciting new city, one I've never before visited. The funk I was slipping into at the airport, when I thought I would be returning to my rut of a life in Chicago with Dana, has been rapidly replaced with possibilities of the unknown with Paris.

Go for what you know, I can hear my older brother Anthony saying in my head. His mac-daddy self would have already bedded her by now, as aggressive as he is with women, even though married with kids. I've just never been that bold. I'll have to find a way to get Paris in bed in my own time. At least now I know she definitely wants me too; it's not just my imagination.

"This is sweet," Dana admits as we enter the #4 Audobon Cottage through the private courtyard.

"I told you," I say, admiring a fireplace in the center of the room, which is replete with antique furnishings.

"It ain't six-hundred bones a night nice," AC huffs setting his huge green duffel sack down with a thud.

"Please! How could you say this is not worth it? Look at this place." Paris stretches her lovely arms before her. "Tennessee Williams wrote *A Streetcar Named Desire* here."

"Who?" Dana asks.

Paris sighs deeply and wanders around the townhouse. "I want to see you guy's room."

"Okay," I say, unable to look her in the eye. "What time is that bus picking us up?"

She glances at her watch. "In about an hour so we better start getting ready."

"Shit, I'm ready to chill." AC bounces on one of the beds.

"Me too," Dana agrees.

AC slaps the space next to him on the bed, but Dana ignores the gesture. I wish she did like him, then maybe that would take some of her attention away from me and Paris. But I know Dana would never go for someone like him. He's not her type.

"You all afraid to go in the swamp?" I tease, adding levity to my voice.

"I ain't afraid of jack," AC jumps up, yelling. "I'll wrestle a fucking alligator in a minute."

"What if they jump in the boat with us?" Dana widens her eyes with her forever-animated expression.

"They won't," Paris says, also now avoiding my glance. I force myself to look her in the eyes, attempting to mask the uneasiness that we both feel.

"Speaking of which," AC pulls a thin joint from his pocket, "we must prepare."

"Okay," she says, and a twang of jealousy actually pops into my heart as I watch her follow her husband back to their suite.

I hate that she smokes herb, and cigarettes for that matter, such a beautiful girl with a bad habit, probably picked up from that no good husband. What does she see in someone so repulsive and mean? To top it all off, the man doesn't have any money and treats her like shit.

Showering and changing quickly, Dana and I meet the group outside at the tour bus. On the 45-minute drive southeast to Honey Island Swamp, I tune out the excited passengers as they chat of mythical swamp monsters.

Upon arrival, we are led to a small boat with a makeshift bench down the middle that sits each group on either side. Luckily, AC walks on first, Paris next and then me followed by Dana. To make room for the other members of the group that can't fit on the opposite side, I slide down until Paris' bare leg is touching mine.

We creep through the eerie marsh, sailing under moss hanging like drapery from gnarled cypress trees. Our tour guide, Dr. Paul Wagner, identifies sounds for us as he tosses marshmallows into the black water, hoping to entice a sweet-toothed alligator into making an appearance.

"Looking for Wookie?" Paris turns to me and asks, referring to the legendary swamp monster Paul has just mentioned.

"Yeah," I laugh.

"See that shack, there?" Paul asks, pointing to an abandoned shadow beyond the trees. "It used to be a trapper's house, people that used to kill the local animals and sell their fur for a living."

Dana begins talking nervously to a couple seated nearby. She is terrified of the dark.

Grateful for her distraction, I long to reach out and feel Paris' baby soft flesh again. If only I can get her alone at some point, I can tell her to meet me somewhere.

But how on Earth will I get rid of Dana? Just then, a thought occurs to me. "I've got some relatives in New Orleans, you know," I say to Dana, placing my arm around her.

"Oh yeah, you told me before. That's why you're so fine, you got that Creole blood in you." She kisses my nose, and I promptly wipe off the spot of orange lipstick I'm sure is there.

"I should look them up, I haven't seen them in years. My Aunt Adrienne, her kids."

"You should."

"I'm gonna call my mother and get their address."

"Yeah, then we could go visit them."

Dammit, I should have known she'd want to go. "Yep, if we have time." I'll have to think of a reason why I must visit them alone.

The guide cuts the motor, allowing more sounds of the night to come alive. Owls and other nighttime creatures make their appearance known as we coast through the green duckweed on the murky surface. I stare at a small deer standing stationary in a clump of grass.

Suddenly, a flash of white rises to the surface of the swamp.

"Look!" Paris shouts, touching my leg as she notices the same white mass, just before it ducks below the water.

"What?" AC asks, seemingly in slow motion.

"I think it was an alligator," Paris says.

"Where?" Dana leans forward and squints into the blackness.

"I saw it too," I confirm. "It was white!"

"An albino?" Paul says, breaking his monotone dialogue. "Those are good luck for anyone who sees them."

Paris and I grin knowingly at each other.

📖

"Today I'm going to read from a section of my book called *The Magic Number*," Paris begins the next afternoon, as Dana, AC and I sit on stiff folding chairs in a poorly ventilated auditorium where several poets and authors are reading from their works to an eclectic crowd.

"The magic number is a nickname I use to refer to the number of sexual partners one has had, and it means very different things to men as opposed to women. This is evidenced by the bragging rights accorded celebrities such as Gene Simmons of the rock group Kiss and Wilt Chamberlain, who have both claimed to have slept with thousands of women. When men speak of the two celebrities, while mentally calculating the possibility of that many liaisons, it is usually with an envious grin.

"Women, however, debate over whether their number should even be exposed. This, of course, is usually only the case when more than one hand is needed to count the number. Some women who have had five or less lovers use the small tally as their bragging right to virtuosity. Others, like me, are more forthright. My number, ladies and gentleman, drumroll please...is 57."

My sharp intake of breath joins a smattering of involuntary gasps and chuckles, some of which come from Dana. Paris places her hand on her abdomen, as if to steady it with a look that pleads for silence. Once the noise subsides, she continues.

"I've felt emotions ranging the gamut regarding my promiscuous past. Sometimes, I reflect on it with a sense of pride, like a brazen Don Juan carving notches of conquests into the proverbial bedpost. Whenever my girlfriends would complain about being unhappily celibate, I would gloat about never having experienced that problem, always being able to find a man. While my needy ego believed that men were continually falling into my lap, I now realize that my friends were being a little more selective and honoring themselves, instead of giving in to every other Joe Blow that came along.

"More often than not, the number embarrasses me, and before writing this book, I kept it fairly hidden. The only time I would offer the truth of my checkered history was when I was beginning a new relationship with someone I truly cared about, like I did with my husband. Even then, I worried about his reaction, but I wanted to give him the knowledge up front as to what he was getting himself into. At least I pride myself on being honest, which is more than I can say for some of my girlfriends, who have counts just as high or even higher than mine but lower them significantly with the justification that their mates could not handle the truth."

Dana shifts in her seat, grabbing at her lower back. "These chairs are horrible," she whines, but I keep my focus on Paris, who has finally looked at me through the throng of people.

"I think the reality is that they can't deal with it themselves, and choose to bury that part of their life like an abuse victim who denies hurtful violations. But, the only way to heal is to claim your past, which in essence, says you accept that part of yourself, you don't label it in chauvinistic terms and have moved beyond the shame of the experience. The past is the past and cannot be changed.

"There are advantages. At least I don't wonder about what I've missed, like some women who married with very limited or no sexual experience. Through the grace of God I never obtained a sexually transmitted disease and am AIDS-free.

"So I can only reflect positively on my past. Afterall, the men I've slept with, some wonderful human beings and some not worth the time of day, meld into a mosaic that, like all the books I've read and places and people I've encountered, make me who I am today. This book would not be here without those experiences, which ultimately taught me that sex does not equal love. Luckily, I no longer look for affection in that vein. No pun intended."

A few people laugh as I chuckle to make it seem as though I get the joke. Paris concludes, still looking to me.

"Good or bad, I am who I am. Take it or leave it."

Several women in the room stand and begin applauding fervently, until the entire group is on their feet cheering. My queasiness over the number of men she has had sex with is tempered by the sheer adulation she is enjoying this very moment, and I realize, like probably many of the men in the room, that I would take it.

Paris is ecstatic after leaving the reading, and literally bounces down the cobblestone street where the four of us are walking. "Let's go to Bourbon Street, we haven't been yet."

"Cool with me," AC says, banging his fresh cigarette pack against the palm of his hand.

"But it's still daylight," Dana says, glancing at her watch. "You always want to drink."

"I just want to celebrate."

"Where to?" I ask, already following Paris and AC in the direction of the bars.

"Pat O'Briens. Home of the dreaded hurricanes!" Paris shouts.

We find the historic bar and get drinks to go, and I think of how I tipped the bartender in Key West to add grain alcohol to the women's drinks, and how they almost caught on. This time I just get normally strong drinks containing Bacardi 151 Rum and hand Dana hers.

"I've never seen you drink this much in your life," she says, eyeing her drink suspiciously.

"I'm on vacation!" I say, and walk fast to catch up with Paris and AC, who are heading into a nearby store.

Inside, risqué T-shirts and drawings hang between painted masks. AC heads directly for the elaborate array of dildos on the wall and picks up a huge black one. "Hey Dana, here you go."

"How disgusting," she says, folding her arms and stepping toward the entrance. *"Men of perverse heart shall be far from me; I will have nothing to do with evil.* Let's go outside."

I walk behind her, but stop just shy of stepping outside, and instead dart over to Paris in another corner of the store.

"How's your drink?" she asks, glancing at me from the corner of her eye while inspecting a T-shirt displaying skeletons in a variety of sexual positions.

"It's good," I say quietly. "I can't get used to walking down the street and drinking liquor. I keep thinking I need to hide it."

"Me too," she laughs. Then, holding her drink out to me, she says, "Taste mine."

I dip my finger into the creamy mixture, but before I can raise it to my mouth, she bends her mouth down and engulfs it with her lips, sucking the length of my flesh and pressing her tongue against the tip. I am speechless, and immediately hard.

Looking away, Paris begins speaking in a loud, forced tone. "I don't know if this stuff is really worth the price."

"It's starting to rain," Dana says, suddenly behind me, panicking. "I don't have an umbrella. We have to go now!"

Paris calls to AC and all of us leave the store in a rush, running back to the hotel. The springtime storm is fast and hard, and by the time we make it safely back in our cottage, we are all soaked to the bone.

"Hey, do you guys want to come to our room to watch a movie? They have a video library here we can rent from. I'll go pick up a couple," Paris declares, leaving the room once again.

"Cool." Anything to keep us together, I think.

"Look at my hair," Dana says, inspecting her wet mop of a bob in the mirror.

"Damn woman, will you stop complaining about your hair?" AC says, removing his shirt and wiping his bald head with it. "If you wouldn't denature yourself with those relaxers, you wouldn't have to worry about it. You need a fade or some dreads or something."

"Negro please," Dana says.

Dana and I change into dry clothes and head back to their room, but Paris is in the bathroom.

"What movies did she get?" I ask.

"Some crazy shit," AC says, lighting a cigarette by the open window. "Love stories, I think."

"Oh no," I say.

"I should have gone," AC says.

"What wrong with love?" Dana asks, her freshly washed hair tied in a scarf.

"What's right with it?" AC asks. "I want to see some blood and guts."

"And explosions," I add, trying to perpetrate a connection with him.

As Paris enters the room, the three of us stop talking and stare. She is wearing a gray romper that is so short, I can see the bottom of her ass. A few buttons are undone and although she has on a bra, the outline of her nipples protruding through the soft cotton is apparent.

"You guys can take the bed; get comfortable," she says, plopping down next to AC. As his ashes fall onto the couch from the jolt, he frowns.

"They had all my favorites," she continues, bounding up again to turn off the light and start the movie. "*The Player, The Professional* and *The Lover*. This is *The Lover*."

"The only one I've heard of is *The Professional*," I say.

"Yeah, let's watch that," AC says.

"No, that one's gross, isn't it?" Dana asks.

"Yeah, it's pretty violent," Paris says above the heavy thud of raindrops falling on the banana leaves outside.

"I don't care, let's watch it," AC says, jumping up and switching movies.

We watch the entire movie, with Dana covering her eyes throughout most of it.

"Okay, now *The Lover*," Paris says, popping out that tape and placing in another.

"I'm sleepy," Dana looks to me with anticipation.

"Take a nap," I tell her, staring at Paris' body, outlined through the snow on the television screen. Her one-piece has ridden farther up her butt as she stoops down to the VCR.

"I know I'm falling asleep on this shit," AC says, stretching out over the length of the sofa.

After starting the movie, Paris tries unsuccessfully to recline in front of him. "Move over," she grumbles.

"I'm all the way back. You know you're too damn big to fit here. Why don't you get on the floor?"

"Forget you," she says, rolling onto the floor.

The movie is good, a tad slow for my pace, but eventually leads up to some very erotic scenes between a well-built Asian actor and a thin, sensuous, youthful woman. I listen and as Dana's breathing turns deeper, Paris and I periodically exchange a glance.

AC, too, has fallen asleep, as witnessed by his loud snoring.

"This floor is so hard," Paris whispers, standing, then turning to make sure AC and Dana are still asleep.

I move the covers back gently for her to slide in next to me. She does, and we both are motionless, pretending to still watch the movie as my heart pounds with excitement and fear.

After inspecting Dana's uniform wheezing for several more minutes, I move my hand to Paris' bare thigh and rest it there. She doesn't move or say a word, so I continue up her legs. Parting them slightly, she provides me with perfect access up the back of her romper.

One by one, I move my fingers onto her bare bottom and squeeze. I hear her moan slightly and rotate her hips a little. Sliding my middle finger between her legs, my heartbeat races as I feel the tickle of her curly hair. In clockwise circles, I play with her until a slight wetness on the tip of my finger hones me inside and makes her body rise.

Suddenly, Dana shifts and Paris tightens around my finger. We both remain still until I hear Dana resume snoring. I thrust deeper, stimulated by warmth and danger. Paris rocks against my hand, then quietly reaches back to caress my hardness.

Just as I reach forth to explore her breasts, Dana stirs. I remove my fingers from inside of Paris and glance back at the television.

"This movie still on?" Dana asks, disjointed.

"Yeah," I say, "it's good."

"Are they still watching it?"

"No, I think they're both sleep."

Dana sits up, realizing Paris is next to me in bed. "We better go."

"Okay," I say, without argument.

Dana and I get out of the bed, waking AC. "Hey, where y'all going?"

"To our room," Dana says, yawning.

"I told you it would put you to sleep."

Paris turns over, stretching, as if she has just awakened. "It's a good movie."

"It was good," I say, then pretending to yawn, place my hand to my mouth. When AC and Dana turn away, I lick my fingers. "The part I saw, it was very good. I've got to see more."

"Yes," Paris smirks, "you must."

Back in our room, I don't have to guess if Dana is mad, I can tell by the way she unties the fabric from her hair and brushes it hard, the way my mother used to slam dishes into the cabinet when my father had made her angry. She doesn't know exactly what happened, but she knows something wasn't right.

As we retire, she kisses me forcefully, as if to seal the affection onto my lips. Then, after a few moments in the darkness, she says stoically, "*For the lips of a strange woman drop as a honeycomb, and her mouth is smoother than oil; but her end is bitter as wormwood, sharp as a two-edged sword.*"

I say nothing, pretending to already be asleep.

📖

The next afternoon, I gaze distractedly at sea lions while Dana locks her arm in mine and shakes, urging to me to be as excited as she. I cannot muster the energy of eagerness, for I don't want to be at the Audubon Zoo, a place where I'd normally love to spend long, languid hours inspecting all species of animals. It's a tourist stop that Dana defied me not to visit with her this morning, after making no mention of attending Paris' bookstore appearance happening simultaneously.

But I am plotting, because after yesterday, there is no way I'm spending the entire day with Dana. I have to have Paris. It's just that simple.

"Let's go see the reptiles," Dana says after the show ends, glancing down at her brochure.

"I have to go to the bathroom first," I say.

"Okay, I think they're over there. I'd better go, too."

I enter the men's room as Dana walks into the opposite door, but turn back and head to the nearby payphone. Dialing the hotel's phone number, I anxiously watch the women's room exit for Dana.

"Maison de Ville, may I help you?" a chipper voice answers.

"Yes, I need to leave a message for Eric Toomey in cottage #4."

"I'll ring that room—"

"No! I just need to leave a note. Just tell him that his Aunt Adrienne called and wants him to come visit her tonight."

"Adrienne? A-d-r-i-"

"Yes, yes," I hurry her along, watching Dana exit the bathroom and walk toward me with a look of confusion.

"Okay, is there a number where you can be reached?" the woman hesitates, waiting for my reply. Instead, I gently set the receiver down.

"Who were you calling?" Dana peers without blinking into my eyes.

"The hotel. I was checking for messages to see if my mother called. You know Stephanie is due any day now and I wanted to see if everything is okay."

"Did they call?"

"No," I pause, taking her hand, "but my Aunt Adrienne called, the one I told you lives here, saying she talked to my mother and found out I was down here and that I better come see her."

"Where does she live?"

"I don't know, I have the address written down. I think it's pretty far away."

"Well, I guess we'll just have to take a cab then."

I hold my breath and grab her hand tighter. "Honey, I don't know if it's such a good idea if you go with me."

"Why?" Dana stops.

"Well, it's just, my aunt is a really religious person, and she has this thing about couples being together without benefit of marriage."

"What? That's stupid. We're just going to visit her, it's not like we'll be sleeping there right?"

"Right, but she's just...I mean, she reads the Bible every day and she says it's wrong for anyone to fornicate. You know that. That's why all her daughters moved away from home so early. She's really strict. I don't want to you to have to suffer through one of her lectures."

"I wouldn't even want to visit someone like that."

"She's my mother's sister, and my mother really wants me to see her. It would make her day, her whole year."

I force a quick smile and check my watch. If I hurry, I can still make it to the bookstore to meet Paris before she leaves.

"When are you going?"

"We really should leave here right now so I can go back to the hotel with you, then catch a cab out there. I want to spend some time with her but I don't want to be all the way out there all night."

"What am I going to do? I don't have anywhere to go." Dana sighs heavily. "I guess I could go see Paris at the bookstore..."

I try to keep my voice even. "No, I don't want you going all the way over there by yourself, this is a dangerous town."

"What am I supposed to do? You'll be gone all night!"

"Maybe you could go somewhere in the French Quarter, close to the hotel. While it's still light outside."

"Okay," she says, looking sad.

"Don't worry," I place my arm around her shoulder, "it won't be that long."

"Better not be," she says I as drag her toward the zoo's exit. "Slow down!"

"Hurry up!" I counter, pulling her into the next available cab.

"Aren't we going to take the ferry back?"

"No, I want to just drop you off and continue on to my aunt's house."

"Okay." Dana looks up to the driver, an older bald Black man resembling B.B. King. "We're going to the Maison de Ville's Audobon Cottages, but then he'll go on to..."

I fish around in my pocket for a fictitious address. "Uhh, where is it? I have it written down. I think it's somewhere near where we went to that swamp."

"Honey Island?" Dana says, losing the sweet tone in her voice.

"That's quite a haul," he says.

"I'm not sure, I'll find it. Let's just go to the hotel first, and I'll find it. I might be wrong."

"You didn't tell me it was that far away."

"I don't know," my voice rises with annoyance as I open my wallet and flip through endless pieces of paper. "I'm not sure where anything is here. I've never been here before."

Throughout the entire ride to the hotel, I continue to search for the fake paper. Stopping in front of the hotel, I urge Dana to exit the cab.

"But if you can't find the address, how will you know where to go? Don't you want to come in and call her?" she stands outside the car, peering through the open window.

"No, I know we need to get on the highway, so I'll find it by that time. If not, I can stop at a pay phone."

"Alright, well just call me when you get there."

"I'll try, but I don't want to be using her phone. I'll just be back here tonight. You be careful if you go anywhere."

"You be careful," she says, leaning into the back seat to kiss me.

"Okay." After the car window is completely closed, I turn to the driver. "Garden District Bookshop, please."

He looks through the rear-view mirror, grins and drives off. Dana waves at me from the curb.

Twisting in the back seat, I pray silently that AC won't be there with her. If he is, I can always duck out before either of them sees me. Wussing out, is what my brother Anthony would say. He's so bold he'd walk right up to a woman with her man and ask for her phone number. And then proceed to talk shit if the guy says anything to defend his honor.

It makes me smile, the way he is, so different from me. Sometimes I wonder if we are actually related, and that I'm not, like he always used to tease, adopted from another family. Shyness was never his problem. Nothing ever seems to be his problem. He was and is the perfect child in the family: the honor roll student, the MVP on our high-school basketball team. The one all the ladies swoon over, even now, though he's a married father.

Anthony needs the attention to feed his ego. Pushing 35-years-old, he still needs the admiration of women and, in a different manner, men, to tell him that he's still the best. He can keep it; I don't even need to compete. I learned to stop trying a long time ago with him. To him, my younger sister Renee and I will always be know-nothing little siblings no matter how much success we've had, in business or in love.

Even though I don't admire his tactics, I must admit that it's his type of aggressiveness that explains why I'm with a mediocre woman like Dana when I want to be with a stunner like Paris. And as the cab pulls up in front of the store where I'll try to steal away another man's wife to make love to her, I feel just like my brother.

I breathe a sigh of relief when I see Paris, without AC, talking with a patron. She smiles a wide-mouthed, Paula Joi Parker grin when she sees me approaching, but continues to speak with the woman, who clutches a copy of *The Sex Files* to her heart.

"...and I never got over that," the woman says, cutting a glance at me.

"Well, it's difficult," Paris says. "We're all prisoners at some point of how we were raised. My best friend never got over not knowing her father. She makes up all these elaborate stories about how he was decapitated when he drove his car under a truck. She has huge abandonment issues."

"Yeah. Well, thank you again. I'm sure you'll be a big success."

"Thank you, and I appreciate your support." The woman walks away and Paris immediately hugs me. "What are you doing here?"

"I came to see you," I say, holding her closely, as long as I want before letting go. "AC's not here, is he?"

"No, he's probably at some strip joint somewhere."

"Good, so it's just you and me."

"Yep, where's Dana?" Paris places her hands on her hips, so that her form-fitting flowered dress rises slightly above her bare thighs.

"I told her I was visiting my aunt."

"Cool, so we can hang out tonight."

"Yeah, are you done here?"

"Yep, you're lucky you caught me, I was just about to leave."

I grab the back of her neck with my open hand. "Well, leave with me."

"Okay, maybe we could go eat. The Pontchartrain Hotel is near here, and everybody tells me how good it is. Are you hungry?"

"I could eat something," I wink.

Paris grins. "Well, I better leave AC a message and make up an excuse first."

She disappears towards the back of store for a few minutes and then comes back out, taking my hand and leading me outside.

"So what'd you say?"

"Surprisingly, he was there. I said the bookstore people were taking me out to dinner and drinks. He wanted to come."

"Uh oh."

"I know, I told him I'd call him later to join up with us but I think it will slip my mind."

We both laugh with the exhilaration of finally being alone, strolling hand in hand like a normal couple past huge mansions with yards overflowing with colorful flowers.

"Isn't it beautiful here?" Paris asks, staring lovingly into my eyes.

"You're beautiful," I say, kissing her hand.

Entering the posh Caribbean Room restaurant of the hotel, Paris is awed by the huge painting of a beach village that takes up nearly an entire wall.

"We're just in time for an early dinner," she says, as our host leads us to a cozy table in a room with exposed brick walls.

"I love these chairs." I sink into the cushy forest green Louis XVI armchair like Alice in Wonderland.

"Let's see what looks good." Paris opens the menu and gushes over the selection. "I don't know where to start, so much good food."

"I think I'll get the 16-ounce porterhouse."

"You mean you're going to eat red meat in New Orleans? With all this delicious fresh seafood?"

"I don't like seafood."

"What? It's so good. It's so...erotic."

"Just like you," I grin.

I reach for a warm piece of the fresh-baked bread from the basket and eat it quickly while Paris blushes.

"I see you like bread."

"Yep. Order whatever you'd like, it's my treat."

Paris looks up, surprised. "That's so sweet."

"You deserve it, you've been so nice to me."

"In that case, let's get a bottle of red wine. Do you drink wine?"

"Yeah. No problem."

Three glasses into the wine we'd ordered, our meals arrive, my sumptuous steak and Paris' butterflied shrimp.

"You don't know what you're missing," she toys, placing the large prawn inside her lips and sucking it before devouring the flesh. "Seafood is so delectable."

"Is it, now?"

"Yeah, especially oysters. But I'm afraid to eat those ever since I saw this report that said they gave some people hepatitis. I've come this far without catching any diseases, and I don't want to tempt fate."

"So, like you said at your reading, you've been tested for HIV?"

"Twice. Have you?"

"Yeah, once by my family doctor. I'm negative."

Paris drinks another gulp of wine. "I know, isn't it great? I felt like that actress in the beginning of that movie *Casual Sex*. She was in her doctor's office waiting for the results of her test and she was on her knees praying it would be negative."

We both giggle and stare, as if we have just given one another permission to go further. With the alcohol making me bolder than usual, I say exactly what is on my mind. "You know, after dinner, I could always get us a room upstairs."

Paris pauses and places her hand on mine. "You know, I've been thinking about us..."

"Uh oh."

"No, seriously," she slurs slightly. "I am really attracted to you. Too much, I think. But what we've done is really wrong. Especially yesterday. I mean, I don't care about AC, he's a jerk, and Dana's no angel but she doesn't deserve this."

"What do you mean?"

"Nothing, it's just, I want you really badly but Dana is just so fragile. If she ever found out, I don't know what she would do."

"Well I guess she just can't find out then."

Paris looks down. "We just can't," she says softly with little conviction.

By the time we leave the restaurant, the sun is going down and sprinkles of rain begin to drop. We hop aboard the rickety St. Charles streetcar, partially to take in a view of the oak-lined district, but mainly because we just can't bear to part. Sitting in the farthest rear seat of the olive green car, we kiss passionately, Paris holding the back of my head and drawing my mouth into hers as the storm strengthens and pounds against the car's roof.

The train bounces us along, stopping to pick up passengers en route. We grope without caution, as if we are the only two people on the car. As I move my finger along the smooth skin of the outside of Paris' hip, she moans onto my tongue and pulls away.

"We'd better get off," she says, suddenly aware of people staring.

"Yeah," I say, wondering when all those people had arrived.

We stand at the streetcar stop for a while in the pouring rain, kissing as the train pulls away. Paris hails a nearby cab and grabs my hand.

"Yeah, let's get dry. Where are we going?" I am dazed in a haze of wine and ardor.

"You'll see," she says, dipping into the cab. "Metairie Cemetery."

"What?"

"It's dangerous there at night, now," the cabby warns.

"Wait for us, please," Paris says, digging in her purse for money.

"No, I'll get it," I stop her and hand the driver a twenty-dollar bill from my wallet.

As soon as we pass I10 and Metairie Road, I catch sight of a huge cross. "What's that?"

"The Moriarity grave. A man built it for his young wife because he felt guilty for not treating her right when she was alive," the cabby says lowly.

"I know the feeling," Paris chuckles.

"You all be careful," the driver warns again as he lets us out at the main entrance.

"Thanks man, don't go nowhere" I say, handing him another twenty.

We get out and wander among the exquisitely structured tombs, snickering at the odd offerings left on them.

"Look at that one," Paris points, stopping to read the epitaph of a tomb of an Army of Northern Virginia veteran.

"Mmnn," I say, drawing her hips to me and kissing the back of her neck.

"You're such a bad boy," she smiles.

Walking farther down the elaborate tombs on millionaire's row, we both pause at a gravesite, with a darkened statue of a woman entering the doors of heaven. Mesmerized by the structure, we walk closer and try to read the name at the top of the monument.

Paris touches the bare foot of the statue. I turn her around and press her against the wet marble. The rain has left droplets of water on the grass, my shoes and clothes. Usually, I hate being wet but at this moment don't give it one thought; my only thought is being inside of Paris.

She places her arms around my neck as we kiss again, this time with the unabashed desire that comes with relative privacy. I lift her by the waist and sit her down on the ledge right near the statue's foot, pushing her dress upwards past her thighs that spread ajar, encompassing my slim hips.

Grabbing the round flesh of her ass, I feel myself grow harder as I slide my hands up her back and lift her dress above her chest to reveal her white lace push-up bra. Pulling down a cup, her breast springs forward as I take the nipple in my lips and suck. Paris whines and pushes my head closer into her chest. I tighten my mouth around her and bite very gently.

"Oh," she moans aloud, and I reach down to unbuckle my belt and unzip my pants. I let them fall down around my ankles as I slide my thigh-length jockey shorts down to my knees and hold my hardness in my right hand, positioning it close to her matching lace thong panties.

Paris looks down and smiles as I push the crotch of her underwear aside to reveal her engorged lips, cleanly shaven. We both moan as I guide the head into the warm wetness of her womb. The coldness of the marble against my knees electrifies the hotness of her as I remove my hand and plunge fully into her depth.

"Uhnn," I yelp uncontrollably as the unfamiliar walls encase me. She is so tight, wet and deep, and feels so impossibly good, I have to train myself not to come immediately. I don't know if it is the newness of her or the thrill of the location but a vibration travels up and down my spine, creeping through me and making me want to explode. I have to stop moving.

"Are you okay?" she says gently, kissing my neck.

"Yes," I pant. "You feel too good."

Paris smirks and hops off the ledge, turns around and bends over the marble, supporting her weight with her elbows on the ledge.

"I love your ass," I say honestly, fondling her round fullness with her lace thong in the middle of her cheeks. I move her panties aside again, this time exposing a different bare view of her full lips, open and ready for me to enter.

I plunge my firmness inside of her again, this time experiencing the charged tightness of her in a new and even better position. Locking my hands around the large handles of her pelvic bones, I move her hips back and forth on me until the building orgasm within me can no longer be contained.

The tip of my head bangs against her insides and I freeze as I feel my warm liquid spurt out of me with a force I've never felt before. I rest against the tomb as she grabs the skirt of the statue to support my weight. We stay like that for a few minutes, both in some sort of suspended state of ecstasy. It is the best sex I've ever had.

I grow limp and extract myself from her, standing back and pulling my underwear and pants back over my hips. As Paris reorganizes her dress, I hear a slight rustling behind me that sounds like footsteps in the wet grass. Before I can turn to see who is there, a look of fear flashes across Paris' face, and a harsh thump on the base of my skull sends me to the damp grass. Everything goes black.

BOOK II

THE LOVER

Chapter 5

Ouray and Denver, Colorado

Faith is the substance of things hoped for, the evidence of things not seen.

Hebrews 11:1

urbulence. The body of the jet lurches left then turns upright, continuing to buck like a rollercoaster. Thick blankets of clouds shield my view through the small oval window, hiding the snow-capped mountains below. I hate this. Squeezing my seat belt tighter across my lower lap, it cuts into my belly. Normally, a view of the scenery comforts me, except for the harbor at Boston, as if knowing what's outside and below will somehow give me greater control of my destiny. But now my only vista is inside the flexible fuselage, contracting and expanding against the force of the rough air, making me dread the unknown and unseen. I gather that we're too close to Montrose Airport to climb to a higher altitude, so I prepare for more roughness as we dive straight through the storm.

It's my ceaseless punishment, penance for sleeping with my best friend's man. Eric paid more dearly than I last night, I recall, cutting a glance at him across the aisle, adopting the brave face of a man hiding his fear. A white gauze pad covers the spot on the back of his head where the stranger hit him, shocking us out of our post-coital bliss.

Just thinking of it makes my tongue go numb. Worse than the terror of the bouncing plane is the thought that Eric and I could be dead.

"I'd just as soon shoot you than piss on you, bitch," the thief's grim voice spat through the darkness, as Eric fell face up on the damp lawn.

Throwing my purse to him, I prayed for our lives as he struggled to get Eric's wallet from his tight back pocket. A rustling nearby scared him, and he gave up and ran away with only my leather handbag dangling from his clenched fist.

I ducked down to Eric, roused him awake and struggled to lift his heavy body before the assailant could return. With my arm around his waist, I limped with him quickly back to the cab and ordered the driver to the nearest hospital. Coming back to full alertness after waiting hour upon hour in the emergency room, Eric suggested we practice what to say to each other this morning in front of Dana and AC.

"What happened to you?" I said to Eric as rehearsed, while AC, Dana and I piled into a charter van on our way to New Orleans airport.

"I got jacked outside the hotel last night," he responded, repeating his line verbatim.

"Oh my God," I said, with all the horrific surprise I could muster. "Did they steal anything?"

"Nope, a cop came nearby so I guess they got scared."

Dana twisted to fondle him. "I don't know why you didn't just come inside and get me before you went off to the hospital."

"I didn't want to faint into that pool trying to get back inside. I just hailed a cab right there."

I paused, awaiting my cue. "I can't believe this. Somebody stole my purse last night in the Garden District."

Dana dropped her hand from Eric's forehead and looked at me with disbelief.

"No way," Eric said. "I'm glad we're outta here. New Orleans is just too dangerous for me."

"I know, that's what it said in my guide book. Sometimes whole groups of sightseers get robbed on those graveyard tours." I threw in the reference to our location despite Eric's plea not to mention it.

"You'd have your purse right now if you would've called me," AC proclaimed, repeating the same lame shit he said when I first told him I'd been robbed.

But Dana remained silent, staring contemptuously at me, rolling her eyes and head up and away from my glance. AC didn't notice, luckily, but even if he had, he wouldn't equate it to what Dana deduced. He was still mad that I didn't call him to come party with me and the bookstore people, never being one to miss a meal or drinks. I told him I just got carried away with the time, and that, when several of us got our purses snatched, we all went to the police station to file a report.

Since AC is still giving me the silent treatment, I clutch the book I'm reading instead of his hand as the jet shudders through its decline. I don't want his hand anyway. I wish I were in Dana's seat, right next to Eric, comforting and consoling him like I did last night. My nurturing instincts came out, and I realized how much I was beginning to care for him.

The plane tail twists to the left and I jerk open my copy of *Conversations with God, book 1* to distract me, to force the thoughts of Eric out of my mind.

My eyes befall a passage: "*...it would truly be your salvation...the idea of a God Who is not to be feared, Who will not judge, and Who has no cause to punish...*"

Suddenly, we are below the vile winds and in the clear, and the plane lands gently on the runway.

📖

"This," I say with a deep inhalation of frosty air, "is God's country."

It is the next morning, and the sun shines brightly over the mountains at the Telluride ski resort where we all stand in line, waiting to purchase lift tickets and rent skis.

"Just get me on those slopes," AC says, squinting at the rays that glare on the white snow, making it glisten with specks of silver.

Eric is behind us, with Dana huddled under him trying to decide which run to try. "I need a beginner's hill," she says, diverting her eyes from mine. We haven't spoken since leaving New Orleans yesterday, and she still seems uncomfortable to even glance in my direction.

"Y'all can do the bunny slopes, I'm going to See Forever," AC says, putting on the wraparound Oakley mirrored sun glasses I'd bought him on a whim, when I still lavished him with unexpected gifts.

"You are not that good," I say. "You'll be seeing forever alright."

"Well you two lovebirds can ski anything you want, Eric and I are going to the easy hills," Dana says.

Eric frowns. "I'm not doing no bunny slopes."

"I don't even think they have bunny hills," I claim with uncertainty. "Look, we can all do this Double Cabin run, it's supposed to be perfect for beginners. It's that lift over there."

After purchasing our tickets and getting the proper skis, we trek awkwardly to the lift.

"I'll do a couple of runs down this one, but I didn't come all the way here not to do some black diamonds," AC says.

"Do what you want," I say.

AC and I hop onto the first lift as Dana and Eric leap on the one behind. I extract my mini-thermos and begin drinking.

"What's that?"

"Hot chocolate."

"That's all? You should have put some liquor in there, some Jim Beam or something."

I exhale, watching smoke stream from my mouth. "I don't need it up here. I can't fuck around and ski into a tree."

"Please. You're turning into a prude."

"Whatever." Eric doesn't think so, I think, staring down at the run carved through a line of forestry.

As soon as we approach the top of the hill and round the corner, AC jumps off and starts down the mountain, tracing perfect S's through the trail. I stand at the top, pretending to fiddle with my thermos until Dana and Eric exit their chair.

"I can't do this," Dana says with clear terror as she sizes up the dips in the path.

"Yes you can, come on!" I say, giving a good-natured pep talk.

Eric skis next to her, picking her up every time she falls, which seems to be every yard or so. I continue down the mountain, falling twice as I try to slalom and accidentally cross my skis in front of each other. At the end of the run, I snowplow straight into a bored AC.

"Man, this bites. I'm going to a better run."

"Okay," I say, searching the hill for Eric, "I'm gonna do this one again."

"Fine."

"We can just meet back here when you're finished."

AC takes off as I get on the lift again, this time solo. Staring below me, I see Dana and Eric about midway in the run, him still helping her each step of the way. When I reach the top, I decide to stay and wait for them again.

After what seems like an eternity, I smile when I see Eric get off the lift by himself.

"Hey," he says, skiing over to me, then kissing me unexpectedly, in the open.

"Where's Dana?"

"She's waiting down at the bottom. She was too scared to go again."

"Oh. AC went to a harder run."

"Cool," Eric says, grabbing me into his arms.

We hold hands and ski the run together, tumbling over each other as I fall on a bump on the edge of the trail, causing both of my skis to fly off my boots.

"Nice job!" Eric says smiling, reaching for one of my errant skis.

"Forget you," I say, lunging forth and throwing a fluff of snow in his face. We tussle on the ground for a few seconds.

"Let's go in there," Eric says, gesturing toward a group of tightly packed trees, removing his skis.

I oblige, covertly following him into the cluster of greenery that hides us from the passing skiers. We kiss deeply and I feel his firmness press into my abdomen. Instinctively, I drop to my knees and unzip his pants, allowing him to fall free into the cold. With a sudden remembrance, I take a swig of the hot chocolate and hold in my mouth for a few seconds.

He is clean and pure and virtually hairless, so unlike AC's jungle of naps. I devour him, vowing to explore every inch of him with my tongue, demonstrating how much I want to pleasure him. Relaxing my throat muscles, I send him deeper, and his groans of delight grow louder. Placing his hand against the back of my head, I direct him to grab my hair tightly, and move my head as he wishes. Probing every facet of my mouth, jaw and throat, he thrills as I place my index finger and thumb around my lips, forming a tighter bond.

I want him completely, I think, glancing up to the altar of his delirious face, backgrounded by fast-moving clouds through a powder-blue sky. He is ready to give and I to receive as I drink in the pulsating liquid from his body. I wait until he releases the death grip from my hair to slide back and lick the residuals like the last traces of ice cream from a Haagen-Dazs carton. This man is happy, and from his unadulterated look of bliss I know Dana wasn't lying when she said she never goes down on him. Ironic how one's own trickery can lead to their demise.

"We've got to go back," I say, wiping away at my lips and gulping the last ounce of hot chocolate from my thermos.

"Okay," Eric says, gathering himself. "You'd better go first, then I'll ski down after you."

"Okay." I turn to clump away in the heavy boots, but he pulls me back for a polite post-fellatio peck. I smile and gingerly head out of hiding, hurriedly placing on my skis and snowplowing down the rest of the run.

"Where's Eric?" Dana says as soon as I'm in earshot. Her panic is close to the surface and her arms are folded defensively across her chest, positioning her poles askew.

"I don't know, I thought he was with you." I peer questioningly up the slope at approaching skiers.

"No, I waited down here for him. He was just going once more."

"Well I didn't see him. Maybe he went to another trail."

"How could he?" her high-pitch tone catches me off-guard as my mind races for excuses. "I would have seen him. He has to come out here."

"Hell, I don't know. These runs are so big. Maybe he fell or something. Did you see the ski patrol go up?"

"No," Dana responds, with a deer-caught-in-the-headlight expression that makes me pity her. The look of pure worry almost prompts me to confess my crimes like the paranoid murderer in Edgar Allen Poe's *The Tell-Tale Heart*.

Yes, I would scream, yes! I did it! Tear open my stomach and see the evidence. Therein lies the semen of your boyfriend!

Instead, we wait in silence with bated breath for our man, wondering into whose arms he will land.

It is now that I realize I'm choosing Eric over my best friend, the only female companion I have left in the world. The last bastion of estrogen I've managed not to exclude from my life because they didn't meet my rigid criteria: not pretty enough, not smart enough, lacking a sense of humor. If only I could clone myself for a friend. Funny that I don't subject the men in my life to such extensive scrutiny.

When Eric finally does come down the hill, and my lips ache with sweet soreness as I break into a grin, I've already decided that I don't need any friends.

📖

"That Palmyra run ruled," AC rambles on in the car ride back, as I eagerly engage his uncharacteristic excitement to cover up Dana's anger.

"Man, how long was it?" I ask, glancing to him in the driver's seat.

"I don't know but I rocked it."

"You should get a snowboard."

"Yeah, I think I will," he shoots back.

I continue asking as many questions as come to mind during the drive back to Box Canyon Lodge & Hot Springs, and praise God AC doesn't notice the dissension in the back seat. It would only take one word from Dana to set him off in the wrong direction, just one murmur of her suspicions and we would all feel the wrath of a madman.

The next afternoon, I'm not surprised when Dana abruptly says she and Eric can't make it to Denver, leaving a lonely me and AC to drive up through the mountains. I tell him that Dana is sick, but I am the one who feels ill, knowing I won't see Eric again until possibly tomorrow night back in Ouray, and then only for one more day before they return home.

Arriving at the Cherry Creek location of the Tattered Cover Book Store, I marvel at the four luxurious floors of books upon books being relished by bibliophiles in overstuffed chairs with reading lamps. But the warmth and hospitality of the staff and cozy atmosphere doesn't take away my yearning for Eric.

Sipping cappuccino and browsing the books, I kill time until my reading. At exactly 7:30 p.m., I sit before a small group of mostly women and AC and turn to the portion of the book called *Needless Things*.

" 'Put your head down'," I begin.

"Those were the words of the lady doctor as she roughly scraped away at my insides. Tears collected in my ears as I placed my head back onto the frigid steel table, unable to stop looking at the blood and tissue beginning to filter into the large glass jar off to my left.

"The suction tube tugged away at my uterus, finally eliminating the unwanted seed that grew inside of me like an alien being. The worst was over, or at least that's what I told myself. Six months later, right around the time the baby would have been born, I cried for my loss.

"Sixteen-years-old, and save for my sister and best friend, primarily alone, I chose to abort my child after the father hung up on me. I didn't want the baby, and still don't, but I can't shake the idea that I didn't do the right thing.

"Pro-choice for years, I now wonder if there isn't a better way. While the words, 'I'm pro-life' get stuck in my throat, I know this is the view probably closest to God's. A friend once argued that slavery was legal at one point but our society grew more morally responsible and had it outlawed. Maybe this will happen again one day with abortion. His words echo in my mind, but so do the visions of women injecting bleach into their wombs to rid themselves of unwanted pregnancies because they have no other means.

"You would think the horror of that day made me smarter. But instead, I made the same mistake again, and again and again. Giving away the precious gifts of God's love like so much waste. Will He ever bless me again? I think so. I've repented, and understand deep down the consequences of my irresponsibility.

"So, is it murder? Definitely. Should a woman have the right to choose? I believe yes. Do some women use it as a form of birth control? I used to vehemently deny that, but the fact that it is an available, viable option, might have had some bearing on the careless decisions I've made.

"I hate being on the fence. I like to take a strong position and stand there. The only thing I do know is that I will teach my daughter to respect her body enough not to abuse it, and no matter what anyone says, birth control is her sole responsibility. The man can too easily walk away. It is for this reason I feel he should have no legal recourse as to the decision the woman makes to keep her child or not. I had a friend whose boyfriend begged on his knees for her not to abort, and now that the little girl is nine years old, where is he? Your guess is as good as mine.

"Maybe we need a new category. Pro-life-choice. Those who believe abortion is essentially wrong, but, to prevent more dangerous outcomes, respect a woman's right to have one."

I close the book and watch as the women stare open-mouthed at me. There is no applause, only a polite rustling about as a few of them approach me to discuss the book. I am uninterested. For all this time I've waited for my coup of coups, a reading at this popular bookstore, I can only concentrate on the empty pit in my stomach. Very appropriate for the passage I just read.

The second AC steps outdoors for a smoke, I excuse myself from the few women surrounding me and call Eric. Brazen and missing him, I don't care if Dana answers the phone. I can pretend I called to speak to her, even though she would immediately see through that lie.

"Hello," his deep voice comes on the line in an almost whisper, and I beam at the sound.

"Eric, it's me."

"Paris? I'm so glad you called. I wanted to call you but I didn't know where you were staying in Denver."

"What's wrong?" I ask, sensing the urgency in his tone.

"Dana changed our plane tickets to go back to Chicago tomorrow."

My heart jumps. "What? But you can't leave. I won't be back from Denver yet."

"I know, that's her intention." He pauses, then continues with soft billows of breath against the receiver. Our lips feel near enough to kiss. "She's in the bathroom right now."

"I've got to see you before you leave."

"Me too."

"I'll come back from Denver tonight."

"Can you?"

"Yes."

Suddenly, Eric begins speaking in a loud, dramatized tone. "So how's Stephanie?"

"Who?" I ask, confused.

"Does she have you running all around town buying pickles and ice cream?"

"Dana's there?"

"Yep. So when are you all going to visit us?"

"Tell Anthony I said hello," I hear Dana sing in the background.

"Dana said hi...Yeah, she's fine."

"Let me talk to him," she continues.

"Oh shit," I say. "Look, I'll get off now."

"A'ight, man."

"Listen, I'll drive back tonight and then let's meet each other in the morning at nine o'clock by the hot springs whirlpool at the hotel. We'll figure out what to do from there. You're going to have to miss that flight tomorrow."

"Definitely. I'll get back with you," he says, and promptly hangs up with Dana still chattering away.

📖

"You ready to eat?" AC asks, when I return to the area where I gave my reading.

"I'm not really that hungry."

"What? You, not hungry? Well, I am."

"Okay," I oblige, staring at the exit. "They have a good restaurant here on the top floor."

"Cool."

Entering the eatery, we are seated at a comfortable table, encased by volumes of books and author's photographs. Meditating on the resplendent clear vista of Pike's Peak, I try to invent a reason to tell AC why I don't want to stay overnight in Denver as planned.

"This food is excellent," I say, fingering the bread on my plate after our dinner arrives.

"It's not bad," he says, gulping down his beer along with mounds of pasta, leaving traces of ruby marinara sauce on his chin.

"Man, I really want to stay here tonight but I think we should go back to Ouray."

He stops mid-bite. "This late? For what?"

"Well, since Dana and Eric just up and decided to stay there tonight, those are more unplanned expenses that I have to deal with."

"But what does it matter if they're there or here? You would have just been paying for one night here instead of there."

"Not necessarily, it would've been cheaper here. Plus, we didn't check out of our room back in Ouray, so that's another waste of money."

"You said we didn't need to."

"I know, I wasn't thinking. So now, since we'd just be spending one day in Denver anyway and not do anything but probably staying in the hotel, I figure we might as well go back."

"Uh huh," he says, swigging the rest of his drink in one fell swoop. "I know the real reason you want to go back there."

I stop breathing. "What?"

"You're broke ain't you? You spent all our money, didn't you?"

I almost laugh at the *our* part but don't, because it isn't far from the truth and is better than what I thought he was about to say. "Almost," I say, hanging my head.

"Dammit," AC says loudly, punctuating the expletive with a slam of his fist on the table, making the plates clatter. My head jolts up, along with several other patrons in the restaurant, wondering who interrupted their peaceful dinner conversations.

"AC, please," I say softly.

"Please my ass. I told you not to bring them with us to New Orleans and here, but you just wouldn't listen to me. You said there would be enough for all of us."

"There will be," I lean forward and whisper, hoping my quiet tone will soothe him and lower his voice. "I'm selling enough books to–"

"That book ain't selling enough for shit," he yells. "How much is left?"

"I have to balance the account."

"*About* how much?"

"I guess...about a thousand."

"What?" he screams with such force, the wait staff notices. "Out of all that money? What the fuck did you buy? I knew I should have just said no to this stupid shit from the beginning..."

AC's shouts continue, and I'm immediately transported to the last time we performed this show, several years ago one 3rd of July on the shores of Lake Michigan in Chicago. I became the unwilling participant in a street play, portraying the role of the embarrassed, cowering wife to his abusive, out-of-control husband character. Hordes of revelers who had valiantly trooped downtown to witness the city's huge annual fireworks display were treated to unexpected bursts when AC decided to unleash all his suppressed frustration that evening.

The night started off innocently enough, with my sister and brother-in-law in town, visiting from San Antonio. I was on a break from my last summer semester of college, and initially AC had been happy to see me. The four of us sat on a small blanket on the grass, trying to keep warm in the unusually chilly summer breeze, impatient for the display to begin.

But AC was seething inside, unable to forget our recent confessions of infidelity to one another. He had divulged his affair with a coed in the Art Department at school, so I revealed I'd also had a brief fling with David, a friend down at FAMU. I guess it was silly of me to assume we were even-Steven, that once we'd argued and confessed and cried, we would be able to put the past behind us. Of course with AC, things are never that simple.

Eternally pissed at me because I didn't confess first, he wouldn't let my family or me nor any of the hundreds of people around us that night forget it. His transgression was somehow excused because he had unburdened his soul first. Since I hadn't, I was the lying bitch who could never be trusted. So when the magnificent Roman candles soared into the air and burst overhead, I didn't see them. Four-letter words instead roared louder than the bangs of the show, dissipating negative energy like sparkles all around us.

Unfortunately, AC had given us all a ride there, and he held the keys to his car, and thus, the power. He ran across Grant Park with me screaming after him not to abandon us. Ever the fighter, my sister picked up the heaviest branch she could find to go after him, while my brother-in-law tried to console my wracks of sobs. Public transportation was the last option, for drunken mobs lined up to take free rides home throughout the city. Besides, he had taken us, and should have brought us home. I couldn't believe AC was treating my family so cruelly, unconcerned with making a good impression so soon after meeting them.

I'd grown accustomed to him regarding me in that manner, just like now, yelling at me at the top of his voice, forcing my throat closed and tears to stream the length of my face. It's bad enough in the privacy of our own home, but in public, it's inexcusable. There is only so much humiliation to which a person will subject herself. It's like he doesn't even care that every eye is on us, and that our waiter is politely handing us our dinner bill prematurely.

"You know I haven't gotten my replacement Visa card yet," I choke out in a defeated whimper.

"Oh yeah," he huffs, finally pausing the tirade to temporarily extract from his wallet the Visa debit card I authorized when I added his name to my checking account. He examines the bill, then reluctantly flips the card onto the table, depicting the bread-winning husband who must once again pay the bill for his penniless wife.

I shake my head and chuckle at the irony; the fact that I got him that card initially in case of emergencies and to give him a sense of self-worth while unemployed. But now AC is using my kindness against me, and berating me in the process for spending all of my own money.

"What the fuck is so funny?"

I tell myself to say nothing, to be meek and mild and becalming and humble. Saying it will only make it worse. But his devilish eyes and condescending tone dare me, and I look straight at him and say, "You."

"Fuck you!"

In one motion he lifts his plate of pasta smothered in red sauce and hurls it at my face. I am too shocked to move for several seconds, but the pain of the steaming food rolling down my neck prompts me to throw a roll at his face, bouncing harmlessly off his shoulder. He picks up his beer bottle and throws it toward me, catching the back of my hand before shattering onto the floor.

I flee from the table into the ladies room, quickly washing my face and clothes as best I can before running outside. Beyond shame, I scurry in any direction, just to get away from him and any witnesses to the debacle.

AC quickly catches up, grabbing and holding me by both arms. "Look," he says, out of breath, "I'm sorry, I'm sorry. Where are you going?"

"I don't know! Anywhere. Away from you!" I scream and cry, frozen within his grasp, praying he will release me.

"I'm sorry. Just come with me. We can go back to Ouray."

I stand still, afraid to move, afraid to speak.

"Come on, I swear I won't hurt you," he says, in a repentant stance that I've never seen before. "You don't have any money or anything, there's nowhere you can go here."

AC slowly releases me, and even though every fiber of my being wants to run away, call my mother for money and go back to Ouray alone, I fear missing my meeting with Eric tomorrow morning.

"Okay," I say, barely audible, and follow AC back to the car.

The entire ride back I sob, holding my hand, wondering if he hasn't chipped a bone because the pain is tremendous. I sense him tiring of my cries, so I crawl into the back seat and curl up, hoping he won't drive us off the nearest cliff.

Thinking only of Eric, I realize that any guilt I felt for sleeping with him because of being married has gone. AC's actions are only pushing me farther away, into Eric's arms. If AC were smarter, he would be treating me like a queen, giving me second thoughts about ever leaving him. Now, the answer is as clear in my mind as black and white.

Under the veil of a sunny new morning, I hurry over to Eric, pacing near the redwood spa. Throwing my arms around his neck, I start crying unavoidably.

"Hey, what's wrong?" he asks, breaking away to look into my eyes.

"Yesterday. It was horrible. AC went off in Denver. He burned my face and hurt my hand," I sputter, holding up my hand for him to inspect the small bump that has risen atop it overnight.

"Oh my God, why?" he places a gentle kiss on the sore area while cradling my hand in his.

"Because he's an asshole."

Eric looks around cautiously. "Where is he now?"

"Oh, probably just finding the letter I wrote him saying that I was flying back to Denver today to talk to an abuse counselor the bookstore set up for me. I wanted him to feel guilty for what he did in front of all those people. He finally got out of bed to go to the bathroom and I slipped him the note and then left so I wouldn't have to face him."

"Good," he says, placing his arm around my shoulder. "When did you say you'd be back?"

"Tomorrow. I know it sounds lame but I didn't know what else to say. I had to get away from him."

"No it's okay, it's perfect. I told Dana I'd be back tomorrow too."

"You did? What did you tell her?"

"Well first, I got pissed off that she changed our plane tickets without telling me, so I changed them back to tomorrow and told her I needed some space. I told her I was flying out to Phoenix to see my grandmother for the day and that I'd be back in time for our flight tomorrow."

"Did she believe you?" I ask, searching his amber-brown eyes.

"Who cares? I couldn't go back home without seeing you again."

I kiss him, then look around to make sure we're still alone. "We better get out of here, then. Maybe we can take a cab somewhere, 'cause I left the car keys with AC–"

"No, it's okay. I got a rental car last night after I talked to you. I figured we'd need one."

"Perfect!"

After Eric leads me to the blue sedan and we enter, he begins driving with trepidation. "Where should we go?"

"Oh, okay...there's a hotel called the Wiesbaden Hot Springs near here somewhere. I was thinking of staying there before I booked our hotel. But, you know, I don't have my credit cards with me." I look at him sheepishly. "I could pay you back, though. As soon as they send–"

He pats my thigh, sending vibrations through my leg. "Girl, don't even worry. I'm taking care of it. Plus, I'll take care of our rooms in Ouray. You've spent way too much on us already."

"No, you don't have to do that, I was the one that invited you guys."

"I know," he grins, "and I've had a really good time. I just want to show you how much I appreciate what you've done."

"Thank you," I whisper, then quickly turn to the window so Eric won't see the tears welling up in my eyes again. I am so overwhelmed by his gesture, so unexpected, so pure. The thought that for once, I'm not the sole provider, trying to figure out ways to get the bills paid, gives me an easy sense of calm.

"It's snowing," he says, forcing me out of my thoughts.

"That's weird," I say, looking at the flakes fall in slow motion on the windshield then melt into spots of water. "I didn't know it still snowed this late in the year."

"I guess anything can happen."

📖

As soon as we find the lodge, check in and enter our rooms, we are pawing at each other and falling onto the bed. We make love with wild abandon, finally being able to experience the completeness of our nakedness without the constraints of space, time or lack of privacy.

Over and over again we consume each other, locked away in the confines of our own love nest. Sneaking away to the hotel's vapor caves, we strip to our underwear to take in the misty steam. Our passion arises again, until we can no longer take it, and run back to our room to finish.

Relaxing in the tub, reveling in the afterglow of our amorous afternoon, I hear the most pleasant, most overwhelming sound that I haven't heard in ages. A knock at the door. A simple action, but loaded with such kindness and respect and meaning that I had forgotten it was how normal couples relate. So accustomed to AC barging in on me, even after I've locked the door, I've always taken baths with the guarded assumption that I could be startled out of my wits any second.

But Eric, he knocked. "Paris?"

"Yes?"

"Do you want me to order room service?"

"Sure, I'll be right out to look at the menu."

I smile at the simplicity of his unknowing gesture, and sink back in the tub for a few more minutes of undisturbed meditation.

📖

"Oh...my...God," I say unbelievably the next morning, after opening the shades and inspecting the white blanket of snow that covers the town.

"What?" Eric says, joining my side.

"Look at this! Can you believe this? It must have snowed all night."

"It's got to be three feet of snow out there. Let me turn on the TV."

After flipping through several stations, we find a local news broadcast.

The announcer says, "...is causing delays with many of the connecting flights in surrounding cities. The last time the Montrose Airport closed was due to a similar surprise storm..."

"Yes!" I scream, hugging Eric while he listens to the rest of the broadcast.

"...and will be closed at least until tomorrow morning. Stay tuned for further details."

"I guess God does work in mysterious ways, looks like He wants us to be together."

"I guess so. I still have to call Dana."

I sigh, "Me too. I better call the jerk. We better do that code to block them from doing a *69. What is it? I always get confused on that one. Shit, I do not feel like talking to him."

"I know, me neither, but I better call her now before she flips out and calls my whole family."

"Has she been really suspicious?"

"Yeah, she keeps asking me if I'm seeing you and if I like you. I just say no."

"I know, if I didn't think she'd blab to AC, I'd tell her the truth about us."

Eric stops and looks at me in shock. "No, don't ever tell her."

"I won't. I just feel guilty that's all."

"I know, me too. But that would only make things worse. Does AC know anything?"

"Nope. He's dumber than a box of rocks. All he cares about is how much money I have."

I listen in silence as Eric makes his call, quietly assuring Dana he will be back whenever the airport opens to go home with her. My stomach drops as he talks about returning to Chicago, and I think about making some loud noise, something that will let Dana know that he is with me now, just to blow the whole thing up, so I can stay with him and not have to see AC's face again.

Instead, I remain quiet, like the dutiful mistress, and steel myself to call AC as soon as he hangs up. Luckily, when I do, AC doesn't answer, so I leave a message with the desk clerk.

"We're free," I sing, bouncing in Eric's arms.

"At least for another day," he says.

This day is a repeat of yesterday, with us holed away in the room making love and eating into the night. We fall asleep embracing, awaking to the news in the morning that the airport has reopened.

"Well, I guess this is it," Eric says, as we stare face to face inches from each other, resting on our sides.

"I can't leave you. I don't want you to go back to Chicago with her. I love you." I watch for his reaction.

Eric touches my arm, then falls onto his back with a loud exhalation of air. "I don't want him to hurt you. These two days together have made me feel so close to you. I care about you too. I don't even want Dana anymore, I've stopped sleeping with her."

"I don't know what to do. I guess we can just see each other back in Chicago after the book tour."

"That's too long. I can't wait that long. I'm not leaving you. That's it, fuck it. I can't let you go without me. I'm coming to Vegas with you."

Chapter 6

Las Vegas, Nevada

If we say that we have fellowship with Him and yet walk in the darkness, we lie and do not practice the truth.

I John 1:6

My heart pounds against my breastbone like a conga drum when I pull a small slip of paper from Eric's wallet and decipher the cobalt-blue handwriting. Realizing it is only some type of sports statistic, I refold the note and place it back in its exact location. Just as I extract what appears to be a credit card receipt, the shower flow stops and brings dead silence to the room. I shove the document inside the billfold, which I quickly return to his pants pocket and hop onto the bed.

Eric emerges from the bathroom clean and freshly shaven, with the aroma of robust citrus cologne wafting behind. He is extremely handsome in his baggy gray shorts and a new canary Nike T-shirt, his hair even more meticulously groomed than usual. I lust after him with the desire of a neglected woman.

"I'm going downstairs to check out the casino," he says, lacing up his gym shoes.

"I want to go. Just let me put on my sandals."

"No, you hate gambling. I don't want you to go against your beliefs. I won't be that long."

Eric dashes out the door, as though another second in my presence would be torture. I stare out the sloped windows of our Luxor suite to the white peaks of frost atop faraway mountains, amazed at coldness juxtapositioned against the heat of the desert.

Snapping myself from the trance, I walk over to the door and lock the deadbolt, then grab Eric's black duffel sac and carry it to the bed. I gingerly remove one item of clothing after another, examining each carefully, deeply inhaling the scent of his undershirts and the crotches of his underwear. The potpourri of sweat and cologne makes it difficult to distinguish Paris' fragrance for sure and I need irrefutable proof—the kind Eric refuses to provide.

I already know in my heart of hearts that they are messing around, by virtue of the fact that we're even here, in Las Vegas. Nothing would convince him to get on that plane to Chicago, and that's when I realized this was probably more than a fling.

The red flags are endless, like his emergency trip to 'visit his Grandmother' coincidentally the same time Paris just happened to fly back to Denver. And that night in New Orleans he stayed gone so long, then they both had the same lame story about getting robbed the next day. They might be fooling AC, but they're not fooling me.

Eric's been showering as soon as he comes back from God-knows-where and he doesn't want to make love. All of a sudden his pager has been vibrating every day with a so-called crisis from one of his car washes.

"That's it," I whisper to myself. "I can check his messages."

After dialing his message retrieval number, I pause when prompted for the access code. If I try long enough, I can probably crack the four digits. First I punch in 0815, his birthday, but that doesn't work. Next I use 0622, my birthday, but that too denies me entry. I hang up, making sure I won't deactivate the code by false attempts. Searching my memory banks, I try his parents' birthdays, his brother's birthday, his baby sister's birthday, his home address and any other significant four digit number that comes to mind, but they all fail.

Frustrated, I hang up and pace the room. An hour has passed and I am getting cabin fever, while Mr. Be-Right-Back is nowhere to be found. I think of leaving to explore this brightly-lit exciting city alone, but stay because I want to be here when he does return. We've spent so much time apart, I've begun to cherish the few moments we do spend together. It's like our first taste of living together, and while I love the closeness, Eric runs away. To be with her.

Entering the bathroom, I spot Eric's wooden handled brush and pick it up. Among the firm ebony bristles is a lone golden hair, much longer and lighter than his. I hold it tightly between my index finger and thumb, knowing I finally have the proof I've been seeking. Back in the bedroom, I place it atop my purple shorts so I won't lose sight of it.

I wait, knowing the minutes that crawl like hours to a dejected girlfriend fly like seconds to a couple lost in passion, stealing that last kiss for the night. I wait. Turning on the television for a distraction, the actor's voices are background noise and the plot lost on my faraway gaze.

When darkness consumes the alpine landscape, I begin to moan a wail of agony. If he leaves me alone the entire night again to be with her, I think I will lose my mind. Yet thankfully, three hours and forty-nine minutes after he left, the prodigal boyfriend returns.

"Whose hair is this?" I demand, thrusting the single shaft in his face as soon as Eric opens the door.

"What?" he asks, squinting.

"I found this in your brush. Whose hair is it?"

Eric plucks the hair from my fingers, briefly inspects it, and then tosses it to the floor. "I don't know, it's probably yours."

"No it isn't." I dive to the rug, searching the patterned carpet for my evidence. "I never use your brush. And it's lighter than my hair."

"I don't know. It's probably my grandmother's. She used my brush when I was in Phoenix."

"Yeah right, your grandmother's hair is gray. That hair was light brown."

"Whatever," he waves his hand down, dismissing me, as he walks into the bathroom.

I run behind him. "What are you doing? You going to take another shower?"

"I was going to pee!"

"Fine, I'll watch you."

Eric frowns. "Are you crazy? What's your problem?"

"I want to see. Do you have something to hide from me? I know you've been with Paris all this time I was here waiting for you. You said you'd be right back."

"I wasn't with her, I was just checking out the hotel. Then I walked down the strip a little bit and turned around and walked back."

"For three hours?"

Eric walks into the bedroom, with me close on his heels. "I didn't know I was gone that long. I stopped and gambled a little bit and then kept walking. Everything looks so close here but when you try and walk to it, it's farther away than you think."

"Couldn't you take a cab? And why didn't you call me?"

"Look, I just wanted to walk. Why are you giving me the third degree?"

"Because!" I scream, my anger spilling forth. "I was here waiting for you all this time. Why don't you just admit it! I know you were with Paris. I know you've been with her. Why don't you just tell me?"

"I was not with her! Stop accusing me of something I didn't do." His nostrils flare as he speaks through clenched teeth. "I just didn't feel like being here because you're always stressing me out about something."

"Don't blame me, just tell me. I know you like her."

"I don't like her."

I suck my teeth. "Right! You're only following her all over the damn country. What are we even doing here?"

"I told you, I've never been to Las Vegas and I wanted to see it. I haven't traveled anywhere; all I've been doing is working my ass off for years with hardly any time off. I thought you like to travel."

"I do, but why can't it be just me and you? You've been running out of the hotel room as soon as we check in. Are you seeing her?"

"I'm not seeing her! Just stop asking me!"

"Why are you getting so mad?"

"Because you keep asking the same stuff over and over. I'm tired of your jealousy. You always do this with other women. You make me want to go out and do something. I'm already guilty."

"This isn't the same. I've seen the way you look at her. I know you find her attractive."

"No I don't."

"Oh, God!" I flip my hands up in frustration. "You don't find her pretty at all?"

"She's alright. I've seen better."

"Give me a break."

"Look," Eric says, walking back into the bathroom. "I don't feel like hearing this right now."

"What are you doing?"

He slams and locks the door before I can open it. I begin pounding, but soon the sounds of the shower running drown out my banging.

"I knew it! You're washing off her scent, huh? Open the door!" I scream, my voice breaking into sobs as I slide down and collapse on the floor. The misty steam seeps beneath the door.

A long time later he exits the door as I lean against it, causing me to topple onto his feet.

"What are you doing down there?"

I stand, inhaling the clean scent of his skin. "Just please, I need to know the truth. You owe me that. We can get past this."

"There is nothing to tell. There is nothing to get past."

"We can work through this."

"Dana, look," he says calmly, "I think we need some time apart."

"No," I groan, like a mother who has just lost her child.

"Yes, it will help. You can go back to Chicago–"

"No, Eric."

"Come on now, I think it's the best thing to do. We're always fighting all the time."

I snap to merriment. "No, look, I'm sorry, I won't fight with you anymore. I won't argue. We can be happy. Please don't do this–"

"We never were really that happy. You can see other people–"

"Don't do this, please," I whimper. "Don't leave me, not for her. Please."

"I'm not leaving you for anybody. I just think we need some time apart."

"Please...Eric, please," I sob harder, recognizing the seriousness in his gaze. The vision of us permanently apart flashes through my head, and the thought returning alone to my tiny roach-infested South-Side apartment sends me reeling. The cries come in jolts that threaten to suffocate me; I can barely breathe.

"Please," I repeat, as Eric places his arms out to steady me. His touch is comforting, so infrequently doled out to me yet lavished on Paris. I gasp for air.

"Are you okay?" he says as I plunge headfirst into his arms.

Several seconds later I awaken from the brief faint, as Eric scoops me up and places me on the bed.

"Don't leave me," my voice quivers through violent shakes. "Please, don't leave me."

Eric is frightened, as if inspecting a deadly wild animal. "Just get some sleep."

I grab his arm and pull it around my waist. "Don't leave me."

"I won't," he says softly, gently removing his arm.

Placing his arm back around me, I lean up to kiss his face. At first he resists, but as my eyes begin to tear again, he wills himself to comply. We make love, and instead of it being a tender moment, it is mercy sex, something done just to appease me. Afterwards, I feel worse than if he would've never touched me at all.

At daybreak, glaring sunlight seeps through my puffy eyes, forcing me to pry them apart. I discover I am alone, that Eric has snuck away like a thief in the night without so much as a goodbye. I fall back on the bed, emotionally exhausted, recalling the languid Saturday mornings we used to spend in bed. With our legs entangled, we'd bask in the daylight and make love, his favorite time for sex.

This morning, he is once again drawn to Paris' lair and repelled by mine like an insect fighting his way out of a Venus flytrap. It's a reality too harsh to bear, especially after he promised not to leave me last night. My first instinct is to call Paris and cry on her shoulder, until I remember she is the source of my problems. I dial my mother instead.

"Hello?" she answers, the lilt in her voice divulging her drunkenness. In Chicago, it isn't yet noon.

"Hi Ma."

"Dana? Where have you been? Why haven't you called me?"

"I'm sorry, we've been traveling. I'm in Las Vegas."

"What?" she yells, forcing me to remove the receiver from my ear. "What are you doing there?"

"Eric brought me here as a surprise."

"Did you all get married?"

"Not yet," I say, adopting a playful tone.

"Good, 'cause I want to be there when you do. Can't you fly me out there? Plus, you know your grandmother's dying wish is to see you get married. I mean, if you have to, do it there, but then come back here and make him throw you a big reception. Did he give you a ring?"

"No."

"What's he waiting on? You'll be thirty soon."

I exhale loudly. "I know, Ma. I think he just wants to surprise me."

"Okay, but just make sure it's a good ring. Get it appraised. Are you sure you're okay?"

Hesitating, I consider succumbing to my sadness and telling her the whole sordid story. My pain traverses the phone line like her inebriation, and for once, I want to tell her the truth. That my man is leaving me and my world is crumbling. I'm scared and lonely, I want to yell, and I'll never find a good man and have a family.

Mother, I'd say, come cradle me as I cry, feed me hot soup and sleep in my bed with me like when I was a little girl. Nurture me, nestle me, love me. Let's have a rational discussion, without your patented solutions. I want to discuss my problems like two adult women, and I want you to be sober and listen.

But alas, that's not the mother I have. Her litany of negative responses is as predictable as a crowing rooster. Dana, I always told you not to bring any girlfriends near your man. Men are no good. Like your son-of-a-bitch father, who left me the second I told him I was pregnant with you. And George after him, who stuck me with that car loan I cosigned. And Tom, who wouldn't divorce his wife and left me hanging on all those years. He's still with that fat bitch today…

She'd rant, working herself into an angry frenzy, sinking me into a deeper depression and leaving me to wonder why I ever brought it up. Before closing, she would proclaim the curse of the Mince women as spinsters.

I love her more than life itself, but I just can't open up.

"No, I'm fine," I say through the lump in my throat.

"Okay. Well, when are you coming back?"

"I'm not sure, soon. I'll call you. Love you," I rush, hanging up the phone as she says goodbye.

I break down and weep fresh teardrops that hurt my tender eyes.

📖

"You look like shit," AC says immediately after opening the door to his room. He stands butt-naked, the fresh imprint of an elastic waistband indenting a ring around his paunchy mid-section.

"You're no prize yourself," I counter, stepping back into the hallway. "Put on some clothes and come with me."

"Where?"

"I want to go find Eric; I'm sure he's with your wife."

"She's at Caesar's Palace giving a reading to some sex addicts or something."

I gaze everywhere but directly at him. "That's what she told you. Come on, hurry up."

"Okay, come on in while I get dressed."

"That's okay, I'll wait out here."

"Please, it ain't nothing you haven't seen before," he says, flicking the door so that it slams loudly in my face.

"And didn't want to see it again," I muffle, turning around to lean against the atrium's railing.

His body sends shivers of repulsion through mine, forcing suppressed visions of past sexual escapades to my mind. How could I have ever been so desperate? I tell myself that it never happened. I would swear it on a stack of bibles to anyone, especially Eric.

"Let's roll," AC says, emerging from the room wearing torn camouflage shorts and a Mettalica T-shirt.

"I bet you a dollar to a donut she's not where she says she is."

"That bitch better be. I'll put one of these hollow point's through her temple." AC pats the gun in his leather fanny pack.

I grin automatically at the image of Paris being harmed—it is the perfect solution. With Paris hospitalized or even dead and AC in jail, it would be just me and Eric back together again. Then she could get a taste of the pain she's put me through.

"And I'd shoot your pretty-boy too, just on GP."

I stop and whirl AC to face me. "No, don't you touch him! Paris is the one that caused all this."

"Shee-et. Your nigga' too. How's he gonna shake my hand, sit up in these hotel rooms I've paid for, and then fuck my wife?"

"But you don't know what Paris has said. She could have told him any kind of lie. You don't know."

"Neither do you," he mumbles as he lights a cigarette. "But whatever's happening, I need to see this shit with my own eyes."

To my dismay, we reach Caesar's Palace only to discover Paris actually is speaking to a group of sex-addicts. AC glares at me as we enter and take seats, while Paris and the entire audience stares at us.

After we are settled, Paris continues. "...and that's why sometimes we still feel horny after we've just had sex, because we are unfulfilled. The act itself has no meaning.

"Sexual addiction can sometimes lead to obsessing over one person," she says, looking up at me. "I've experienced such compulsion in the past. My sophomore year of college I met this gorgeous guy named Kenny outside of the Kappa Alpha Psi fraternity house where he lived. I was flattered that such a handsome, athletic guy would pay me any attention, so I began a love affair with him that lazy summer semester of school.

"He was physical perfection, with taut strong calves honed from hours spent swimming laps in the Olympic-sized pool and riding his bike around the city's steep hills. I considered it an honor when he came to visit me, mostly to have sex. At least in the beginning he stayed the whole night.

"After only two weeks of dating, his birthday rolled around and I spent my last dollars on a cake and the Le Coq Sportif sportswear he loved. I even decorated my bedroom, not the living room, with crepe paper and balloons. The location of that private party should have been a major clue to the nature of our relationship.

"Following that night, he'd visit less often, and then only for a few hours of sex. I could see what was happening, but I allowed it to continue because I didn't value my precious body. I'd beg his darkened silhouette in the hallway not to leave, but he always found an excuse to go away.

"Then I went home to Chicago for Labor Day weekend. He sang while driving me to the airport, delighted that I was leaving. The summer was ending, and soon all the regular students would be back on campus and he would have his pick of the litter, not just a substitute. I sensed it was the end but didn't want to believe it.

"After the holiday weekend, I was anxious to see him, but couldn't get in touch with him. Things had obviously changed. He disappeared, but I didn't want it to end. I kept calling until one day he finally admitted that he had met someone else and wanted to see her now. I couldn't take it, and pleaded with him to stay with me. During our conversation, the other woman called. He clicked over, and then back to me, saying it was she and that he had to go. I wouldn't say goodbye, and after patiently asking me to let him go a billion times, he hung up. I sat there with the dead phone in my hands.

"Unrelenting, I called him back, but of course he didn't answer. I tried calling his fraternity brothers to get him to talk to me, but thankfully, none of them answered. The Lord spared me from making an even bigger fool of myself.

"I continued to invent reasons to see him, like the time I made a federal case of returning the laundry basket he left at my apartment.

"Then, one night, by happenstance, his Subaru was in front of mine, and he had a female companion in the front seat. I just knew it was she, the woman he dumped me for. What did she look like? Was she prettier than I was? Was she from Chicago? How did she dress? All these questions entered my mind as I struggled to get a better look. The red light turned green and they proceeded forward, driving straight past the corner that was my planned destination.

"For a split second I contemplated following them, to get a good look at her and find out where they were going. Nearing the intersection, I knew I had to make a choice. Luckily, reason overcame me, and I realized that to tail them would be a waste of my time and self-esteem. It was obviously over between us, and no matter who she was, it was his loss. I had more class than that. So, on that fateful night, I turned the corner, literally and figuratively. Ladies and gentlemen, I invite you to do the same. Look within the depths of your being and realize that you have the strength to overcome your fixation. Turn the corner."

The audience explodes into applause, then gravitates to Paris.

"I can't believe that shit," I say, standing.

"What? She was here like she said. And I don't see Eric anywhere around here."

"They're probably gonna meet somewhere later."

AC rises. "We can wait and follow her when she leaves."

"Dammit. Look at all these people, she'll be here forever."

"We can go to the casino and come back."

"This is messed up. She'll know we're following her. We need a better game plan. You were in the military; you should know how to spy on someone."

"That wasn't my area. What are you so pissed for?"

"Because," I sigh as we walk out of the room and past the Forum shops to the casino, "I can't believe she read that shit about turning the corner. Paris was telling me basically to give it up and leave Eric alone."

"No she wasn't, that really happened."

"I know it happened. She told me all about Kenny. Hell, she called me and cried that night he hung up on her. She was using it as a message to me about Eric."

"I don't know, Dana. Are you sure you're not being paranoid?"

"Look, I know what I know. Let's go figure out how to get you some proof."

The continual ding of the slot machines assaults us as we enter the game floor.

"I need some money," AC announces, seeking out the nearest ATM machine. I watch him extract $200 from the cash slot, then remove the printed receipt and toss it in the nearest garbage can. "Let's go play."

We find an empty section of dollar slots and sit next to each other. AC slips a crisp hundred-dollar bill in the opening, then scrutinizes the red light that counts his credits. When it stops at one hundred, he begins punching the Bet Max button repeatedly.

"Aren't you gonna play?" he says, as red, white and blue sevens whirl on independent reels.

"I don't believe in gambling."

"Yeah, right. You don't believe in spending your own money. And don't look at me, 'cause Paris already spent too much money on y'alls ass. I ain't gonna shell out the duckets like your wuss-ass man."

"I didn't ask you for nothing," I roll my eyes. If I didn't need him to rough up Paris, I'd be gone by now. "I bet they have tons of surveillance here." I crane my neck up, inspecting the ceiling.

"They have to. People steal here all the time."

"That's what we need, to go to one of those spy shops and buy some stuff to watch Paris and Eric."

AC stops pressing the button and laughs at me. "Girl, do you know how much that shit costs? You need some serious dollars for that."

"We should look anyway. Maybe we can find something cheap."

"Okay, but I doubt it."

AC and I sit at the slots for a stretch of time, both of us watching as his winnings periodically increase and then decrease. After an hour, the initial hundred dollars is lost.

"Man, let's go to another machine. These aren't paying shit."

"Okay," I answer, following him into an isolated section with more comfortable chairs.

"This is what I'm talking about," he says, sitting down.

"These are $5 machines! You're going to play these?"

"Might as well. You spend big, but you win big. They have $100 machines in here, too."

"That's just crazy."

"Crazy for you," he says. "Because you can't see fit to come up off a dollar."

AC repeats the scenario, but this time the machine stops at only twenty credits. As he carefully presses the button, this time only betting one credit per pull, I think of Eric. He would never let me sit and watch him play without instinctively offering me a twenty from his wallet so I could join in the fun. Unlike AC, who wouldn't know what the word *gentleman* meant even if he looked it up in the dictionary.

"Dag nabbit," AC screams, pounding a fist into the machine as three identical symbols stop almost perfectly on the line, except for the center one.

"Let's just go," I say, standing. "We don't want to miss Paris."

"Alright, just let me finish out these credits."

I glance at the screen, which shows 14 credits left. "You'd be better off cashing that in right now and putting it in your pocket."

AC ignores me and keeps playing. Suddenly, his machine produces an unfamiliar song, and the top beige light starts blinking.

"Did you win something?" I ask, squinting at two symbols aligned perfectly with a mismatched third symbol.

"Yeah," AC says, reading the legend on the top of the machine.

With his specific combination, with two credits played, I determine he's won four times $2,500.

"Oh my God. Did you just win $10,000?"

"Yep," he says smugly. "I'm glad I didn't listen to you."

"Oh my God!" I scream, bending down to hug him.

"Oh, now you love me?" he laughs, pulling back and brushing his hand against the side of my breast.

My first instinct is to smack him, but I stop myself. "Now we can really buy some spy stuff," I say excitedly.

"Yeah," he nods, circling his tongue around his dry lips.

After some time spent completing forms, AC collects his money in cash, deciding against taking any portion of it in a check.

"Paris will just spend it all if I put it in our account," he complains in the cab to The Spy Factory, a surveillance store we found in the phone book.

The more money you can spend on spy equipment, I think. When we reach the store I nearly run inside as AC pays the cab driver.

When he enters the store, I am already getting help from a man behind the counter.

"This is the Ear 200 Wall Probe. You can hear sounds through walls, windows, metal, air ducts, plumbing, anything."

"How much is it?" AC asks, finally next to me.

"$249.95."

"That's too much."

"Come on AC, please," I whine, amazed at his cheapness. Finally he relents and directs the man to remove it from the case for his inspection.

I nod for the salesman to continue.

"Also, if you have the person's permission, this is your best bet: a two-way telephone recorder with automatic start and stop. You can connect it to a single-line telephone, and the TA-229 recording control will start the recorder and tape both sides of the conversation. When they hang up, it stops and waits for the next call. It's only $24.95."

"We'll take that too," I say, smiling sweetly at AC.

"But you need to get either the micro cassette recorder or request a GE recorder to go with it. They're both $49.95."

AC reluctantly nods his approval once again, as I gaze up at him with puppy-dog eyes.

"Now, how do I get inside somewhere if I don't have a key?" I ask, the panorama of equipment dizzying my eyes.

"Walk down here. We've got lock pick sets, or, what's probably easiest for you is this lock pick gun. No experience necessary."

I shake my head without even asking the price. "Okay, we'll take that too."

"Great, just keep looking around and let me know if you have any more questions."

"Thanks, I will."

I am giddy with excitement when we make it back to my room and pour the equipment onto the bed. I barely notice how empty and extraordinarily neat the room seems.

"We've got to hurry up before Eric gets back," I say, noticing a note left on the nightstand.

"Shit, I ain't afraid of your little boyfriend. I'll call our room and see if Paris is back yet."

I take the paper into the bathroom while AC picks up the phone and dials. My hands shake so badly, I have to place the letter on the counter to read.

Dana,

I've checked into another hotel. I don't want to hurt you, but I need this time apart to figure out what I want to do. I bought you a plane ticket back to Chicago on Continental under your name, leaving tomorrow morning, but you can change the time or date if you wish. I love you, but I don't think we should be together right now. Just give me some time, and maybe we can be friends one day.

Eric

I reread the note several times, hoping it doesn't say what I just read. The tiny room whirls, and I clutch the sink for support. I am sinking, and the only thing that snaps me back to reality is AC screaming in the other room. Summoning the strength, I enter the bedroom to eavesdrop.

"No, you stay there 'cause I'm not coming back tonight. And I'm definitely not paying for that shit either, so you might as well stay there. I'm getting my own room. I ought to kick your mother-fucking ass–"

He stops screaming, then slams down the receiver and looks up at me with a scowl.

"That fucking trick. I told her about the money I won and she had the nerve to ask me to pay for our rent at home and give her some money for the rest of her book tour. Then, in the same breath, she's talking 'bout maybe I should go back to Chicago to give her some space."

"You see," I say, thrusting the letter at him. "That's the same thing Eric said. They want to get us out of the way so they can be together. I told you!"

"That bitch is tripping," he says, tossing his purchases back into the bag and walking out of the room.

"Wait!" I trot to keep up with AC as he runs down the hallway and boards the elevator to their floor. Once inside their room, we see that Paris is gone.

"I knew she'd run away," he says, pacing about the room in frustration. He picks up a copy of her book and rips the pages out. I join him, grabbing several clothing items strewn about the floor and ripping the seams.

"Just wait till she sees this."

"She's not coming back," AC huffs, short of breath, as he tears the cover off another book.

"I don't know. She was probably in a rush to get Eric out of here."

"That bitch better not ever bring him up in this room. She said she's not coming back in here anyway."

"She'll come get her books."

After destroying everything of Paris' that we can find, we fall down onto the bed in twisted laughter. When I notice AC giving me a hungry look, I sit up, but he grabs my arm and pulls me back down.

"Where do you think you're going?"

"Back to my room. Maybe Eric will call."

"Right, Dana. Didn't you read that note? He left you. Besides," he says, lowering his voice and running his hand up my thigh, "you haven't thanked me for all this stuff I bought you."

"You got this for both of us. This is gonna help you find out about your sleazy wife."

"Hey, I could care less. Eric can have that bitch for all I care. I'm doing this for you. Unless of course you don't want all this stuff. I can take it right back to the store."

He leans his head down and glances up at me in an effort to appear sexy. I sit still, looking from the spy equipment to AC, thinking of my empty hotel room and feel myself descending once again. After several minutes I walk over to the mini-bar and extract every miniature bottle of alcohol and place it on the table.

"Let's get bubbly," AC says, taking a bottle of Jack Daniel's from the stack and gulping it down, followed by a swig of Coke.

I pick up each bottle and tilt the strong liquid down my throat, refusing the soda AC offers as a chaser.

"Oh you're trying to get real nice," he says, removing his shoes.

I don't respond. After emptying seven bottles down my throat, I stand and remove all my clothes, then slide under the covers. AC plops down on top of me, forcing his rough lips against mine then his tongue in my mouth. I think only of Eric as I shut my eyes and feel myself being penetrated prematurely. I envision myself in a beautiful white wedding gown as both of our families watch us get married. Then we sail off on a honeymoon cruise, with Eric apologizing about ever thinking of breaking up with me. He tells me he was a fool, that he found out what a horrible person Paris was and immediately dumped her. We smile and laugh as we go back to our room, making the love that eventually leads to our first child.

"You were like a dead fish," AC says, snapping me back to the present moment.

He rolls off of me to reach for a cigarette and another mini-bottle on the nightstand. The phone rings but AC doesn't answer. I curl onto my side and hold my stomach, feeling ill from the liquor and sex. Before long, I fall asleep into a drunken stupor.

I am awakened from my deep slumber by a sharp pain inside, and realize it is AC, pounding away at my dry insides once again. I shut my eyes in the darkness, allowing him to continue pumping while I envision Eric. It doesn't work, for I could never mistake Eric's gentle touch for this ruffian, so I open my eyes. Looking towards the foot of the bed, I see what appears to be a figure standing over us.

"Stop," I whine to AC, leaning up against the force of his body. "Stop."

"What?"

"Someone's here." I push him off just as the lights are flicked on, making me shield my eyes against the brightness.

It is Paris, watching us with her mouth agape.

"Why the fuck did you bring him in our room?" AC yells, and I am confused for a split second until I see another person at the door.

It is Eric. At that moment I catch sight of him staring at me, and I pull the cover up to my chest. His look is indescribable, a melee of disappointment, disbelief and pure disgust.

"No," I mumble.

"Let's go," Paris says, leaping toward the door and pushing Eric out with her.

AC jumps out of bed and hurriedly places on his underwear. "Come on! We have to follow them."

"It's too late," I say, motionless. "He's gone."

Chapter 7

San Francisco and Napa Valley, California

...if her husband nullifies them...none of the vows or pledges that came from her lips will stand.

Numbers 30:12

"He's gone."

"Would you stop fucking saying that?" I explode, momentarily glancing away from the monotonous highway to Dana, who's staring catatonic through the windshield. "If it wasn't for your slow ass, we'd be right behind them now. You better hope Paris shows up at her reading on Saturday so you can catch up with Eric then."

Looking back at the road, I try to gage her reaction to my last comment through my peripheral vision. But it's as if she doesn't hear me at all; she gazes silently into the distance.

The white lane markings blur into a continuous streak as my stomach dances with nervous anticipation and anger. I'm exhausted, but I know I can make it to San Francisco without stopping except for gas. I've done drives three times as long with my eyes barely open.

Those trips were always for Paris, especially after a big fight. When the strain of the distance and other lovers threatened to break us up, I'd hop onto 65 South headed to Florida where we'd feverishly reclaim our love.

It's the same thing now, her testing the boundaries and running away while I come to the rescue. I'm almost addicted to the thrill of the chase, this sick cat-and-mouse game that lends drama to our marriage. I smile unavoidably when I think of it, the ebb and flow of this relationship as tumultuous yet eternal as the sea.

That's why I'm not even gonna trip. We've been through this shit before and have always recovered. This is the last time, though. We're getting too old to keep playing these damn mind games. I'm just going to let her know that we gotta settle down and have a normal marriage.

No more dalliances with other people just to keep things interesting. Most of the females I've screwed, including Dana, were just diversions to pass time while Paris was away at school. In the end, none of them compared to Paris, which is why we always stayed together. And I'm sure this clown Eric is just her way of getting back at me for how I've been treating her lately.

I've been an asshole, I know, but things just haven't been going my way since I graduated. I did so well with my art in college, and having it prominently displayed in Cobb Hall, I just naturally assumed I'd be able to get work easily. But that didn't happen and I guess I took it out on Paris, seeing her spend money freely on all the stuff she wanted while I couldn't buy anything.

Once we get back to Chicago, though, I'll show her. I'll get serious about pounding the pavement and finding a job, even if it's not in my field. Then we won't be so strapped for money and arguing all the time. I need her. There's no way she can up and leave me now with that mortgage to pay by myself, which is only in my name. I'd be up shit's creek.

Yeah, Paris has to come back. Because there is absolutely no way in the fucking world I'm calling my ol' girl and begging her to pay for my crib again. I'd never hear the end of it.

This is all about the Benjamins anyway. Paris probably flipped over wuss-boy just because he threw a few duckets her way. Two can play that game. Now I have the edge 'cause I've got the money and history on my side. She'll get all gushy and romantic, waxing nostalgic like she always does and we'll make up. Women love that crap.

"Our Deluxe room is $355 dollars a night," snips the man behind the desk at the Westin St. Francis hotel, as if I'll walk out.

I plop the entire wad of hundreds onto the counter and begin to count. "I'll pay cash for two nights now–I'm not really sure how long we'll be staying."

"Alright, let me see what's available," he says, tapping lightly on the keyboard.

Inside our room, the extravagant fancy chandeliers and plush flower curtains speak of the type of indulgence Paris craves. I see why it immediately appealed to her all those months ago when she looked it up on the Internet and made reservations. She loves comfy, safe environments. Even though I'm sure her and lover-boy have chosen a different San Francisco hotel, it can't hurt to stay here just in case.

Dana saunters to the bed and collapses. I walk over and plop beside her, thrilled to finally rest. Turning over, I begin to rub her hairy arms lightly. She stirs, then emits a moaning sound. I become excited, until her body convulses and I realize she's crying.

"What's wrong with you now?" I ask, pulling her over onto her back.

"Don't you get it? Eric saw us together. He saw us. There's nothing I can say now to get him back."

"That's not true. He's been fucking Paris," I offer, watching her face contort at the name. "He should be apologizing to you."

"I wish."

"No, for real. Once you see him, just rap to him, you know, a little blasé- skippy, and explain the whole thing. He'll forgive you." My voice conveys genuine concern, hoping there is a snowball's chance in hell for them to reunite.

"No, you don't know him. The look on his face when he saw us–" her words catch in a lump in her throat.

"Come on," I say, stroking her stomach. "It'll be okay. I'll make you feel better. We can chill out in here for a couple of days until the reading."

I lean down to kiss her, but she pushes me up and runs into the bathroom. Gagging sounds escape through the door and I realize she is vomiting.

"Man o' man." I sigh, sitting up on the bed, holding my head in my hands. Fighting fatigue, I stand up and leave the room.

I don't know where I'm walking, I just know I gotta get away from her sadness before it envelops and swallows me whole. There are enough crazy thoughts swirling in my own mind, abundant feelings of emptiness tugging away like hunger at my insides, without having to commiserate with that bitch's misery.

As soon as I spot the hotel bar, I enter and take a seat at a small table near the door. I order a glass of Johnny Walker Black straight and sip it, entertained by the assorted characters coming and going.

One catches my eye–a petite stylishly dressed Asian female who enters the bar alone. I smile at her instinctively, and to my shock, she walks straight to my table.

"Are you partying tonight?" she asks through narrow slits of heavily made-up eyes. Exotic and gorgeous, her unexpected attention causes me to stumble over my words as I respond.

"Pity-partying."

"Well, we can't have that. May I join you?"

"Sure." I feel as though I'm hallucinating without the acid.

"I'm Miyon," she says, extending a tiny arm.

"AC. What are you drinking?"

"I'd love champagne."

I motion for the waiter. "A bottle of your best champagne, please." I laugh as the words I've always wanted to say trickle from my mouth. Before he can even question me, I remove several bills from my wallet and place them on the table.

Miyon grins widely, her deep burgundy lipstick offsetting perfectly aligned teeth. "You really know how to treat a girl. So, are you in town for business?"

"How'd you know I was from out of town?"

"Woman's intuition, I guess."

"No," I say, contemplating hiding my wedding band for a split second. Then I recall how much more action I got after I got married, so instead I place my left hand conspicuously on the table. "I'm just here kinda visiting my wife. We've had some problems but I think we'll work it out."

"That's good," she says, touching my hand.

Bingo. The married thing always works like a charm. Took me a long time to figure out that a taken man is infinitely more appealing to women. Just look at Paris' obsession with Eric.

"So, are you from here?" I query, leaning closer.

"Born and raised. I love it here."

"I can see why." I pause to accept the champagne being presented to us in an ice-filled silver bucket. Pouring our flutes to the top and toasting, I grin at Miyon through the sheer crystal design traversing the rim of my glass.

She is so elegant; I can hardly believe my luck. Paris doesn't realize what she's giving up. It's not like I haven't always been able to get women, but rarely someone this good-looking and Korean, no less, as I learn during our extended conversation.

"Man, I wish I knew where to get some snow," I find myself exclaiming, growing tipsier and my tongue looser.

"I've got you covered," Miyon says, tapping her small handbag. "And if you need to buy some, I've got connections."

"Man, you are perfect. I've got the weed up in my room, you've got the budda, sounds like a perfect match."

"So you have a room here?"

"Yep. Do you want to go up? I've just got to get rid of my friend up there and we'll be straight."

"Are you sure it's cool?"

"Yeah. Come on," I say standing and holding my arm out for her to stand. "After you."

Watching Miyon's slender figure in the slinky black short skirt as she follows me into the elevator, I can hardly contain myself. Even with her slightly flat behind she is still hot as hell, and my dick prays that she's not teasing me.

"Get up," I say loudly, rousing Dana from sleep once we enter the room. Miyon stands off to the side, unsure.

"Why?"

"I have company. I need you to leave for awhile. Preferable all night," I whisper close to Dana's ear.

"But I'm sick. Where am I going to go?"

I huff and look up at the ceiling. "Here," I groan, throwing a one hundred dollar bill at her. "Find somewhere, please. I don't want you staying here."

"Fine," she says, deliberately dragging herself off the bed and out the door.

Miyon then takes a small brown vial from her purse as I prepare a joint and direct her to a smooth surface on the table. With a crisp, tightly rolled bill, we take turns doing a couple of lines.

"This is the ultimate high," I say, lighting the joint and puffing it, feeling the rush overtake my body.

"I know."

As soon as we finish smoking, I can no longer hold back from touching her. I'm already fully erect as I kiss her small mouth, overjoyed that she doesn't pull away. Leading her to the bed, I hurriedly unbutton her blouse and slide off her skirt.

Miyon's matching purple and black lace underwear accentuates her diminutive frame, and I pause to press her breasts together in her bra before removing it. Sliding her panties down and ripping off my clothes, I am so hard at the sight her completely naked except for slim black heels, that it almost hurts. This woman really knows how to turn on a man.

I bend down to suck her large nipples, brown and perky, almost bigger than her tiny breasts. She is delicate and absorbing, so different than any woman I've felt in a long time. Plunging into her, I immediately hit the top without being fully inside. This only excites me more. Paris was deep and endless. Pumping away, I begin to wonder if I'll even need to seek out Paris. With a woman like Miyon, I can easily see myself forgetting all others.

Thanks to the cocaine I remain firm and repeat the act several times. Hours later, I'm physically exhausted, but nowhere near sleep. Tooting more blow, the numbing drain oozes down the back of my throat as I recline against the pillow.

Miyon snorts a bit more, then begins to dress.

"Where're you going? Can't you stay all night? You got a boyfriend?"

"No, not exactly," she smiles wickedly, clasping her bra behind her back. "I could stay if you want me to, but all night is five thousand dollars."

"What?" I chuckle.

"Really. I'm pretty expensive. High-maintenance call-girl."

"Are you serious?"

"Of course." She slips on her blouse and skirt. "What'd you think I was?"

"I don't know. Not a hooker. You don't look like one," I stand, my voice growing serious. Miyon grabs her purse from the side table and walks closer to the door. "You didn't tell me up front."

"I asked if you were partying, I thought you knew the terminology. I can't just come right out and ask if you want to fuck for 800 bucks. You could be a cop."

"800 bones? Are you kidding? I've never paid that much for a piece of pussy in my life."

"Well, darling. I'm just not any old piece of pussy. I'm a professional."

I reach for my wallet. "Yeah, professional con-artist," I say, counting out eight bills. I open the door and throw the money into the hall on the floor. "Get the fuck out."

Miyon gawks with genuine shock, then darts into the hallway to pick up the money. Running down the hall, she glances back while stuffing the bills in her purse. I recognize Dana sitting in the corridor on the floor against the wall, and as Miyon passes her, she lifts herself to her feet and comes inside.

Dana looks slightly smug, the first hint of a smile I've seen on her face all day.

"Don't say a fucking word," I mumble, slamming the door with force after she walks in. "And gimme my money back."

📖

Today is finally the day, I exhale, lighting another Kool and blowing the smoke out of the open car window. Dana coughs in the seat next to me but I ignore her. I'm getting fed up with her ass. All she's done for the past two days is sleep, and when she is awake she bitches and moans about everything. Not that I'm in the mood to see all the tourist traps of this city or anything, but she could've at least dragged her lazy ass out of bed long enough to go somewhere.

Mainly, I just walked around by myself in the area close to the hotel. I wasn't in the mood for clubbing or shopping or anything. And after the incident with that whore, I figured I'd better just hold tight until I could see Paris again. Which should be any minute now, I think, glancing at my wristwatch. Paris always arrives at her readings early, to give her enough time to set up. And with the prime parking space right across the street from Great Expectations, the quirky bookstore that was listed on the itinerary she gave me months ago, I knew I couldn't miss her.

"There they are," Dana says without emotion, and I almost disregard her until I see Paris and Eric pulling into the space directly in front of us in a dark green Altima.

"Get down," I say, pressing Dana's head down near mine toward the center console as they exit the car.

After a few seconds I peek up to see Eric unloading display props from the trunk of the car. He slams it, and they trot together across the street, careful to dodge approaching traffic.

"What a fucking gentleman." I fling my lit cigarette butt onto the sidewalk through the window as Dana and I lift our heads. "I wish I'd brought my knife; I'd gut his ass like a fish."

Dana leans farther out her window and stares wistfully, as if to try and get closer to them.

I watch also, noticing that Paris is wearing a new dress, a silky flowery number that billows behind her in the wind as she runs. My abdomen tightens at the thought of her having new clothes that I've never seen before. I bet he bought it for her. It's like she's continuing to live without me, getting a fresh start and discarding her old life.

Being apart from her for a few days, coupled with her oddly conservative attire, I feel like she is a stranger. Yet and still, I think as Paris enters the door Eric holds open, she is the same woman I met so long ago, possessing that same svelte long-leggedness that first captivated me.

Seven years. How do you let someone go after all that time? They become more than your spouse; they're your best friend, lover, caregiver and sparing partner. They flow through your system as much as the blood in your veins. You can't throw that away. You can't go from seeing them every day to never again. It's like they drop off the face of the Earth.

Reaching into the back seat for the shopping bag full of spy stuff, I take out the Tracking Transmitter Kit, then cautiously open the car door. Ducking between the two cars, I attach the device to the underbelly of their car, then slink back to ours.

"Okay, now all we have to do is wait. And don't sleep, 'cause we gotta duck as soon as they come back out. We're lucky they didn't see us the first time."

"Yeah, thanks to me," Dana says, rolling her eyes.

Two antsy hours later, Paris and Eric emerge from the store and walk to the car. Once again, we hide until I hear the sound of doors slamming and the engine starting and fading away. I turn our ignition and take off, listening as the signal from the transmitter is engaged. Their car is a few hundred feet away, and I can easily follow as they twist and turn through the steep city streets until after a short while they stop in front of Golden Gate Park on Haight Street.

Paris pulls over at a corner and waits while Eric jumps out of the car. I pass them, stopping a safe distance away. Eric enters the red-bricked hotel and returns shortly, carrying luggage. Once he's inside the car, they take off again.

Driving across the Golden Gate Bridge, I wonder how long of a drive I'm in for. I pray that they're not about to drive all the way to Phoenix today for her next book tour stop. There's no way I'm in for that long haul tonight, and definitely no way I'm letting schizo Dana take the wheel. At least the transmitter will let me fall a safe distance behind, but not that far. I begin to wish I'd jacked some of that skeezer's cocaine the other night before kicking her out.

📖

I'm relieved when not that much later Paris and Eric exit the highway, then drive to a group of cottages on a hill and stop. I stay several hundred yards behind as they enter what looks like a lobby and reemerge several minutes later. Turning off my headlights, I snake behind them as they park and carry their belongings to a bungalow partially enveloped by trees.

Noting their cottage number, I drive back to the management office and get the one right across the way from theirs. Returning to our carriage house, I hide the car around the corner so that Dana and I can exit the car out of their line of sight.

"Wake up," I say, jostling Dana. "We're staying right across the street from them."

"Where are we?" she says, squinting and rubbing her eyes in the darkness.

"Auberge du Soleil, in the wine country. This better be worth it."

Ducking into our cottage, I'm impressed with the fireplace and Jacuzzi. After examining the entire villa, I keel onto the bed next to Dana and fall asleep.

Soon after daybreak I'm awake, opening the French doors and stepping onto the terrace. I crouch into a corner and light a cigarette and wait. I know Paris and Eric probably won't awaken for several hours, but I want to make extra sure I don't miss them.

As the sun rises and paints silvery rays over the vine-studded valley, I marvel at the symmetry of the rows of grapes. My gut aches with envy at their order, wishing my life had such direction. In such a short time my stable yet fun existence has whirled out of control. I didn't think Paris would let me down like the rest of the women I've been with. I never thought we'd be in this situation.

Thinking of it tightens my throat and I quickly run to the bathroom to pee so I won't cry. There's no way that woman's gonna make me break down like a wuss. Going back into the bedroom, I pop on the TV, still keeping one eye on their door.

I nearly fall back asleep before I realize there's movement in my side vision. Standing, I peek through the blinds to see Eric and Paris get into their car and pull off.

"Come on," I say, rousing Dana. "They just left. Let's go over there."

"Can't you go yourself?"

"Get your lazy ass up. I need you to be a lookout."

I grab the bag of spy equipment as Dana slowly pulls herself from the bed.

"Hurry up! We don't know how long they'll be gone."

Using the lock-pick gun to enter their cottage, I work quickly to set up the wireless video camera that looks like a clock directly in front of their bed. Being new lovers, I'm sure this is where they'll spend most of their time. I can only hope they don't realize the device wasn't there last night.

Dana picks up Eric's shirt and inhales deeply, holding it in her arms.

"Let's go," I say, watching as she carries the shirt with her.

I snatch it from her and throw it back on the floor.

"We can't make them any more suspicious that someone's been in here. That'll blow the whole deal."

Back in our cottage, I turn on the television and play around with the transmitter until I get a clear image of their bedroom. I can't test the voice transmission until someone speaks, so I sit back and wait for them to return, studying the unchanging screen like a piece of modern artwork. Still life in black and white. As poignant as Warhol's soup can.

Becoming antsy after a long time, I exit to the balcony to smoke a joint, a departure from my usual bathroom hideaway. I don't care–I'd rather risk someone smelling the odor than miss Paris and Eric. The patio door opens, and I turn to see Dana standing in the doorway.

"You scared the shit out of me," I say, holding my heart. "I thought you were asleep."

"No," she says, closing the door behind her and walking close to me. She removes the joint from my fingers, and before I realize what's happening, places it to her lips.

"What are you doing, Miss Holier-Than-Thou?"

"Fuck it," Dana says, inhaling slowly and deeply, forcing vapors from her mouth like a long drawn-out yawn.

She looks bad. I scrutinize her for the first time in days, noticing the bags that have grown under her eyes. Her face is plain and sallow, unusual for a woman who has always worn makeup. Her hair is pulled back in tangled clumps, exposing her broad forehead. Dana's pain has consumed her countenance, etching anguish on a once pleasant appearance, like a riot-torn neighborhood.

To think, I went along with this whole trip just so I could get closer to her, to see if I could get with her one more time. Now that I have, and now that she's here with me, I don't even want her anymore.

"Don't get carried away," I say, taking the joint back. "Where's your God now?"

She chuckles half-heartedly, her shoulders raising for a brief moment then falling. The witty retorts are gone, along with her spunk. "Nowhere, I guess."

We finish the joint and stare off into the distance in uncharacteristic silence.

📖

"I'm buzzed from all that wine." Paris' voice sounds deeper through the television when they finally arrive back in their villa.

I increase the volume while Dana sits next to me on the bed.

"You don't need to drink," Eric says. "You get crazy."

"No I don't. I'm in control. I wasn't the one flirting with the tour guide."

"What? Who me? I wasn't flirting with no tour guide."

Paris passes before the camera, removing her shirt. "I don't care. Don't get so defensive, I'm not Dana."

Dana inhales sharply, staring intently at the screen.

"I didn't say you were."

"It doesn't matter. You can be honest with me. Just tell me what you want," she says, posing in front of him in her underwear. "I just want to make you happy."

"You do make me happy," he says, hugging her closely.

"Good, but I'm not the jealous type. You can tell me. If you want another woman you can bring her home."

Eric pulls back. "I don't want that. You want that? Just like you did with AC and Dana?"

"No, not like that. I'm just saying, if you wanted another woman, you can tell me."

"Well I don't. You're the only woman I need."

They fall into each other's arms again, kissing for what seems like an eternity. Moving like clockwork to the bed, Paris removes Eric's shirt and shorts. Soon they are naked, rolling atop each other and making love.

"Turn it off!" Dana screams, rising. She reaches for the television but I push her out of the way.

"Leave it alone."

"Turn it off! Turn it off!" she repeats, running into the bathroom.

I ignore her, continuing to peer at the real-life X-rated scene before my eyes. The guttural sounds of Dana puking once again escape from the other room. I turn up the volume.

Paris' familiar curves arouse me, prompting me to reach into my pants and tug at my semi-hardness. They continue, with her riding atop him, briefly stopping to turn away from him and face the camera directly as she places him inside her again. I pump harder, fascinated by this new and strange position that she never tried with me.

Imagining myself underneath her, I want to run across the street and burst inside. Into the room and her in one fell swoop. I can't, I know. She'd run away faster than anything. If I could only be within her one more time, feel those walls surrounding me.

But, I have to be patient and do this the right way. I must follow my plan. And if it works, it'll be worth all this shit she's putting me through. Damn bitch, I grit my teeth, exploding onto my hand and thigh.

Grabbing a T-shirt to clean myself, I watch them finish as well.

"Oohh!" Paris says excitedly, popping herself off of him. "We should take a balloon ride in the morning!"

"I'm not getting up in one of those things."

"Fine, I'll go without you."

Eric squeezes her closely. "No you're not. You're staying right here with me."

"Come on," she giggles. "We only have two more days before we go to Phoenix. And it's so pretty here, I want to see more of the valley."

"We saw it today. Besides, we need to be keeping a low profile. We don't even need to go to Phoenix. You don't know where your lunatic husband is."

I tighten my fist and grin.

"Please, he's probably back in Chicago by now. And we definitely don't want to go back there and run into him. We might as well go to Phoenix."

"Whatever, but you gotta just stop telling everybody where you're gonna be. Like that woman at that bookstore we just left. You shouldn't have told her we were coming here."

"That was the manager! She might need to contact me. You never know, people like that could help me get an agent or a contract or something."

"Whatever. You just need to be safe because I don't want anything to happen to you."

Paris adopts a baby voice. "Aw, that's so sweet. You're worried about me."

They begin kissing and making love once again with renewed intensity. I smile, connecting the final dots of my scheme.

147

I'm up with the birds the next morning, excited to start my plan of attack. First, I search the Yellow Pages for the nearest men's clothing store and call for directions. Once there, I drop $480 on a sleek, black pinstriped suit with a three-button single-breasted jacket. I also buy a starched white shirt and a colorful tie, not losing my artistic edge completely. Shiny patent leather tasseled shoes complete the package.

Staring in the dressing room mirror, I can't help but admire myself. It's been forever since I've worn anything so business-like, let alone a nice suit like this. Paris has got to love it. All those times she begged me to get a suit in hopes of finding a job, and me always refusing because I didn't want to conform. Maybe I would have long ago if I knew I'd look this distinguished.

On the way back to the hotel, I pick up a dozen roses from a unique florist in a small store.

"Don't say a word," I say to Dana as soon as I enter the room.

"Why?"

Hanging the suit on the closet rack and placing the flowers on the dresser, I turn to her. "Because, it's important. I need you to be absolutely silent for a few minutes. Don't even get up, flush the toilet or nothing."

"Fine."

Digging through the spy bag full of goodies, I take out the Voice Changer II and read the instructions before I hook it onto our phone. I pick up the receiver, but then put it down again and walk over to the television and turn it off, just in case of reverb.

Sitting back on the bed, I force my breathing to an even tone, then turn to Dana and place my finger up to my lip as a final shushing signal. After a few moments, I dial and wait.

"Hello?" Paris answers, her voice as sweet as a songstress.

"Yes," I respond, remembering to speak in a normal tone, knowing the voice changer alters my inflection and pitch to an unrecognizable state. "Paris Gibbins, please."

"Who is this?"

"This is Danny Duda, with the San Francisco Chronicle."

"Oh my God."

"I got your number from the manager at Great Expectations, I hope you don't mind the intrusion."

"No…not at all."

"Well, the reason I'm calling is that I've heard a lot of buzz about your book and I wanted to set up an interview with you."

Paris gasps. "That would be great. Where are you located?"

"Huh, my office is on Montgomery Street," I stammer, recalling a random street name I'd seen in the city. "But actually, I was thinking it would be easier for me to come to you."

"Really? In Napa Valley?"

"Yes, that fits in my schedule perfectly. My wife and I are planning to be there later this evening so I thought I could sneak in the interview sometime tonight."

"That sounds great."

"Good. Actually, I'm very familiar with Auberge du Soleil. They have one of my most favorite restaurants in the valley. I was thinking we could dine there, on the company, of course, around seven o'clock?"

"That's fine with me."

"Okay, it's all set then. I'll be the man in the pin-stripped suit. And, a couple of ground rules: I'd like to interview you alone, and I'll be taping the conversation."

"No problem. Thanks so much for calling me; I can't believe this. I'll see you there."

We exchange a few more pleasantries then hang up. I turn to Dana and grin.

I force myself to stay in the room until ten minutes after seven, making sure Paris will already be there waiting for me. Spraying on a little more of the spicy cologne she always favored, I pick up the roses and walk to the door.

"Just tell me," Dana says, following me outside. "What does she have that I don't have? Why do men go falling head over feet for her?"

I give her a pathetic look and shake my head. "Can't call it."

Approaching the restaurant, I feel like a giddy teenager at prom. I spot her first, sitting pretty at the edge of the deck, at the table I tipped the host extra to guarantee for tonight. As I inch closer, she sits straight up, then stands and grabs her purse.

"Please," I say, "just sit."

"No, AC. You have to leave. I'm waiting for a very important..." her voice trails off as she examines my suit. "Aw shit."

"I had to, I knew it was the only way you'd see me."

"Dammit, I really thought I had a good interview. How'd you do that?"

"Never mind, please, just sit down."

"Fine," she says, plopping down at the table. "Talk."

"First, these are for you." I thrust the flowers toward her but she waves her hands.

"I don't want them. Don't you understand that it's over?"

"That's why I brought you here. I thought we could talk about that. I want to treat you to a nice dinner tonight, and tomorrow, I can take you for a hot air balloon ride."

Paris squints. "Look, I don't want any of this. And anyway, I am glad you're here. I need to talk to you."

"Yeah," I say, hopeful.

"I really do love you, AC, but I just don't think we were meant to be together. I think...we should get a divorce."

Her words sting my cheek like the cool night air.

"You don't mean that. You're just saying that now because you're mad at me. But I've changed. I messed up before, but I'm gonna make it up to you."

Paris shakes her head.

"I will, I swear. I know now what I need to do. I won't be mean anymore. I promise. I'll go to counseling. Just give me another chance."

"AC, I have already. I've given you fifth and sixth chances."

"I know, but I just want to..." I reach out and touch her hand on the table. "I've just got to make love to you again."

Paris snatches her hand away and stands. I notice her ring finger is now bare. "No. That's never going to happen again. It's over. Don't you get it? It's over. Please, just leave me alone."

She walks off quickly, almost running, with a few people staring after her. I want to get up and chase her, but I refuse to be humiliated anymore tonight in public. Stupid bitch. How in the world does she think she can leave me sitting here alone like a damn fool, holding a fucking dozen red roses?

Paris didn't even give me a chance to explain. I'm laying it all out on the line, telling her all the stuff I'll do to make her happy and all she can say is she wants a divorce? After I've gone through all this money to make this night perfect? I don't think so.

That's alright. I'm keeping my cool. I ain't gonna make a scene like in Denver. She's not making an idiot out of me. Leave her alone. Yeah, we'll see about that. I don't fucking need her. She thinks she can do this bullshit to me? Just wait. Fuck this shit. No more nicey-nice. All bets are off. That bitch is gonna pay.

Chapter 8

Phoenix and Sedona, Arizona

Be still, and know that I am God.

Psalm 46:10

"Grandma!" I say, taking her shrunken yet sturdy frame into my arms.

"Eric," she drawls warmly, giving me a tight squeeze. "I can't believe you're here."

"This is my sweetie-pie."

"Well hello sweetie-pie."

"Nice to meet you," Paris smiles and they exchange a brief embrace.

"She's gorgeous," Ruby proclaims to me, as if Paris isn't standing there. "Come on in."

She leads us inside her salmon-colored adobe home, the bottom of her bright tunic and matching flare-legged pants dancing behind her as she takes small steps. Stucco walls open to an expansive great room, and my memory takes me back to summer vacations spent sliding across the mosaic floors with my brother and sister.

"It's just like I remember it," I say, plopping down next to Paris on a plush sofa that sits low to the ground. The mass of hanging plants, none of them southwestern in origin, gives the home the feeling of an oasis in the desert.

"I haven't changed much since you last came out. And that's been years now."

"Yep," I agree, thinking back. "I guess the last time was Grandpa's funeral."

"Wow. That was nine years ago. Good thing I visit Chicago every year or else I wouldn't know what you looked like."

Ruby grins at me, her face an older replica of my mother's, strong yet feminine and much younger in appearance than her 81 years. Her voice is warm and soothing as always, its delicate timbre swaddling me in safety. Such a smart and accomplished woman, I chuckle when I think of how I worried about her well-being after losing Papa. Yet her drive and determination has kept her going better than anyone could imagine.

"So, I hear you're a writer," she says to Paris.

"Yes. I'm on a book tour right now."

"What's the name of your book?"

"*The Files*," I say quickly. Paris glances at me but then looks down. "It's a work of fiction about different people's lives. She's really good. I'm so proud of her."

"That sounds fascinating. I'd love to read it. I love reading."

"Me too," Paris says. "I'll make sure to get you a copy."

Letting out an exaggerated yawn, I stretch my arm around Paris. "We are so pooped. I drove all night from Napa Valley."

"You must be. I've got your room all ready right through there so you two just go get some sleep."

"Thank you," Paris stands. She walks into the room, and my grandmother sits next to me after Paris is out of earshot.

"I didn't want to say anything in front of Paris, but Dana called last night," she whispers, barely audible.

"What?" I bolt upright. "How did she get your number?"

"I have no idea, I didn't even ask. She just went on and on about how you left her stranded in Las Vegas and how you broke up her friendship with Paris..."

I raise my hands to stop her. "Grandma, I swear. Don't listen to anything that girl says. She has problems, and right now she'll make up any kind of lie to get me back."

"Well I was uncomfortable talking to her. I've only met her that one time, and now she calls out of the blue and tells me all these personal matters. She even had the gall to ask me not to let Paris stay here."

"She said that?" I crinkle my brow, becoming anxious and angry at Dana's indignation, wondering what else she told my grandmother.

"That and a lot more. I had to finally force her off the phone."

"Good. I'm so sorry she called you. I never gave her your phone number. She's just desperate to get back into my life because she messed up and she knows it."

"She sounded desperate. She sounded...I don't know."

"She is so totally different than the person I thought she was. Over two years you think you know a person but Dana had me totally fooled."

"In what way?"

"Every way, I guess. She lied so much. It just goes to show you that you can't trust people."

"Oh, now I wouldn't go that far. One bad apple shouldn't spoil the whole bunch."

"I know. I'm just saying, I'm going to be a lot more careful from now on."

"Well, Paris seems lovely. You two look like brother and sister."

I smile. "Everybody says that. I really like her."

Reclining my head against the sofa, I stare at the sparkling blue water of the pool in the searing afternoon heat. I take comfort in the fact that dingle-berry hopefully only called my grandmother and not my parents. Ruby is more like a caring, interested friend who doesn't judge me, something I've always treasured.

"I wish we could just get away from this craziness for awhile."

"You're not in trouble, are you?" Ruby says, with a fearful expression.

"No, I'm fine. I just don't want Dana bothering us."

"Well, you know you can stay here as long as you'd like."

"I know," I say, envisioning AC and Dana showing up at my grandmother's house and causing a ruckus. "No, we don't want to put you out. I just wanna chill out somewhere for a little vacation before going back home."

"I know the perfect place. You remember my friends' daughter Toni?"

I nod yes.

"She has that place in Sedona she never uses. She lets me use it all the time. I'll call her, but I'm sure she won't mind if you two stayed there. It's very nice."

"Really? Could you?"

"I'll call her today."

"Thanks," I stand and hug her, all the while glancing down the hallway at the front door.

📖

That night the rains came like an unwelcome intruder in the still of the evening. Such an oddity in the desert, I think, resting face up with my hands perched behind my head, listening to the drops beat mercilessly against the window.

"What's wrong?" Paris stirs, rolling over.

"Nothing. Go back to sleep."

"No, really. What is it?"

I pause, staring at shadows on the ceiling. "We need to leave tomorrow morning and go to Sedona."

"Why?"

"My grandmother's friend said we can stay in her house. It's empty."

"Cool," she murmurs, "but we can't go until day after tomorrow. Remember I have that talk show to do."

"We should skip that. We need to get out of here right away."

"Why? We just got here."

"Dana called here. She knows we're here."

Paris sits up on her elbow. "How'd she find out?"

"I don't know. I never gave her this number. I know my parents would never give it to her."

"What's going on? How are they finding out where we are?"

"I don't know, but I don't want her or AC coming anywhere near here."

"Shoot, if he knows, we need to be here so your grandmother won't be by herself."

I shake my head. "No. I just want to go and get my grandmother out of this mess."

"Okay, but can't we just wait until right after the show? That would only be one more day."

I sit straight up. "Is that all you care about? Don't you care about my family being hurt?"

"Of course I do," she squeals. "We can cancel all the rest of the tour stops, but since we're already here, we might as well do this one. It's important."

"It's not like it's Oprah."

"I know, but I can still get some orders. I need it to pay for my second printing, especially since they fucked up all the books I had with me and Lord knows how many back in our apartment."

"What's the show about?"

"Pre-teen sex."

"What do you have to talk about?"

"I was gonna talk about how I had sex too early at 12, and try to convince the–"

"What? You're going to say that on TV? What if my grandmother watches?"

"Oh, she's not gonna watch. You said yourself, it's not Oprah. It's taped anyway."

"Is that true?"

"What?"

"You were 12-years-old?"

"Yeah. Didn't you read the copy of the book I gave you?"

"I couldn't. Dana took it."

Paris huffs. "Great, I'll have to dig up another copy somehow."

"I don't want it, and I definitely don't want my family to find out this kind of stuff. Dana calling here was bad enough."

"Look, this is who I am."

"What?" I say, no longer to contain my shame. "A freak-of-the-week? That's what you want everybody to know?"

Paris stops, seemingly too shocked to reply, and when she does, the words are forced out of her throat in broken fragments. "No. What...I was trying to say...was...that I want to let these young girls know that they don't have to have sex as young as I did. They watch videos with Lil' Kim and Foxy Brown parading around in nothing and think their body is all they have to offer. I want them to know that their mind and heart are so much more valuable."

"Well that's fine, but why do you have to tell them everything about yourself?"

"Real life experience is the best teacher. They'll be more receptive if I share my story and not just sit there and say, 'Don't do this, don't do that,' like my mother did."

"So fine, do it in a novel. You can write anything you want in fiction, I don't care. Then you don't have to tell my personal business to everyone in the street. You're my business now."

"Maybe the next book will be fiction. But for now, this is the book I have. And it was here before you even came into the picture."

"Fine, keep your damn book. But I can't live with a person who's gonna spread my business all over the street."

"Oh, what? You'd rather have–"

"Lower your voice," I say sternly. "My grandmother can hear you."

Paris whispers loudly. "You'd rather have a woman like Dana, who plays all goody-goody in front of you but is off doing any and everything behind your back? You don't even know the shit she did while y'all were together. At least I don't lie to you. I'm putting it all on the line."

"I don't care about her. She's out of the picture. And I want the truth, but I just want it between you and me. If you can't handle that, then…"

"Then what?"

"Then maybe you're not the person for me and I'm not the man you need."

"How could you say that?" Paris moans, then falls onto the bed with her back facing me, sobbing.

I turn my back to her and face the window, watching the sprinkles streak down the pane. Getting up, I twist the shades closed.

📖

"Hey sleepy-head," my grandmother teases the next morning as I stumble into the living room and kiss her cheek.

"I can't believe I slept so late. Where's Paris?"

"She's out by the pool. We let you sleep because we knew you were tired from driving so long. Do you want some breakfast?"

"No thanks, I'm going to go out and talk to her."

I slide open the patio door and step onto the deck, and Paris glances at me through pitch-black shades then back at her book.

"What're you doing?" I ask, sitting on the lounger next to her.

"Sunbathing," she says solemnly, staring at the pages.

"Look," I touch her arm, "I'm sorry about last night. We can stay one more day. But we have to leave right after the show tomorrow."

Paris drops her book into her lap and hugs me. "Thank you. You really hurt me when you said I wasn't the woman for you."

"I didn't mean that; I was just mad. You are definitely the woman for me; I just worry about everyone knowing everything about us. Can't you understand that?"

"Yes, I understand. I'll tone it down on the show."

"I love you," I say finally, allowing my building surge of emotions to release.

"I love you, too." Paris hugs me even harder and cries onto my shoulder before breaking away suddenly. "Oh! Look what I found this morning. You are not going to believe this."

"What?"

She twists to grab something from the other side of the ground and opens her palm, displaying a small gadget. "A tracking device."

"Where was that?"

"On our car. I knew there had to be some way they found us in Napa Valley, and something told me to check the car."

"Aw, man," I take it from her and examine the device. "I never even thought of that."

"Only the minds of maniacs would do something like that. We can't put anything past them."

I carry the contraption into the house and quietly riffle through drawers and cabinets until I find a hammer. Going back onto the pool area, I set it on the concrete and smash it with one heavy blow.

📖

"Good morning ladies and gentleman, I'm Maria King and this is Eye on Community," begins the raven-haired hostess, speaking with a slight Spanish accent. "Today we are talking about pre-teen sex and have several guests with us to shed some light on the topic.

"First is Maya, a fifteen-year-old who has engaged in sex since she was eleven–" the crowd lets out a predictable gasp as the host continues, "–and says old rules don't apply to her generation.

"Next we have Staci, who is twelve and has already had several lovers. Beside her is Natasha, who says the only pre-teens that aren't doing it nowadays are either lying or nerds.

"And lastly, we have Paris Gibbins, who wrote a book called *The Sex Files* where she details losing her virginity at twelve-years-old but now says she regrets that decision. Welcome all."

Forcing myself to applaud along with the mass of vacationers and senior citizens, I sink farther into my seat as the spectacle begins. The thought suddenly occurs to me that since I'm seated in the front row, Paris might refer to me, and I could be placed on television. I should have never agreed to this.

"So, Maya," Maria says, glancing at a shuffled stack of blue note cards, "what made you want to have sex at eleven?"

"I was ready," the young girl says bluntly, cocking her head to one side and crossing her arms in front of her thin torso.

"At age eleven? Were you pressured into it?"

"No, I was the one who wanted it. I was curious."

"Do you think the fact that all your girlfriends were not virgins played any part in that?"

"Not really. I followed my own mind."

The talk show host sighs and the audience follows suit, mocking the teenager.

"I can understand that," Paris jumps in. I hold my breath as I wait for her to make her point. "That's the same way I felt. In fact, my best friend tried to talk me out of it before I did it. But I wouldn't listen. It's like I had made up my mind that that was what I wanted to do and there was no stopping me."

"And how was it?"

Paris turns her attention to the host and then to me, her mouth ajar. A few uncomfortable seconds pass without her saying a word.

"Paris?" the host asks, but she is quiet, seemingly frozen.

Is she afraid to speak? Does she want me to say something? I nod for her to continue but she doesn't. I've never seen her suffer from stage fright before. What's wrong with her?

All of a sudden I realize she is not looking directly at me, but above my head. I turn around and look up, following her line of sight.

Then I see them. AC and a woman stand behind the glass partition on the viewing balcony above us. He wears fatigues and scowls at Paris. My eyes widen farther as I see the woman is actually Dana, dressed in the tight spandex tank top and purple Daisy Duke's that I forbade her to wear ever since I first saw them two years ago. I'm unable to move as I take in her image.

Her hair stands wildly on end and bright red lipstick adorns her mouth; she is a caricature of herself. The imprint of her ribs and concave stomach show through the flimsy material, and her breasts shrink in the bra-like top. Smiling deviously down at me, she slings an arm loosely around AC's hips and rests her head on his shoulder, as if to say, "Look at my new man."

However, AC pays her no mind, unintentionally knocking her away as he starts to beat on the glass with clenched fists. The entire audience and cameras swing to look at the unexpected noise, and I finally force my feet from their locked stance and run to Paris.

"Come on," I say, grabbing her hand and running towards the back stage.

Something stops her in her tracks, and I glance back to see her struggling with a microphone that is snaked under her blouse and attached to her lapel. "I'm stuck!"

I turn back to help, both of us fumbling and grabbing the microphone, trying to pull it off.

AC rattles the glass harder and screams, "Paris!" while the stunned viewers stare. It is a scene straight out of *The Graduate*, yet the woman being sought isn't calling her suitor's name, she is running away from him.

Suddenly, AC takes both fists and pounds hard, shattering the partition and sending shards of glass onto the crowd. Bedlam breaks out as he steps onto the ledge and searches for a clear path to land. He jumps down, toppling people and chairs to the ground.

Paris finally rips the cord free from her blouse and we run together through the backstage hallway and out to the parking lot. I tug the car keys from my pants and quickly open the doors, start the car and throw it into reverse while watching the exit door.

As I put it in drive, the stage door flings open, and groups of people rush out screaming. I don't see AC in the bunch, but I focus on getting out of the parking lot and onto the street without getting hit or hitting anyone.

"You see why I didn't want to come? You see!" I scream, as Paris places on her seatbelt.

"I'm sorry," she whimpers in a shaken voice, turning to look behind us.

I run several red lights, halfway hoping a policeman will stop us so we can tell him a madman is after us. No such luck, so I barrel onto the first highway I see and zoom to the farthest left lane, pushing the pedal to the ground until the steering wheel vibrates.

"We shoulda left yesterday like I said."

"I'm know, I'm sorry. I didn't know he would do that. I'm sorry," Paris says, curling against the passenger-side door.

"That's all you are is sorry!"

I check the rear-view mirror every couple of seconds, fearing that every car racing up to my tail is AC. When I confirm that they aren't, my bearings return and I find the correct road to Sedona, but still exit and enter the highway a few times, driving a convoluted path to ensure no one follows us.

After an hour racing through the cactus-laden drylands, I'm a little calmer and my heart rate and breathing have returned to their normal state, a necessity to negotiate the steeper slopes ahead.

Paris still cowers in the corner, her legs shifted away from me. I feel bad for yelling, because I know she is just as scared as I am.

Wanting to apologize, I don't, for I can't admit to my lady that I'm afraid. I'm supposed to be her protection, the knight in shining armor that fights for her honor. Instead, I'm running away like a coward. She might even be mad that I didn't stand up to AC right then and there and force him to leave her alone.

A real man would have done that. Like my brother Anthony. "Fight like a man," he would always say to me, drawing his body up to his full six feet four inch height.

He never walked away from a fight, in fact, he even started several of them. Sometimes, he would take up for me and Renee when we were little, but as he grew older, it would mostly be just him fighting over some woman he messed around with.

162

Even when he got his ass kicked, he was still talking shit. I was never like that. I always shied away from brawling, and have only had two fights in my whole life. The first was just a playground thing, but the second one happened in college with an annoying friend who always took his practical jokes too far.

At least he was an equal match of medium build, and our friends broke it up before it really got started. That was nothing like the formidable opponent I now face, a lunatic husband with an arsenal of weapons and fire in his eyes. How do you fight that? With one shot to the head he could kill me or Paris. I should get a gun; I need at least a fighting chance.

I also need to call my grandmother. Dana and AC could've found out where she lives and gone there to ask her where we are. I don't even want to think of what they might do when she refuses, especially after what I just saw AC do to those old people in the audience. I'm so stupid. I should have placed that tracking device on some other car instead of destroying it right at her house.

And what is up with Dana dressed like a whore and leaning on AC? Did I drive her that insane? With her sick mind directing AC, who knows what kind of harm might come to anyone of us.

I press the gas pedal harder, gliding swiftly up and down the hills until the red rocks of Sedona come into view.

📖

"Oh my God," Paris gasps, breaking her silence as we enter the driveway of the massive wooden home. "Is this the right house?"

"Yeah," I say, directing the car into the underground three-car space. "This is it."

"Sweet."

"Let me go in first."

I enter the home cautiously with Paris behind me gawking at the extensive view of the mountainous valley provided by floor-to-ceiling windows that continue into skylights.

"We've got to cover these up."

"They are scary. How?"

"We'll find some newspaper or something. Come on, let's do it now."

"Okay," she says, inspecting the rest of the house.

I gather a ladder from the storage room and find tape and newspaper in the garage. She returns to the room to help, but stops at the sliding glass door to inspect the pool.

"This is unbelievable."

"It's nice. I knew Toni was doing well, but not this well."

"Thank God she let us stay here. This is the nicest home I've ever been in."

Paris unlocks the latch and begins to slide open the door.

"Don't go out there," I yell, startling her.

"I was just checking it out."

"Look," I say, leaning against the ladder. "We do not need to leave this house."

"But I wasn't leaving, I was just looking at the pool."

"I know. But you don't know if AC was right behind us or not. He might have put another transmitter on the car we didn't see and he could be staring at us right now. Let's just stay inside."

"Okay," she says, closing the door shut and twisting the blinds closed. "But we don't know how long we'll be here. We have to get food sometime."

"I saw food in the cabinets, and we can just drink tap water. We have to really be careful to stay out of sight. And don't use the phone, you never know if it's tapped."

"Okay. I'm sorry. I won't go outside or call anyone."

Climbing the ladder, I attach newspaper to all the windows I can reach, leaving the highest windows uncovered. Stepping down, I try to think of a way to cover the rest.

"She didn't have a taller ladder?" Paris asks, placing her arms through the spaces formed from my hands on my hips.

"Nope."

"Well, that's not bad. At least you got all the ground level ones covered and then some. We should be okay. She has an alarm."

"I know what I can do," I say, breaking from her embrace. Retrieving the long-handled dusting mop from the garage, I return to the living room.

"Be careful," Paris says, watching as I attempt to stick a sheet of newspaper onto the window from the mop. However, the tape that is stuck to the mop wins out, and every time I press it against the window and remove the mop, it's still stuck to the mop.

I climb down in frustration. "We just need to stay out of this room."

"At night?"

"All the time. At least the other rooms don't have these tall windows."

Inspecting each room of the house, I make sure every door is locked and all shades are closed. I put cans in front of the windows to alert me of an intruder in case the real alarm fails.

At night I take to bed with me the largest butcher knife and hammer I can find in the house. As Paris snores, I sit awake, poised and ready for any shadow or noise that enters the room.

Each time my head droops in sleep, I snap it back to alertness. By sunlight, I'm dead tired but I don't want to succumb to sleep and wake up being attacked. Later in the afternoon I can no longer hold back and fall asleep for several hours. When I awaken, Paris and I entertain ourselves by watching television and playing board games that we find in the study.

After just 24 hours in the house, we are already bored. We make love, talk and eat but nothing keeps us occupied for very long. I never realized how imprisoned one feels without going outside.

"You can take a swim," I relent, watching Paris' face light up like a candle.

"For real?"

"Yeah, I'll go out there with you."

I go outside first, searching the hills with binoculars I found in the drawer, making sure no shadowy figures are standing in the landscape.

"What are you doing?" I ask as she begins taking off her clothes.

"I don't have a bathing suit. I have to swim in my underwear."

"Just leave your T-shirt on."

"Why? My underwear is just like a bikini."

"Just do what I say."

"Fine," she snaps, jumping in the pool with a loud squeal.

I shush her when she resurfaces, smoothing the water from her round face.

"Aren't you coming in?"

"No, I'll just stand here."

The cool blueness beckons me in the stifling heat, but I remain on the edge. I refuse to let my guard down for one moment and allow AC and Dana to sneak up on us like in Phoenix.

After a half-hour, I cajole Paris, frolicking like a child, out of the pool. Pouting, she obliges, kissing me before barely drying herself and going into the house to shower.

"Eric! Come here!" she shouts soon after entering the master bedroom.

The urgency in her scream sends me lunging toward her, unarmed but ready to break up a battle.

"What?" I say, annoyed at finding her safe and alone. My irritation is soon allayed when she points to the big screen television and I see a grainy videotaped image of AC at the Phoenix studio. They show him pounding then shattering the glass.

"The surprised crowd of mostly elderly citizens scrambled to their feet," the announcer says dramatically, "but not soon enough to escape the hurtling glass that sent many to the hospital with lacerations. One man is in serious condition after suffering a concussion caused by the attacker landing on him.

"The enraged man was after this woman," Paris gasps at seeing her image highlighted in a freeze-frame shot, "his estranged wife, who was on the show to promote her book *The Sex Files*."

Next appears footage of AC being led away in handcuffs by police. "Fortunately, a few good Samaritans were able to detain the attacker until cops arrived and carted him off to jail."

AC struggles like a trapped animal against the two men holding him, his face a twisted shouting mass beneath streaks of blood.

Paris and I are motionless, continuing to stare at the screen as the announcer introduces the next segment.

"Well, at least they mentioned my book," she laughs nervously.

"What show is this?"

"Real TV. You've never seen it?"

I shake my head. "No."

"Thank God he's in jail."

"That don't mean nothing. They could have let him out after a couple of hours. You know how they let murderers out now in months."

"Naw, a Black man hurting old White people? He's still in jail."

"We don't know that. And if he is in jail, then he's still close to us, right in Phoenix waiting to be set free. We still have to keep a low profile."

"I know," she says, exacerbated.

I lean over and hug her, but break quickly to return to the living room and retrieve the butcher knife.

📖

While Paris grows seemingly more comfortable with each passing day without incident, I become increasingly paranoid. The image of AC's bloodstained face haunts me day and night.

"I wonder what that cross is up there," Paris says, appearing next to me in the forbidden room, disrupting my thoughts as we peer through the top windows at the scenery.

"I don't know."

"Let's go see it."

Here we go again. "No, we don't need to go up there."

"Come on, it's not like we haven't been outside. We've gone to the grocery store."

"That was a necessity. We don't have time for sightseeing."

"Fine," she snaps, going into the bedroom.

I stand alone for some time, thinking of how much I miss my family and wish I could call them. I know Paris probably wants to call her mother and sister, too.

I follow her and sit on the bed. "Alright, let's go. But not for long."

Driving in the general direction of the cross, I am excited to get out of the house. As nice as the place is, I admit I'm getting cabin fever as well.

When we finally find the structure, we learn it is a church named The Chapel of the Holy Cross, a popular tourist stop. Paris pleads to go inside, so we enter the small building as I look around guardedly.

"This is great. We stick out like a sore thumb," I say, noticing we are the only Blacks in the mass of sightseers.

Paris walks to the front left of the temple, lights a candle then sits down in the pew. After a few silent moments, she kneels and holds her head against her hands. I wait as patiently as possible, then gently touch her arm to signal it's time to go. Her face is wet with tears.

"What's wrong?" I ask.

"Nothing, I'm just happy, that's all."

📖

"I want to go back there," Paris says the first thing upon waking the very next morning.

"We will sometime."

"No," she gets out of bed. "I mean now."

"Why?"

"I don't know, I just felt so good when we went there yesterday. So at peace. I want to go. If you don't want to go, please let me use the car because I want to."

"I'll go," I sigh, regretting I ever agreed to take her there yesterday. "What are you bringing that for?"

Paris brushes dust from her laptop and slides it in its case. "I want to jot down some notes."

We return to the church and sit, with Paris clicking away at the keyboard as I stare through the glass windows at the red rocks. I find myself getting lost in them, so I turn around to watch people enter the chapel.

"Are you sure you should be doing that here?" I ask, causing her to stop typing momentarily.

"Why not?" she asks, the screen casting a glow on her pretty face.

I don't answer, and Paris looks back to her laptop and types.

It becomes our daily ritual, visiting the church in the morning when it is less crowded. Every day I drag Paris away, and as we leave, she forces a bill into the stuffed collection box at the entrance.

"Don't give all your money away," I say one morning when I am too exhausted to get up, so I let her go alone. Handing her my cell phone, I instruct, "Page me at the slightest hint of trouble."

"Thank you," she grins, kissing me with enthusiasm.

After that day, Paris trods up to the chapel alone, laptop in hand, then returns a happy camper.

📖

"Look at this," she says, one afternoon after logging onto AOL. "I have emails from publishers wanting to buy my book!"

"How do you know those are for real?"

"I can check Book Wire."

"What?"

She types furiously and taps her thigh as she waits for the site to load. "Oh my God, it's true. Look!"

I read aloud the headlines on the screen. "Publishers seek elusive author of *The Sex Files*."

"I can't believe this," she says, turning the screen back to read more about the story. "I bet you they heard about the book on Real TV and since they couldn't get in touch with me, they assumed I was playing hard to get."

"That'll be the day."

"Shut up," she says, slapping me gently and smiling.

"Well, this doesn't mean you should call them. This could be a scam."

"No way, this is a reputable site."

"But you can't. It's too risky."

Paris looks down at the screen and continues to read. "But they want me now! This is what I've been waiting for. It could mean a lot of money."

"Lot of good that'll do you when you're dead."

Paris jerks her head up, then continues to click around the site. After some time, she logs off and closes the laptop and curls into a ball on the bed.

📖

"We have to go to New York," she says bluntly one morning, weeks past the day we read the news on the net.

"We can't. It's still too soon to go. We don't know where AC is."

"I don't care. I can't give up this opportunity any longer. We need to strike while the iron is hot. These people won't want me forever."

"But you have to be alive to enjoy the money."

Paris sits downs and adopts a serious tone.

"Do you know what I've been doing up at that church every morning?"

I remain defiantly silent at her question.

"I've been writing about us, everything that's happened since we started this book tour. And I realized God wants me to make it into a novel. "

"So?"

"So everyday, I've gone up there and typed like a maniac. Sometimes the words come to me so fast that I can't even type them. It's like I'm taking dictation from a higher place. Like I have a holy-ghostwriter."

I don't laugh at her pun.

"Anyway, today I went up there and I couldn't type anything. Nothing came to me. I sat there but the words didn't come. And I realized that I can't write anymore."

"Why not?"

"Because I'm at this point of the story, hiding away in Sedona. I can't go any further because I don't know how it ends. I need to live out the rest of the story to write it."

"Even if it means you die?"

"Yes. But that won't happen. Because I know I have a higher calling. God wants this book to be published, more than my first one. He's made this clear in my heart. And I have to do His will."

"But why would you risk your life? I'm not going."

Paris jumps up. "Come on, we can't stay here forever. I'm sure this lady is going to want to come back sometime and I know we've worn out our welcome."

"She doesn't care," I say. "My grandmother said she might sell the place because she never comes here."

"Yet and still, as much as I love this place, it's time to go. I was sitting in the church and I looked up and saw a plane, the first one I've seen since we've been here. It was a sign."

"That's just a coincidence."

"There are no coincidences. God wants me to leave. And as much as I love you, if you won't go with me, I'll have to go by myself."

"Where did all this religion come from all of a sudden?"

"It came from God. It's not like I just started believing in Him, I always have, but now I feel it stronger than I've ever felt it before. This isn't fakery. I'm not fronting like Dana. I really mean this."

I sit down on the bed and sigh. "So you're leaving me?"

"I'm not leaving you. This isn't about us. This is about following God's plan. And if you're asking me to choose your wishes above His will, that's not going to happen. I choose Him."

BOOK III

THE COMFORTER

Chapter 9

Manhattan, New York

The LORD is my light and my salvation–whom shall I fear? The LORD is the stronghold of my life–of whom shall I be afraid?

Psalm 27:1

AC emerges from his stowed-away position in the first class lavatory shortly after take-off, stalking the aisles like a lion poised to pounce a defenseless gazelle. Sitting in the rear of the jet, I decide to hide before he passes the long line of rows and spots me.

Unbuckling my seatbelt and diving to the floor, it is too late. My rustling must have attracted his attention, because the thud of his footsteps increases in speed and intensity, echoing beneath me in the hollow of the plane's luggage compartment, then stops at my row.

Defeated, I lift my head with trepidation and watch as he points his gun to my face and fires. Luckily, the shot misses but tears through the side panel of the plane, forcing daylight and a blast of frigid air inside. Passengers scream as canary-colored oxygen masks fall to their faces.

AC moves closer, and steadying himself, shoots the next hollow-point bullet through my chest. I marvel at the power of the ammunition, which blasts a huge gaping hole through my torso just like he always bragged it could. The third shot rips through my neck, and the fourth…

Damn this writer's imagination, I curse, literally shaking the violent image from my head. As the plane quietly ascends through the bright blue sky, I focus on the cabin, which is inert with post-takeoff tranquillity.

Thank you, God, for a safe flight and a safe landing at JFK. Also, thank you, for protecting me from AC while I'm there, and in fact forever.

Turning back to the small black bible in my hands, my head jerks up as a passenger stands. You can't live in fear, Paris. You've got to have faith in God to protect you.

And He will, I think, discretely smiling to myself. I wish Eric were right here next to me, though, holding my hand. I'll have to hold my own hand; I can't keep being a baby wanting him to protect me. Besides, most of the men who said they'd protect me are the ones I've ended up needing protection from. Just look at AC. He always said he'd die for me. Now he wants to kill me.

I still miss Eric. Hiding away with him for almost three months made us closer than I realized now that we're apart. Save for my time at the chapel, we were never separated. I began to feel like one person with him, and now it feels like half of me is missing.

But I have a mission to fulfill. If only Eric could understand. How can I explain my profound love for God to him? It's almost something that I can't put into words myself, probably similar to the love a mother feels for her child. Only when one experiences it will they know.

I'm changing. I used to find people who read bibles on buses a bit odd. Now I get it. I can't get enough of His word and I want to be much closer to Him. Finally, I've picked up the right book!

In the Chapel of the Holy Cross I definitely felt His presence, sometimes coursing through my fingers and heart so strongly that it broke me down in tears.

Throughout the writing of this new book He's shown me myself—warts and all. *The Sex Files* described what happened and this new book delves into why, making sense of all my stupid actions of the past. By writing it I discovered that the only thing I thought I needed was to get away from AC and find a good man. I was right, but little did I know that man was Jesus.

Eric is the perfect earthly man, and I'm more attuned to God's grace and kindness for blessing me with him. I finally understand the culmination of all the hurt and pain I've experienced in past relationships, which is the ability to now delight in a man who treats me well. It's God showing His love for me through Eric.

If only I would've learned this lesson earlier. All those fancy negligees and sexy clothes I wore and sweaty workouts I performed in the past, just in an effort to attract the ideal man were for naught, because God was already right there. He was just waiting for me to recognize Him.

The Lord must have cringed every time I gave my precious body to unworthy men in search of that missing Daddy-love. I already had the perfect Father there with me, patiently waiting for me to come to Him and take comfort in His arms. By flirting with all those men, I was crying out to God unconsciously, pleading for the love I so desperately longed for.

When I thought I was enticing a new lover, I was really calling out to the Spirit for help. When I gained false pride from stealing another woman's man, I showed God how lost and in need of guidance I was. When I poured the sweet-smelling bath oil, lit the candles and entrapped an admirer into my lair, only to be hurt by them in return, it was my Creator who spent the night with me after they left. It was my Savior who rocked me to sleep and wiped away the tears. The Almighty was the only one left when all other lovers abandoned me.

I made myself alluring, I thought, for the man I was dating at the time. I had no idea I was really drawing the Lord closer to me, who in His perfect omnipotence understood what I needed. I sought sex but received unconditional love from above. Through my earthly mating dance, I was

177

actually begging for the fulfilling love of Christ to make itself known. I wasn't attracting another flesh-based affair, I was seducing God.

Hence the title of my new book, *Seducing God*. The whole reason for me finally getting up the nerve to call an agent and come to New York, so that I could strike a deal for both books. More important than the first, *Seducing God* is what the world needs to read. *The Sex Files* was just practice, a necessary step in the evolutionary writing process to bring the new book to fruition. God wants this message to be heard, and me to deliver it.

Which is why I had to leave Eric back in Sedona. It really disappoints me, but then again, humans will always fail you and hurt your feelings. God never will. His is a most perfect love, and I'm overjoyed He gave me the desire to follow Him and fulfill His divine will for my life. To think of His compassion brings tears to my eyes, even now, as I look down to begin reading again.

📖

The New York noise is disorienting after the serenity of a Sedona summer. Cabbies form a line along the curb outside the airport, scooping up waiting passengers like an assembly line. When my turn comes, I bogart my body through the harried travelers and hop into the next available taxi.

The cab driver looks at me through the rear view mirror, and asks with a weary expression where I'm going.

"The Four Seasons, please."

"Okay," he says, slinging the gear into drive with sudden alertness.

The whole ride is short and uneventful, until we enter the city and are stalled by bumper-to-bumper traffic. Placidly exiting the cab, the driver screams at the top of his lungs and gets back in. I don't even budge, because I fully understand his need for release. I too, have a scream welling inside of me that longs to come forth.

The Four Seasons is fabulous, but I barely notice its beauty because once inside my suite I throw my bags down and walk directly to the phone to call Eric in Sedona. He looked so desperate as he watched me board my plane in Phoenix that I almost caved in and stayed there with him.

The phone rings five long times before the owner's answering machine picks up. I hang up, wondering aloud where he could be, following his instructions not to leave a message.

Studying the artwork on two of the room's walls, I am reminded of Picasso's block style, his women with heads askew, their six-fingered hands representing the motion of masturbation. Lost in the paintings, my hand remains perched on the receiver, building the nerve to make the call that I know I must.

Sheer curtains provide a hazy, surrealistic view of the city below and of the sharp-leafed plant in the corner that captures my gaze and holds it for several seconds before I pick up the receiver again.

First I press *82 and then dial the number. The number that is etched into my memory like a first kiss. The digits that I never need to reference from a phone book, the one that I called many nights years ago, beseeching the occupant to come out and play.

"Hello?" answers the familiar voice.

"Lauren?"

"This is she."

"It's Paris," I say, in a withering tone of guilt.

"Paris," she repeats, expressing utter disdain and repulsion all in one word. "Where are you?"

"I'm on the road. I just called to see how Dana was doing."

"How could you do that to her? How could you abandon my daughter like that?"

"I know," I whine, reverting to the twelve-year-old who first met Dana's mother and sought her approval.

"I spent my last nickel flying out to Phoenix to get her and fly her back here. It broke my heart to pick up my daughter from a shelter out there like she's homeless. All dirty and stained with her own urine. You were supposed to be her *friend*, Paris."

"Oh my God, I had no idea. I'm sorry. That's why I'm calling, I want to make it right with her, and you."

"Where's Eric?" she asks sternly, demanding to be answered.

"I don't know, I'm not with him right now."

Her huff of disapproval is loud and drawn out. "You all were wrong. You know this is not right to do to her."

"I want to help. I'm going to send you some money so she can get treatment and get better."

"Good, because she needs it. She is still a mess. She's not much better than when I got her. Dana's still too thin and she won't eat enough food. She throws up almost every day, which is to be expected, but she has to gain weight."

"Yeah," I sympathize, wondering why nausea is to be expected.

"If she doesn't eat right the baby won't be healthy."

"What baby?"

"She's pregnant."

"By whom?"

"Eric, who else?"

I stand. "How many months?"

"Three. She's been to the doctor–"

"*Exactly* how many weeks?" I stretch for my purse, extracting my checkbook and opening it to the small calendar.

"Uh, twelve weeks exactly. Why?"

I silently count back the weeks then release an audible sigh of relief. "Because this isn't his baby. There's no way."

"What do you mean? It can't be anyone else's."

"Look, Lauren, I'm not trying to upset you but there was someone else since that time."

"My daughter is not lying to me. Now if you see Eric you tell him that he needs to take care of his responsibilities," she proclaims, adopting the same self-righteous indignation she displayed in front of my mother the time they caught me and Dana drunk with our friends near The Point.

That night Lauren played the role of the concerned mother to the hilt, lecturing Dana about the evils of liquor as she walked her to their car. The next night, Dana told me she had to pick up her mother from a bar because Lauren was too drunk to drive home.

I think of this as I listen to her now, transforming my vision of parental superiority into a clearer adult view of alcoholism.

"I'll still send the money for Dana's treatment," I say staunchly, "but as soon as possible Eric can take a paternity test. Then you'll know the truth about your daughter."

I hang up, not wanting to drag out the argument any further. After a few more seconds I dial Eric again, but the phone rings incessantly, only to be answered by a machine.

📖

By 10:30 p.m., I'm on pins and needles, and the softly hued peach walls and lamps do little to subdue my anguish. If he doesn't answer that phone by midnight, I'm calling his grandmother, even though that'll probably worry her too. But then again maybe she can have someone drive up to the Sedona house to check on him.

He'd better not be doing this because he's mad at me for leaving–if he is, I'll kill him. At least I'd know he was okay though, which is better than the vision of him sprawled out dead on the floor of that huge Sedona home, all alone. Oh God, I stop and clutch my hands together tightly, thank You for him being safe and sound somewhere. I should have never left him.

A bold knock at the door stops my pacing in its tracks and I stare at it in shock. No one identifies themselves as housekeeping or hotel personnel, so I creep over to the door, wishing the noise from the television didn't betray my presence.

Quietly leaning to the peephole, I break into a huge grin and throw the door open.

"Eric!" I scream, flinging my arms around his neck. "I was so worried about you. How'd you find my room?"

He pushes past me into the room and closes the door. "I have my ways."

"You should have called me! I can't believe you're here."

"I was on a plane," he says, allowing me to hug him closely. "I drove back to the house after I dropped you off but it felt so empty. I just packed and caught a flight here."

"I'm so glad you're here." I hold him to my bosom for a while longer before releasing him.

"Me too," he stares into my eyes, "I couldn't be apart from you. Even if you can."

"I can't. I was just thinking that I shouldn't have left you. I'll never leave you again."

We kiss with the hunger of reunited lovers. After a few minutes, I gather myself and sit him down on the bed next to me.

"What?" he asks anxiously.

"Now, before you say anything I want you to know I used complete caller ID blocking." I hand him a sheet of information I printed from the web.

"Oh boy, what did you do?"

"I called Dana."

"Paris!" he admonishes, flicking the paper against his thigh. "Why?"

"I wanted to check up on her. But listen, it's a good thing I did because I talked to her mother and guess what she said?"

"What?"

"Dana's pregnant!"

Eric shakes his head and jumps up. "That's a lie."

"I know," I smile uncontrollably, "it probably is. But anyway, even if it isn't, I know there's no way it could be yours because she told me she was exactly twelve weeks pregnant and I counted back and that was while we were in Colorado so it couldn't be yours."

"Right," he says, unconvincingly, reading the page of laser paper.

"What?"

"Nothing."

I stand and face him. "No, you need to know this for certain because she'll try and take you to court on this. I told her you'll take a paternity test as soon as possible."

"Why? I don't want to see that girl."

"You don't have to see her at all. You just need to give blood."

"I don't want to give my blood. That girl probably ain't even pregnant."

I cross my arms. "I know. But if she is, why wouldn't you do everything to prove it's not yours?"

"I don't know."

I stand there, my eyebrows crinkled at his strange behavior. "Eric, what's going on?"

"Nothing."

"Tell me the truth."

"Nothing!"

"Swear to God?" I ask, and he shifts his body weight onto his left foot.

"I slept with Dana in Las Vegas, before I found out about her and AC."

His response kicks me in the midsection, and I slump slightly, like Ally McBeal when the cannonball sails through her stomach. "What?"

"I told you about it."

"No you didn't. You told me that you let her give you head because you felt sorry for her, but that you didn't fuck her."

"I don't remember saying that."

"Yes you did!" I whine, pacing in a circle.

"What's the difference?"

"Oral sex is more impersonal, and more than that, you lied to me. That's the difference."

"I don't remember what I said. It was the last time anyway so what does it matter?"

"You lied to me!" I scream, directly in his face. "And now you're acting like it means nothing."

"Don't scream at me. I'm not talking to you when you're like this."

"Oh, no," I yell even louder, "don't put this on me. You fucking lied to me and you know it and now you're acting like you don't remember instead of telling the truth."

"I am telling the truth. I'm not with her, I'm with you, so stop making a big deal out of it. You should have never called her anyway," he says, once again reading the paper I gave him.

"Stop changing the subject. You won't admit that you lied."

"Paris, I'm telling you, get out of my face," he says, holding his palm up while focusing on the printout. "Wait, what number did you use to do the blocking?"

"*82. Why are you changing the subject?"

"That's the wrong number. That's complete blocking but it displays the number on caller ID boxes and Dana's mom has caller ID."

I snatch the sheet from his fingers, verifying what he's said is true, but too angry to show remorse for my mistake. "Oh well, fuck it. There's nothing I can do about it now."

"Well now Dana can find out exactly where we're staying with one of those reverse directories."

"So what!" I scream again. "I made a mistake, I admit it. At least I admit my mistakes and I don't lie about them."

"Fuck this!" Eric screams, finally exploding. "I didn't fly all the way out here for this shit! I'm going home to Chicago!"

"Fine! Leave! You're turning this all around when you're the one who fucked Dana and lied to me about it!"

"I didn't lie!" Eric turns and kicks the side of the nightstand, causing the lamp to vibrate. He punches the wall with a slightly open fist then grabs his bag and walks to the door.

Slightly afraid, I watch him, yet am strangely comforted by the fact that this is the extent of his anger. He's more pissed than I've ever seen him, and although he's displayed rage, nothing is damaged and most importantly, he didn't once turn to hit me.

I grab his arm as he opens the door and pulls away from me. "Please don't leave," I say. "I won't yell anymore, I just don't want you to go."

He turns and releases the door, allowing it to slam shut.

📖

During the night I awake in fits and starts, my anger evolving to sadness at the thought that I might not be the first and only woman to carry Eric's child. It makes me shiver to think that Dana might be a part of our lives forever.

"I'm sorry," he says in the morning, touching my face tenderly.

I ponder over whether he's sorry he lied or the fact that he genuinely can't remember what he told me. I decide to let the matter go, so happy am I that we always make up easily, all debts forgiven by morning. Unlike AC, who would hold his grudges for days. Or forever.

After making love gently, we go to Central Park and take a carriage ride, resigning ourselves to the fact that whatever will be will be. The clack of the horse's shoes against the pavement creates a resounding echo as we enter the park at Grand Army Plaza.

"My book is being auctioned as we speak," I beam, snuggling close to him.

"Don't you need to be there?"

"Actually, there's nowhere to be. I used to think it was like a Christie's auction where publishers show up and raise placards and the guy slams the gavel for the highest bidder. But it's really all done by phone by my agent."

"Then why did you come to New York?"

"Well, I still need to sign the contract and stuff when it's over. We gotta hammer out the details."

He grins at me with a look of distraction. "Will you marry me?"

"Yes," I respond instantly to his surprising proposal.

Overjoyed at the fact that Eric would even entertain the thought of marrying me, my happiness is dampened as I wonder when I'll ever be free from AC. I want to be rid of him. Why would he want to stay married to someone who doesn't want him? Maybe I can file for abandonment or something, I don't know, anything to get free from him. I can't take being linked with him any longer. More urgently, I can't let Eric get away.

"$575,000?" I repeat loudly into the phone the next morning, making sure I've heard Peter correctly.

"That's it," my agent confirms. "Now I need you to come down to my office so we can finalize the paperwork."

"I'll be right down."

I hang up and scream to Eric. "We did it! We got it sold!"

"I didn't do anything," he says, returning my hug.

"Yes you did. I couldn't have done this without you. We need to go down to Peter's office so I can sign some papers, but after that we are going to celebrate!" I kiss him hard and fast before breaking away to take a shower.

Giddy the entire taxi ride, tears cloud my vision as I reflect on how all my hard work of the past two years has culminated with this moment.

Upon arriving in the lobby of the modern offices, I greet the exotic brown-skinned receptionist with an enthusiastic smile and she guides me and Eric down the hall to a modest corner office where Peter sits buried behind a mass of manuscripts and books.

"Where's your bathroom?" Eric asks urgently, having held it ever since we left the hotel.

"Right down the hall and to your left," Peter answers, pointing back down the corridor we just walked.

Eric exits, closing the door behind him.

"Congratulations," he says to me, shaking my hand from across the desk.

"Thanks. And thank you so much for all your hard work with this."

"Hey, the book sold itself. Okay, now it's time to get down to brass tacks."

"Alright."

"We've already discussed the advance. That breaks down to $200,000 on signing, $200,000 on delivery of the manuscript and the remaining $175,000 on publication. Publication by us, that is."

"Right," I say, checking off that item from my notes.

"How many will you print on the first run?"

"This is hot, people want this. We're doing two-hundred thousand off the bat."

"So that means two-hundred thousand dollars on promotion, right?"

"Not quite that much. I'd say around twenty-five thousand. Everyone already knows about the book, besides, it's not a hardcover."

I smile, resolving not to press him. "Good. Okay, next, I want to buy copies of the book at sixty-percent off."

"You've been doing your homework. Look, Paris, we'll do whatever it takes to close this deal today."

"Me too. What about royalty percents?"

"That's standard. Ten percent on the first twenty thousand, twelve and a half–" Peter stops mid-sentence as the door to his office opens.

I glance back, expecting to direct Eric into the seat beside me so Peter and I can continue our deal. Instead, my stomach surges toward my throat as I see AC enter the office, then hurriedly close and lock the door behind him.

"How did you get in here?" I gasp, moving behind the desk next to a bewildered Peter.

"I told the lady I was your husband," he sputters, his crimson red eyes revealing his lack of soberness.

Peter freezes, having seen the Phoenix videotape, he realizes the danger we are in. Just then, AC removes an unfamiliar large black 9mm gun from a holster under his vest and points it at me.

"Get over here and sit down!" he screams, slurring.

I move cautiously, trying not to disturb his volatile state, and sit in one of the seats in front of Peter's desk.

"You sit down too!" AC shouts, and Peter pulls his large leather chair behind him and sits. "Now you're scared, you dumb bitch," he turns back to me, moving closer until the barrel of his gun is pressed against the back of my head. "Did you think you could just dog me and walk away?"

"Please, AC" I whisper, my voice wavering, "don't do this."

"Don't do what? You don't know what I'm going to do."

"Look buddy, just don't hurt us–" Peter begins, holding his hands in the air.

"Shut the fuck up man! Nobody's talking to your faggot ass!"

I recall a boy from high school, so distraught that he shot himself in the head, but ironically, he survived. I wonder if I can survive a blast to the head. I would have to. Yet I'm sure that guy didn't have as powerful a weapon as the one AC holds. How cruel would it be to die now, just as I'm realizing success as a writer and true love with Eric?

"Paris?" Eric calls through the door, knocking and twisting the knob.

AC swings the weapon toward the door and looks at me.

"Yeah, honey," I say loudly, forcing my voice to an even keel, "we need to go over this stuff alone if you don't mind. Could you just wait in the lobby?"

"If you want," he says questioningly.

"Just have the receptionist call po-po and tell her to meet us here."

"Who?"

"Po-po. She has the number. Thanks!" I yell brightly, hoping Eric or the receptionist will catch my clue to call the police.

I'm confident that AC doesn't know the slang word for police, because he never listens to rap or keeps up with new sayings. Eric and I always do, and hopefully the receptionist will tell him that AC is back here and they'll put two and two together.

My fear is somewhat abated, knowing there is a chance of survival, if I can keep AC as calm as possible until the police arrive.

"I'll kill that motherfucker, too," AC says, after a short period of silence.

"It's not his fault that this happened. It's mine. I'm the one who committed adultery and lied to you, and I hope you can find it in your heart to forgive me."

"Now you're sorry, just because I have a fucking gun to your head," he says, clumsily swaying back to me.

"No, I've been sorry for a while now, I just haven't had the opportunity to tell you."

"Bullshit!"

"It's true. I pray for you to heal yourself. I don't want to see you unhappy."

"I don't need no damn prayers. You're wasting your breath."

With caution, I turn my head to search his expression. "I'm not. God can help you if you just ask Him. He loves you and wants you to be happy."

"Oh, what the fuck are you turning into another Dana? Just because you're with her man now you gotta preach all this bullshit?"

"It's not bullshit. Our marriage didn't work, AC. As much as we loved one another, it wasn't a holy union. There was infidelity, lack of trust and cruelty. We didn't have a marriage. So don't despair over something that never was."

"It was according to the law."

"I know, but now at least we can both recognize we made a mistake and heal from it. Why can't we just give each other the chance to move on and have fulfilling lives?"

He moans loudly, lowering the gun and walking to the corner of the room to gaze out of the window. I see Peter in my peripheral vision moving toward the phone, but I shake my head.

"Easy for you to say. You've got it made now. You'll be getting paid with the book that you wrote when you were with me."

I decide not to argue the fact that he didn't want me to spend money on printing it in the first place. "I know, and you've developed a lot of artwork during our marriage which is brilliant. A lot of people would buy it."

"Don't nobody want to buy shit from me."

"You just have to work hard to sell it, the same way I did with my book. You can do it. With God, all things are possible and you need to turn to Him to heal the hurts of your past that are holding you back."

AC looks to me, his face distorted with anger. "The only thing holding me back is your lying ass. Who the fuck wants a wife like you?"

"Exactly," I agree, staring at the gun which is again a few inches from my face. "Who wants a marriage where the partners aren't healthy and supportive of one another? I don't. I need time to heal myself and walk closer with the Lord, and you need to do the same so that you can overcome the pain your parents caused you."

"Fuck them!" he rants, swirling around uncontrollably. "I don't give a shit about them!"

"You do, AC, that's why it's causing you so much agony. You have unresolved anger toward your father for killing himself and your mother for leaving you."

"Shut up bitch! Don't fucking analyze me!"

"The Bible says we should look inward and do self-examination. That's the only way we can gauge how we're living our lives," I say, surprised at my own calmness and the reasoning spewing from my mouth. "Your parents did things that wounded you, things that no child should have endured, but you need to find a way to forgive them and move on."

"Not this same old shit again. When are you going to get it? It's not easy to just forgive and forget. Life isn't that simple."

"Yes, but it's not impossible. And look at the antithesis. You're stuck in a loop, reliving the nightmare of your childhood because you haven't moved past it and healed."

"You think you know everything," AC begins but is interrupted by a loud pounding on the door.

"Police! Open up or we're coming in!" the demanding voice of a male officer sends AC whirling around the room, unsure of what to do.

He grabs me, wrapping an arm around my waist and pressing the gun to my temple as we all listen to the door being broken down.

"Step away from her," the officer commands, creeping one foot at a time into the room with his gun held tightly in his outstretched hands.

AC is silent, his hand shaking violently against my head. He reeks of rancid smoke and alcohol.

"AC please," I say softly, "give yourself up. It'll be okay. You won't have to hurt anyone anymore."

"I know. I'll just hurt myself."

Feeling the gun move away from my flesh, I tense up, then turn to see AC place it in his mouth and fire.

"No!" the cop yells as AC falls to the ground, and his death grip around my body sends me landing on top of him.

I pull his arm off of me, then turn to his disfigured face, still gurgling through a puddle of blood. "AC, accept the Lord Jesus Christ as your savior. Accept Him now!"

AC's eyes lock on the ceiling and I know he is gone. The policeman pulls me away from his body as the emergency medical technicians try to revive him. Eric enters the room and grabs me, holding me closely.

"It's over," I cry. "It's finally over. God have mercy on his soul."

📖

"Are you sure you're okay?" Eric asks again, once we've finally made it back to our hotel room that evening, after hours of questioning and interviewing by the police.

"Yeah, I just need to take a bath and wash this blood off."

Turning on the faucet, I pick up the bottle of ION's anti-frizz glosser on the side of the tub and instinctively throw it away. I allow the water to run through my hair and body, and I feel baptized by a spirit of purity.

It is unfathomable to me that AC is dead and I am now a widow. With all his faults, he still had so much potential, so much more life to live. I can't believe that with the blink of an eye he could have taken me with him.

Thank you God, I sob, for sparing my life. Please forgive all my sins.

Please forgive the times I've hurt other people, especially the adultery I committed against AC and the lying and pain I caused Dana and other women in my life. Please forgive the abortions, the stealing, the envy and any other wrongful deeds I've done but can't remember or haven't named.

The tub fills completely with water and bubbles, and I recline my head back, my palms outstretched to God. The temperature of the water and my body are the same, and I feel suspended in mid-air.

My audible deep breathing calms until I can hear it no more, and I cry silently for God's grace-filled forgiving nature. Tingling waves of holiness enter my body through my uplifted finger and travel down to my toes and back up, cleansing me with the purity of His spirit.

I am renewed, and reborn an anointed child of God. This is real.

Chapter 10

Heaven's Gate and the Abyss

"Truly I say to you, unless you are converted and become like children, you will not enter the kingdom of heaven."

Matthew 18:3

Emerging from the birth canal and wailing at the light. Lying awake on my cot at nap-time during nursery school, watching my teacher and her daughter rummage through the children's lunches. Running wildly across the street to catch my mother after she dropped me off at grammar school because I thought she had my lunch. Sitting alone on the sofa peering through the torn window screen the day she left.

Talking to Renee Bouillon through the forest-green iron gates of her private school, then hurriedly misplacing a kiss on her nose before running away to catch a city bus.

The first time my father slapped me across the face hard enough to draw blood.

Seeing Pink Floyd's *The Wall* with my friends while tripping off acid then going home and shaving my eyebrows. Partying within the steaming walls of the Music Box as house music pulsated in time with a blue strobe light.

Fluid leaking from my father's head onto the wooden floor.

Attempting to paint *The Scream* alone in my loft, then slashing the artwork to shreds when it didn't turn out right.

The feeling of pleasure as I squeezed the airways of that Marine closed and watched him turn red.

The birth of my son Tyson, so perfect and innocent.

Enjoying a picnic with Paris on the desolate Mexico Beach, then killing the sand crab that stood and watched her as she slept.

Sneaking Dana into the condo and painting her nude body while Paris was at work.

Spying as Paris made love to Eric on the television screen.

Pacing the jail cell, so angered that I thought I would explode.

Sailing above my blood-soaked body through the ceiling of the office building into a field of blazing alabaster.

These and other images flip before my eyes like a brilliant slide show, sequential yet concurrent, instantaneous yet complete.

Feeling more calm and at peace than I've ever felt in life, I am weightless and free from the restraints of my earthly body.

I land before an ornamented throne of gold, inlaid with diamonds, rubies, emeralds and other precious stones that sparkle with indescribable sheen. Taller than the famous Statue of Lincoln, I shrink in comparison.

Behind the elaborate chair are towering gates of iridescent pearls, through which I see two rows of trees with an abundance of fruits hanging from their limbs.

A gentle breeze ripples the surface of the crystal sea that flows between the lush greenery, and I drink in the perfumery of the plush flowers that line the water's edge. Angels luxuriate in velvety clouds above, strumming melodious tunes on harps of gold.

The Lord appears without warning on the throne, His face illuminated, radiating a warmth and holiness that surprisingly makes me want to draw nearer to Him.

"The day of your judgment has come AC," He says in the most comforting voice my ears have ever beheld.

"Yes," I kneel, noticing that I have the ability to speak even though I just shot myself in the mouth.

"As you know, there comes a time when every man will be judged, and all his deeds, good and bad, will be brought to task."

"I know," I sigh, remembering the many times the nuns in my grammar school used that line to get us to behave.

"Good, then let us begin."

All of a sudden the brightness and beauty falls away in pieces and I stand in the dimmed viewing room of a funeral home. Gliding to the front of the room, I notice an old picture of myself as a young boy resting atop a closed burgundy casket. My mother stands in the front, her weeping the only sound in the otherwise silent room. Gloria's face is slackened with the passage of time, yet still possesses the graceful allure etched into my memory.

"Where is everyone?" I ask without speaking, and I'm dumbfounded when I receive an answer.

"That's the reason for her sadness," the fatherly voice explains. "Your mother hasn't spoken with you in so long, she didn't know how to contact your friends and tell them you died. Most of all she weeps out of regret for the manner in which she treated you as a child."

"Good," I say, standing next to Gloria as she stares at my photograph, then dabs her eyes with a wad of tissue.

"Do not delight in the sadness of others."

"But she left me! She should be sorry."

"Gloria deserted you, it's true, and for this she will be judged, but were your parenting skills much better?"

195

"What? I loved my son."

"This I don't doubt. Your mother also loved you, but she made an error by leaving you when her relationship with your father soured. All of your life, she tried to make it up to you by sending money in place of herself. And you too, suffered from this lack of judgment."

Before I can protest, the funeral home morphs into the cluttered bedroom of a child, his toys strewn about the thin knotted carpet. My son Tyson rests on his race-car bed, engrossed in a cartoon playing on a small television set.

His lanky legs appear a lot longer than the last time I'd seen him. Smiling, I am compelled to reach out and pick him up when I realize I can't.

"Tyson!" booms the voice of a slight man entering his bedroom. "Didn't I tell you to take out the garbage?"

"Who's that?" I ask, witnessing Tyson jump to attention, his tiny muscles tensing.

"Your son's new step-father," the Lord answers.

"Yes," the little boy whispers, cowering past the figure looming over him.

"Well then, do what I say!"

"I'm sorry."

As Tyson passes, the man smacks him hard on the back of the head, causing him to fall against the doorway.

"If you don't keep your fucking hands off my son," I scream, sending a fist to the face of the stout man, only to have it dissipate through his skin like the wind.

"Be a man! Stop crying like a little sissy!"

Tyson runs to the kitchen and the scene fades to the blazing glory of the judgment space, but my anger is still close to the surface.

"I can't believe he hit my son! Who the fuck is he?"

"Right now, and for a long time to come, he'll be the only father your son knows."

I shake my head. "I can't believe that bitch is letting him hurt my son. He's not his father. I'm his father. I'll always be his father."

"You didn't act like a father to him when you were alive. You assumed that your mother sending money to pay for child support was enough. You didn't visit him or become any type of role model in his life. Now tragically, he is destined to face the same fate as you, and will grow into a hateful misogynist who abhors his mother for letting his father abuse him, and in turn will abuse women himself."

I stare off into the distance, listening to the trees rustle in the comfortable breeze. "I thought we were supposed to cover the good things I've done too. All you've talked about is the bad stuff."

"We may. This is to be a fair examination. There were countless good deeds you performed over your lifetime."

My attention is directed to images that appear suspended in mid-air, as if projected on an invisible movie screen.

Scenes of myself as a child, moments long forgotten by my conscious mind, begin playing. In one I'm protecting this undersized kid in my neighborhood that always got beat up by bullies. He reminded me of myself, defenseless against larger foes.

In another, I give my lunch to Cathy Spillman, a poor girl in my class, even though I'm starving.

The setting switches to my high school years, when I let a homeless guy stay in my loft for a few weeks because I empathized with his loneliness and despair.

Next, I'm pictured driving the long haul from Chicago to Tallahassee to visit Paris, surprising her with gifts when we were on the verge of a break up.

The display evaporates.

"See," I say, "I've done good things."

"Yes, AC, even more than we've shown. But unfortunately, many more deeds have been reflective of this," He says, pointing a shimmery sword once again to the unseen screen.

Paris and I are in our condo during a heated argument.

"Fucking leave then! Nobody wants your ass."

"I will," she screams, pulling her suitcase from the closet.

"I'll help you pack," I say, ripping a handful of clothes from their hangers and throwing them in the bag.

I watch as I then look to the open window with a smirk, pull my butterfly knife from my jeans pocket and slit the screen until it flips backward.

"No!" Paris screams, grabbing my arm as I take the garments and fling them through the opening and laugh as they sail onto the street below. "You asshole!"

She hits me on the back out of frustration, a meager tap that doesn't hurt. I turn and punch her in the chest, taking her breath away and sending her to the floor.

"Don't ever fucking touch me!" I yell over her body, curled into a ball and sobbing.

I walk out of the room while Paris continues to cry.

📖

"Okay, enough already," I complain, after watching several more scenes of me and my wife fighting. "It's not like Paris was perfect."

"At this moment we will only hold accountable your deeds, no one else's. Just as when their day comes, only their deeds will be discussed.

"Unfortunately, scenes like the last outweighed the good times in your marriage, and that was one reason it didn't continue. It wasn't based on *this* kind of love…"

I look to the movie screen, but my entire surroundings dissolve to blackness. Standing atop a small mountain at a resort nestled in hills, the light from the bubbling blue waters of a Jacuzzi emanates through an alcove.

"This one's empty," I hear Paris' voice say, ascending a flight of stairs with Eric.

Dressed in swimwear, they sit on the edge of the hot tub, dangling their feet and legs in the percolating water.

"This is perfect. Thank you so much for bringing me here, it's exactly what I needed."

"I didn't know if you wanted to come back to Phoenix," Eric says, "but I thought if we came to this hotel it would be different."

"No, I love this place. I needed to come back here. I needed to see that Phoenix was really a friendly place, not some town where awful things happen. Just like Manhattan."

"It's not. Nothing awful will ever happen to you again."

"Thank the Lord." Paris sighs and tilts her face to the multitude of constellations easily seen against the pitch-black sky. "I mean, look at this. The stars are so clear. There's a nice gentle breeze. What else could I ask for?"

"Well, there is one thing missing."

"What?" she asks, turning back to him in wonderment.

Eric takes a miniature velvet box from his red swim trunks and flips it open. "This evening will only be complete if you do me the honor of becoming my wife."

Paris' mouth drops wide open, and looking from the box to his eyes, she starts crying.

"Is that a yes?" he asks, placing the brilliant emerald-cut diamond on her left hand.

She shakes her head up and down, unable to speak, and buries her face in his chest. They sit silently for a few seconds, then Paris leans up and kisses him.

"Ain't that about a bitch? My body isn't even cold yet," I say, the bright light shining through the scenario once again.

"Time is non-existent in this realm. It's been months since your death. But that fact is insignificant. Paris' heart left your marriage long before you died. The point is, Eric doesn't harbor ill will towards her. He will never raise his hand to her, and that should have been your duty as a husband as well."

"How long is this gonna take?" I huff, crossing my arms. "I don't want to keep hearing about my faults all day."

"Since you didn't face them and try to heal from them while you were alive, you must face them today. Tragically, Paris wasn't the last woman you harmed. There is another who suffers greatly."

199

I am shifted to a dingy hospital room, where a lone figure is strapped by its ankles and wrists to a steel bed railing.

"Who is that?" I murmur, afraid to move closer.

"It's Dana, shackled and sedated in a mental hospital. You must account for the role you played in placing her here."

"What did I do? Paris and Eric were the one's that really dogged her out."

"Yes, and they will–"

"I know," I interrupt. "They'll get their own judgment."

"If only you had learned from Me so quickly in life. Dana was at her lowest point when you chose to take advantage of her, just like the first time you persuaded her to soil the sanctity of your marital bed."

"Paris wanted it."

"Just as Eve charmed Adam with the forbidden fruit, it was ultimately his choice as the spiritual head of the household not to give in to temptation.

"Paris wanted to please you, not believing she alone was enough to satisfy your sexual and emotional needs. Yours was a heart filled with lust. Dana had many problems that were intensified by your treatment of her in the last days you were together. Instead of helping her lift herself from the depths of despair, you took advantage of the situation to gratify your carnal cravings. You were the straw that broke the camel's back, sending her to her breaking point."

I look down at Dana's skeletal body, clearly outlined in the dingy nightgown that covers her. "It's not like I was in the position to help anyone. I was in despair too."

"Yes, I know," the Father continues, "and you should have turned *to* Me, not away from Me."

The hospital room fades away and scenes of my suicide begin playing on the screen. I watch as I place the gun in my mouth and pull the trigger.

"Your life was a precious gift, not to be rudely taken away by your own hand."

"At least I didn't kill anybody else!"

"This is true, but it doesn't nullify the fact that you didn't persevere. I know just how much my children can bear. You could have pressed on through the hurt and pain and I would have comforted you. You didn't trust that I would do that for you."

"But you haven't."

"I did, and if you only had an ounce of faith and stepped closer to Me you would have reveled in My glory each day. But you allowed your inner rage to consume you, and reflected it back upon everyone you met. By giving your soul to the devil, you committed the same sin as your father."

Incensed at the comparison, I begin to yell. "I am not like him! I am nothing like him!"

"Ah, but you are AC. You both turned the pain you suffered at your own father's hand against others, then chose to take your own lives. You both turned against Me when you should have called out to Me. You both blamed Me for your pain and cursed Me in your hearts."

"Because you didn't protect me! You let my father do all those things to me!"

"I didn't want those things to happen to you. Humans have free will and as a result, horrible things will happen, but it allows you to see how wonderful life can be when you experience kindness and grace."

"But I didn't," I whine.

"You did, many times. I sent Paris to you so that you might know love, and through it, heal the demons of your past. But instead of forgiving your parents and moving on as she urged, you wallowed in your self-pity and regret."

"She thought it was too easy."

God pauses. "I spoke through her to you, because I know your heart had the capacity to forgive. You could have used your pain to fuel your artwork, and healed others by your graphic representations, yet you chose not to pursue it since you didn't see immediate monetary gains."

"I couldn't get a job. I tried."

"Not hard enough. I would have given you all the desires of your heart if you had trusted Me. Since you've taken your own life, it has been cut short many years and your Spirit is confused. It is too earthbound, clinging to the memory of Paris and what could have been. Yet and still, your suicide wasn't your greatest sin."

"Oh man, what could possibly be worse?"

"What is worse is that your knowledge of Scripture was broad and far-reaching yet you still turned away from Me. This is a greater sin than your father's was because his biblical wisdom was very limited. You knew right from wrong and still chose to turn away from what was good. You knew My word but hardened your heart not to accept it."

"I thought it was fiction, make-believe. Something that the nuns threatened us with."

"On one level, maybe, but deep inside you knew it was Me you turned against that night your father touched you, the night you swore no good God would let that happen to you. That night you made a pact with Satan to serve him and no longer serve Me."

"No," I say, breaking down into a heap on the floor as memories of my father's abuse come rushing back.

It is so clear and fresh in my mind, I feel like I'm experiencing it all over again. Him stumbling into the room, touching me, trying to suck me and then walking out.

"It was Me who guided Him from your room that night, and put it in his heart to never abuse you in that manner again. But you wallowed in the pain, and instead of telling others of your molestation in an effort to heal from it, you became obsessed with women as sexual objects and defiled your own body as an adult."

"I didn't know!"

"But it is for none of these reasons that you will suffer a worse fate than your father–"

"No, please. I understand now," I sob, my body shaking in a lump on the floor.

"I'm sorry, most people comprehend at this point but it is too late to convert. More than any of the sins we've discussed, or the fact that you never accepted Jesus as your personal savior, is the simple truth that you never repented."

"I repent!" I scream, crawling over to the foot of the throne. "I repent now! I couldn't see it this clearly before."

"For I am sorry, it is too late. I gave you many chances to repent on Earth, I sent many people to help that you turned away in self-righteous indignation. Your stubbornness brought you to this point, and will have to be your companion in Hades."

"No!" I scream, spitting tears in front of me. "I believe now! I don't want to go to hell! Now I believe!"

"You must. For you sealed your own fate. It is your destiny."

Suddenly, a hole beneath my feet opens and I begin falling into a pit of darkness. Swirling fast in a downward spiral, I become nauseated and place my hands on my head to try and gain my bearings.

The faint sound of screams increases as I descend, finally landing with a hard thud that crushes my ankles and shoots needles of pain up my shins. I begin choking on the horrible stench of burning flesh that overtakes my nostrils and the heat that sears my lungs.

When I place my hand to my eyes to peer through the blackness, I discover it is dripping with the muddy filth that covers the ground.

"That landing is a bitch ain't it?"

"Who is that?" I say guardedly, making out the slouched form of an aged, decrepit man standing over me.

I stare for a long time, sensing something familiar in his sly smile through the obscurity, ultimately recognizing the man as my father.

Charging out of the oozing slime, I grab the tattered skin of his arms and he falls to the ground. Pounding him with my dirty fists, I open fresh wounds on his face, mixing his blood with the mud from my hands.

He chuckles, and as I hit him harder, he emits loud bursts of uncontrolled, psychotic laughter.

"Keep on, son. Compared to what I've been through these are love taps."

"Why are you the first person I have to see?" I ask, rolling off of him and rubbing my ankles to soothe the hurt.

"The devil's got a sick sense of humor like that. I'm your escort. The person you couldn't stand the most on earth? They'll be your bunk-mate if they're here. Remember how I much I hated jazz?"

"Yeah."

"Miles Davis all day long in my ears. Come on, I'm taking you to your final resting place."

"Isn't this it?" I ask as my eyes traverse the bleak pit, watching cadaverous bodies wander aimlessly.

"Oh, no," he says, rising to his feet with difficulty. "This is paradise compared to where you're going. This is only the first level, for the goody-goodies who just did miss making it heaven. We've got a ways to go."

"Shit."

"Yep, just like there are echelons in heaven, with the highest for the saints, there are also levels to hell, with the lowest sinners going to the center."

"I can't believe this. You look like you're eighty-years-old."

"That's what a few years in this place'll do to you. You'll see. What I wouldn't give to turn back the hands of time…ah well, we better get going."

The old man shuffles off, turning back to me as I remain seated in the slop.

"Come on."

"What's the rush? Don't we have forever?" I quip.

"Yeah, but you don't want to piss off the big guy. Tardiness for meeting him will get you the kind of torture you don't want to know about."

I force myself to my feet, hobbling along in agony next to him.

"Besides," he says, "we should get out of this level before your Aunt Joyce sees you here. It would break her heart to know–"

"She's here? This is bogus. She was the most church-going woman I knew."

"Yeah, Joyce went to church every Sunday, even tithed and everything. But to her it was mostly a fashion show, a thing to do just so other people would see her doing it. She did it all for the wrong reasons. The Bible says not to do good stuff only because you know someone is watching."

"How do you know what the Bible says? You never picked up a bible a day in your life."

"I know, which I regret. Unfortunately, we have to study it down here as kind of an I-told-you-so punishment, finding out now that the key to life was right there on Earth all along. Tell me son," he stops, "what did the gates of heaven look like? It's been so long since my judgment but I think of it every day."

I keep walking. "It wasn't nothin' special. And don't call me son."

"You might not like it, but that's exactly what you are. Like father, like son."

I would run ahead, except without him I have no idea where I'm going. Feeling utterly alone and helpless, I wish I could do something to escape the rising heat and burning thirst in my throat.

"I wanted to warn you," he continues, catching up behind me. "I tried to send word of how horrible it is down here, but I couldn't. It was too late."

We enter a narrow cavern of catacombs, filled with emaciated zombie-like figures groping us. Turning sideways, I walk hurriedly down the path to get out of the area.

"It only gets worse as we go, AC," he calls out. "Yep, they think of all kinds of torment down here that you can't even imagine. They don't feed us–that's why I'm as skinny as a rail. You're starving, but you don't die, because you're already dead!"

He releases that distorted heckle once again, and it echoes throughout the hall.

"Oh my God," I say unconsciously as I step into the next room. It is brightly aflame with fires around the edge and the floor crawls with thousands of poisonous snakes atop each other.

"Don't say that word here. We have to walk across them, it's the only way. They'll bite, but you just have to deal with it."

Stepping assuredly on top of the reptiles, their movement causes me to lose my balance and fall on them. Groups slither to me as I hit the ground, stinging me quickly and sharply with their forked tongues. I dart up and run to the next entrance, eager to get away from the snakes, but fearful of what creature I'll encounter next.

📖

Passing through several more channels, I'm somewhat relieved as my father and I enter a den of moaning sufferers, each in the process of being systematically tortured by their own personal dominatrix. I avoid their eyes as the victims reach out to me, as if somehow I can end their agony.

"This is the holding place for the serious sinners," he says, talking louder and walking slower than I prefer. "You know, the murderers, rapists, hate-mongers, and perverts."

"Oh," is all I can offer, hobbling through the thick drudge.

"Especially the people who hurt children. Child-abusers and killers are considered among the worst type of sinners," he pauses, then points to an unoccupied torture rack. "That's why I'm here. There's my home."

"So this is where you stop?"

"Yep. Look son, for what it's worth, I'm very sorry for what I did to you. I feel responsible for this whole thing, and how you turned out."

Afraid, I look around for the next level. "Where do I go now?"

"It'll be right through that passageway. There's a small lake you must swim before coming to an island, where you'll meet Lucifer himself. That's where he keeps all his children close to him."

"Why do I have to be that close?"

"Because yours is among the most serious of sins. Not just suicide, but knowing it was against God's word and doing it anyway. That's the only difference between you and me. I actually thought it would be easier for me to kill myself. Now look at me, doomed to a tortuous existence for eternity," he snickers, then looks away.

I peer down the tunnel. "Isn't there like time off for good behavior around here? Can't you move up levels if you do good stuff?"

"Unfortunately, no. We used up all our chances on Earth. When I think back to all the times your mother tried to get me to go to church with her, or tried to read the Bible to me. I was just too busy."

He shakes his head, and suddenly, his punisher appears behind him and signals that it's time to leave.

"Son, I'm sorry," he touches my arm. "I didn't realize what I was doing. I was just so lost in the alcohol and misery after your mother left that I took it all out on you. You can choose to accept my apology or not, it doesn't matter."

The burly man begins dragging him away and straps him into the circular rack.

"That's the worst part of it," he yells. "It doesn't matter. I can repent all I want to now and it just doesn't matter!"

The man thrashes a long black whip against his bare chest, adding to the cacophony of music and tortuous screams in the chamber. My father chortles, but as the beating grows, he begins a deafening scream that reverberates down the darkened hallway in which I creep.

Soon, a glowing crimson light emanates through the unlit space and I hear the muted sound of rushing waves. The temperature is unbearable, and when I turn a final corner, a lake of firey sulfur rumbles at my feet.

"Come, my son, I've been waiting for you," says the most wretched voice I've ever heard, and I focus on a crimson figure sitting amidst the rolling heat on a throne of flames.

"I can't!" I scream above the raging waves, terrified.

"You will! It won't hurt but a bit," he grins, flashing eyes of fireballs at me.

Shaking my head, I watch him beckon with an outstretched hand of razor-sharp nails, and as he does, I feel myself being involuntarily pulled into the fire.

I scream and a wave of flames hits me in the mouth. Scorched, I begin swimming, feeling as if my flesh is being burned off with every stroke. Creatures arise from the deep inferno and bite me along the way.

Finally, I make it to the island, and stand before the Prince of Darkness with sulfuric lava dripping from my body.

"You're finally home," he says proudly, enclosing me in his red cape as I disappear into his arms.

I sob, waves of utter despair filling the depths of my soul, knowing I can never escape the madman. At this moment, I feel my most lonely and hopeless, not because I am usurped within evil and in the depths of the underworld, but because I finally realize that my true hell is being away from God.

Chapter 11

Charleston and Hilton Head Island, South Carolina

For what does it profit a man to gain the whole world, and forfeit his soul?

Mark 8:36

loating to the open window, I spy a naked woman perched on the ledge of a towering building, her thin brown body exposed before the world. On the ground below, a miniature dog with curly white hair leaps higher and higher, trying to reach us. Somehow I know the dog is mine, even though I don't have a pet, and it's my responsibility to catch him. Once I do, he turns into a McDonald's bag full of food.

Sirens blare constantly, and the woman tells me they're due to a massive bombing in Minneapolis where the overrun of victims had to be sent to our city, wherever that is. The alarms wail without ceasing, like the endless sorrow in my soul.

Stepping through the window, I'm confronted by an ocean, and to make it to safe land I must cross the jagged rocks. I turn back out of fear, but the house has disappeared and I'm stranded on the rugged cliff.

I awaken to the sound of swaying moss brushing against the roof of the wooden house that serves as a psycho ward. The eerie shadows formed on the walls are like long fingers threatening to grab me. Reality, it seems, is scarier than my nightmare.

Succumbing to the powerful muscle relaxants traversing my veins, I sleep once again, this time dreaming of Eric. No matter what I say or do to show him how much I love him, he won't listen. He ignores me like so much background noise. I'm right next to him in bed as he makes love to Paris, and I try to no avail to pull him away.

Waking again slightly before daybreak, I can't breathe. The restraints on my wrists and ankles allow me to turn on my side, but the pressure on my chest isn't alleviated. It is the physical feeling of sadness, sitting on my chest like a heavy object, weighing me down. I wake up with it and sleep with it, day and night. It does not go away.

The next time I open my eyes it is to the harsh daylight and an even harsher supposed nurse shoving a needle into my vein.

"Please call my mother," I murmur through cracked lips.

"We have," she snaps, snatching the syringe from my arm. "She must not want to be bothered."

Before I can say another word, she shoves a spoonful of thick oatmeal in my mouth, making me gag. The cereal feels like sand against my dry tongue, and I spit it out to prevent choking.

"Fine," she slams the bowl next to me on the side table, toppling a plastic cup of water onto the floor. "You can starve for all I care."

With that, she stomps out of the room, her white shoes squeaking against the floor. I want to cry out in desperation, wondering if in fact my mother has truly left me here without calling to check on me.

I am not getting better, and feel more miserable and thinner by the day. The moisture of my tears eases the dryness of my eyes but increases their tenderness. I want to scream, I feel so helpless, but don't have the energy. The new dose of whatever subduing force she's just put into my bloodstream has already taken effect, and once again I drift off to sleep.

📖

There is a strange tugging at my wrist. Peering through the darkness, I see a woman standing over my bed, cutting off my restraints with what looks like garden shears until all my limbs are free. As she gently lifts me off the bed and holds my frail body next to her bosom, I realize it's Paris.

"We've got to get out of here," she whispers, walking to the window, her chunky heels echoing loudly against the hard floor.

Twisting the lock atop the window, she struggles to lift it. After leaning me against the wall and grunting with all her strength, the window breaks its painted bond with the sill and slides up, filtering whips of wind into the room. The air is frigid against my semi-nakedness, and I am weak as she collects me in her arms again.

Just as she finagles my curled frame gingerly through the opening, we both turn to a noise from inside the room, and see the night nurse enter.

"Oh no, you can't take her outta her like that!" cries the sturdy woman in a hefty voice.

Paris sets me down quickly on the ground outside, hitting my head gently against the dirt. The blow is mild yet makes me pass out nonetheless, and when I come to, she is carrying me as she runs through the dark forest behind the facility.

"Oh," I moan, as each jog shakes my atrophied muscles.

"I'm sorry," Paris says, glancing back to see the woman exiting through the rear door and scurrying down the stairs.

After what feels like a mile but is really only a few yards, Paris opens the passenger side door of a blue Grand Prix and deposits me in the seat. She runs around to the driver's side, enters and starts the car while throwing it into drive.

The nurse reaches the car and bangs so hard on my side of the glass that I think she will break it. Paris speeds away into the darkness, turning on the headlights to light her path.

The rushing scenery, coldness and commotion are too much stimulation after staring at the bare walls of my room for such a long time. I close my eyes and sleep as Paris reaches over me and locks my safety belt in place.

📖

"Hi," Paris says gently when I wake up, as if speaking to a baby.

I am in the brightly-lit room of a real hospital, but as I try to ask which one, the words catch in the aridity of my throat.

"Here," she coos, tipping the edge of a small paper cup into my mouth.

The icy water traces a refreshing path down my esophagus to my stomach, like the first rainstorm of the season anointing a desert. Heeding my motion for more, she fills five more cups, which I devour, until I'm finally satiated enough to speak.

"Where are we?"

"The Medical University of South Carolina."

"Where's Eric?" I ask, hoping he's right outside the room.

Paris looks at her lap. "He's back in Chicago."

I don't say anything, my disappointment evident.

"The doctor told me you'll feel a lot better when you get more fluids in you. You were really dehydrated."

"I do feel more alert," I say, looking at clear liquid dripping into a tube attached to a needle taped to my hand.

"I'm so glad I called your mother. She called that place but they never gave her any information about you. Now I know why."

"I knew it. They told me she didn't even call."

Paris shakes her head. "I had no idea it was that bad. They didn't even want us to take you out of there. That's why I had to steal you. I'm gonna file a complaint about them when I get back home."

"Good."

"Dana," she says, touching my arm, "there is some bad news. The doctor said you're not pregnant anymore."

"Oh," I frown, confused at why I was pregnant in the first place. I turn my head away, wondering if I've suffered amnesia or been raped in that horrible place. Something, however, tells me otherwise, that somehow my mother is behind this mystery.

"I already called your mother and told her you're here. I said you'd probably call her when you felt up to talking."

"I think I feel up to it now," I hint, sitting up.

"Okay, well, let me give you some privacy," she says, standing and dialing the phone. Paris hands me the receiver and quickly whispers, "I'll go back to the hotel and come visit you tomorrow."

"Thanks."

Paris walks to the door, and as I listen to the phone ringing on the other end, I notice how out of season her fine knit burgundy sweater and matching silk shantung pants are to me. Having slept away most of the summer and missed the beginning of fall, I feel like the world has continued while I've stood still.

"Hello?"

"Hey, Ma."

"Dana," she responds dramatically. "You still in the hospital?"

"Yeah, I'm okay. Paris told me you were trying to call me."

"I did. That damn place. If I knew they were that bad I would have never sent you down there. I would have used that money Paris gave us to put you some place here."

"What money?" I ask.

"I told you about it. Oh, you were so out of it you probably don't remember anything. Anyway, just as I was trying to scrounge up enough money to fly down and get you, Paris called and said she would fly down there."

"Well, I'm okay now."

"Is Paris going to pay your hospital bill?"

I hesitate. "I don't know, I assume she is since she checked me in here. I hadn't thought about it."

"You better start thinking about it. I don't have any money, and you don't have a job."

"I know, Ma. I'm sure she will."

"She better. She's got enough money. You know all that drama with AC killing himself just made her richer once the newspapers found out about it. Paris and Eric bought a nice big house in Olympia Fields, right near R. Kelly's."

"What?" I ask, feeling my heart pump stronger.

"It's out there near where your cousin Rafael lives."

"I know where it is. Did you tell her I was pregnant?"

"Mmn," she giggles. "You should have heard how upset she was."

"Ma! I'm not pregnant. The doctor already told her so."

"Well get him to tell her you had a miscarriage or something. That'll make her feel even more guilty."

"I'm not doing that!"

"You need to! You lost your job following her all around the country and now she's rich and has your man. I would say she owes you a lot, wouldn't you?"

"I guess so."

"You better know so. She can't just foot your hospital bill for a few days and then drop you back off in Chicago while she goes on and lives her merry life. You need money for your pain and suffering."

"But I really am hurting!" I say, my own declaration of distress bringing me to the verge of tears.

"Exactly. It's the truth. You do whatever you can to get paid."

"Okay, I'll call you in a few days."

"Alright, sweetie. Take care."

As I hang up, visions of Paris and Eric in a spacious new home dance in my head. It was my fantasy that she swiped, erasing my image in the picture of a perfect suburban family and posting her cheesing face there instead. And she already had a husband! This just isn't fair. Now she's down here trying to ease her own conscience, hoping to buy me off with a quick hospital stay then get rid of me. My mother's right, I shouldn't make it that easy.

◫

"Check out time!" Paris bounds in the room several days later, holding two plane tickets in her hand. "Since our flight doesn't leave until 4:30, I thought we could go to Magnolia Plantation Gardens, if you feel up to it."

"Okay," I shake my head, attributing her newfound excitement today to the fact that she'll be back home with Eric by nightfall.

Tucked away and cozy in their fancy house, I wonder how many dinner invitations they'll extend me to provide an escape from my mother's tiny apartment. As if things aren't bad enough, I don't even have my own shabby place to look forward to since my mother already rented it out in my absence.

◫

Paris settles the bill and we leave the building, the sunny fall afternoon beckoning me outside. Driving around the city, we admire the architecture as I read directions to Paris from a map. A canopied road casts a shadow on the concrete beneath, forcing me look away from the map and at its beauty, and at the tunnel of light formed at the end. As we enter the sunshine again, I allow it to beam down on my face, realizing how much I've missed its warmth.

Arriving at the plantation, we park and walk along the grass with handfuls of other tourists.

Wandering the grounds is like stepping into the Garden of Eden, with huge fragrant calla lilies and freshly cut grass scenting our path and tickling my nose. We stroll along a curved bridge of wood and I grimace at my image in the smooth clear water, boldly reflecting my nappy hair and wearied face. I feel totally ugly, especially compared to Paris, glowing with love, her hair neatly done in a flattering cut.

She guides me to a bench in a quiet spot covered by a white gazebo.

"We better rest. You don't want to expend too much energy," she says, placing her hand on my back to steady me.

"I'm tired of taking it easy. I've lost so much weight. I'm too skinny."

"Shoot, I wish I had that problem," she laughs, patting her hips. "Don't worry, it'll come back. Once you get back to Chicago and start eating that deep-dish pizza and those Polish sausages and stuff, it'll be back in no time."

"Yeah," I exhale drowsily. "I don't know if I really want to go back to Chicago right now."

"Why not? You've got your mother, and I'm sure we can find a better facility where you can get some real help this time."

Paris moves a stray hair from her face, and as she does, I notice a glint of sunlight catch her hand. My eyes follow her hand back down to her lap, and there on her finger sits a huge diamond of at least 1.5 carats, its multiple facets reflecting a rainbow of colors in the brilliant sun. She stops speaking, and tracing my line of vision, instinctively curls her hand away.

I'm speechless. Even though my rational mind has always warned me that they might marry one day, I can't wrap my emotions around the idea. Seeing the ring as plain as day on her finger–the ring that should've been mine–drives all my pent-up rage to the surface.

I lunge toward her on the bench. "I hate you! How could you do this to me? He was mine and you stole him!"

"Dana, please," Paris rises easily out of my grasp.

"You're a bitch!" I scream, jumping up and slapping her face. She grabs my hand, but not before I lock onto a handful of her hair and pull it.

"Stop it," she yells, sliding the hair from my grasp and holding my hands to my side. "We don't need to do this."

Our commotion shatters the tranquillity of our surroundings, prompting other tourists to stare.

"Let's get out of here," she says, holding me as we walk back to the car.

"Let me go," I snatch away, nearly falling as I do.

"Okay. Calm down. We can talk about this."

"I don't want to talk about anything!"

"Fine. We don't have to go to Chicago. Let's just get in the car and drive and we'll figure out what to do next."

📖

After staring at the map for a few minutes, Paris drives distractedly toward the coast and eventually over a bridge that takes us to Hilton Head Island. Spotting a pay phone, she gets out of the car, fans through the Yellow Pages and makes several calls. Then she gets behind the wheel and drives without saying a word.

I bet she's found another mental institution to lock me away in for good, and neither her nor my mother will ever come rescue me.

My fears are calmed when we stop in front of a realty office and Paris goes inside, coming back after some time with a set of papers and keys. I'm still too angry to question what's going on, so I remain silent until we pull up shortly in the rear of a large beachfront home.

"Okay," she finally speaks, "we can stay here for a while until you feel up to going back home."

"Whose house is this?"

"I don't know, they rent it out to people."

I follow her inside as she hauls her carry-on bag into the house. The interior is spectacular, the living room highlighted by a view of the deserted beach. My mother is right, Paris has to be paid to be able to rent a house like this at the drop of a hat. Must be nice.

Paris immediately picks up the phone and dials. I don't have to guess who she's calling.

"Hello?" she pauses, "It's me. I'm in Hilton Head with Dana."

I hear the loud reaction of a male voice, Eric's voice, from the other end of the line, but I can't make out what he's saying.

"I know, we couldn't….She didn't want to come home…But I couldn't leave her here…I don't know, I'll have to call you back….At least a few days."

Paris continues to whine into the phone, as I plop onto one of two sofas facing each other, perpendicular to a huge fireplace in the center of two sliding glass doors.

"I love you," she says, then hangs up.

"I love you," I mock openly. "He couldn't stand to be without you for a whole week, huh?"

Paris twists her mouth uncomfortably and sits on the opposite couch. "Dana, I didn't come down here to fight with you."

"No, you came to just move me from one crazy house to the next then go about your life with my man."

"He not your man anymore."

I lurch forward. "He woulda been if it wasn't for you stealing him!"

"Eric's not some piece of property on a store shelf that can be stolen. He made up his own mind."

I roll my eyes to the cathedral ceiling. "Please! You did everything you could behind my back to get him. I saw the way you looked at him and flirted with him."

"He flirted with me too!"

"But you started it! And you were my best friend. *Supposed* to be my best friend."

Paris takes a deep breath and waves her palms downward. "I know. I'm sorry. I didn't mean to hurt you. I didn't know I would fall in love with him. But either way, I shouldn't have lied to you about the whole thing. That's why I'm here."

"Well I don't accept your apology."

"It would mean a lot to me if you did. I don't want to feel responsible for all that's happened to you."

I laugh. "See, all you care about is clearing your conscience. You always do that, screw up then expect me to forgive you. Just like with Miles."

"What? Miles Kerry?"

"Yes, Miles Kerry. You knew I really liked him but you just had to fuck him to prove you could."

"I went out with him first. Then y'all got together, and after that we got back together. You said you didn't care."

"I don't remember saying that but you knew I liked him and you came along and flaunted your ass back in his face knowing he'd come running back to you."

"I'm sorry, Dana. I honestly didn't know. You see this is good, we need to clear the air so we can move on with our lives."

"What life? You can go back to your mansion with Eric and start a family, but what am I supposed to do?"

"There are plenty of things you can do. You can get a new job, or go back to school. I can help you."

I stand up. "I'm sick of your help. I'm sick of your handouts and leftovers."

"Look, I'm willing to do whatever it takes to get your forgiveness. I lied to you, and that was wrong."

"Whatever it takes?" I say, pacing the drafty space with my arms folded. "Leave Eric."

Paris tilts her head. "I can't do that. Even if I did, he wouldn't come back to you."

"How do you know?" I scream, leaning closer to her, wishing I had long nails to scratch her face.

"Dana, come on. It wasn't meant to be. You knew it, I knew it. You always said you were just waiting for the other shoe to drop and the right woman to come along for him."

"That don't mean it's you!"

"I think it is."

"That ring don't mean shit. He bought me one too! I just gave it back."

"Right, Dana," she says, huffing her disbelief, "let's just go to bed for now because it's been a long day. We'll just pray on it and deal with it tomorrow."

"Fuck you! Fuck you!" I scream, running into the first bedroom I find at the top of the stairs and locking myself inside.

Shivering on the bed, I refuse to answer when Paris offers warm clothes, and instead, I curl into a ball and sob.

📖

By the morning, Paris seems desperate to get me back in her favor, so she takes me to a beauty salon she found that does Black hair, knowing I wouldn't refuse. We both get our hair done, and after the stylist relaxes and cuts mine into a sleek shoulder-length style, I am amazed at how long it is due to months without a touch up.

We then visit a day spa where Paris treats us to manicures, pedicures and facials.

She urges me to get my full set of acrylic nails put back on and I do, directing the manicurist to paint them a goldish-green OPI color. When we complete the salon visit with full makeup applications, I see a new me staring back in the mirror. It is the good-looking girl that I missed and was afraid might never come back.

📖

"We should go to that Baptist church the hairdresser told us about," Paris urges, as we walk along the marina, stopping in various stores to buy autumn wardrobes.

"What for?" I shrug, uninterested.

She stops in her tracks and looks at me. "For healing, for strength. To thank God for all this," she says, holding up the shopping bags in her hand and nodding to my face.

"You have reasons to thank God. Your life is perfect."

"Just because your life isn't what you think it should be doesn't mean you should turn away from Him. In fact, right now is when you should be turning *to* Him."

"I don't know," I start walking, anxious for her to stop talking and get into another store.

"Dana, you're foul. All this time you sat up here and claimed to be saved and recited lines from the Bible like you were so into God, it was just to get Eric to think you were a goody-two-shoes."

"Yeah, and it didn't work, did it? So I don't need it now."

"How could you say that? We all need God and His Word. You just used it for the wrong reasons. If you follow it and use it for the right reasons, it will work for your life. The Bible says to pray to the Father in secret, and he will bless you in public."

"It also says don't lie, cheat, steal, or covet your neighbor's husband. I'm sure they mean boyfriends too."

"I know, and I've repented for that by asking God's forgiveness and your forgiveness. And ever since I've been following the Spirit and doing His will, my life has been wonderful."

"Well whoop-de-do for you. You deal with it your way, and I'll deal with it mine. Let's go in here," I say, opening the door to a boutique that has a fierce form-fitting black dress in the window that has my name written all over it.

Paris is still going on and on about God later that night as we recline on the couches sipping red wine and watching flames roar in the fireplace.

Without warning, a loud boom against the picture window silences us both, and we try to make out the perpetrator concealed in the nighttime darkness. Pressing his face to the glass, Eric's distorted image comes into view and we both exhale a sigh of relief and smile.

Paris unlocks the sliding glass door, and I sit up, smoothing my new silk mahogany nightgown against my skin.

"What are you doing here?" she asks, hugging him. "I just called you."

"I came down here to get you," he declares, shooting an uncomfortable glance my way while returning her hug.

"You scared us half to death banging on the window like that. Why didn't you just ring the doorbell?"

Eric doesn't say anything else as he takes her hand and leads her up the staircase and into a bedroom.

I lean back on the couch, my heart racing a mile a minute at the thought of him seeing me with so little clothes on. The way he tried to keep from looking at my body, probably out of respect for Paris, brings a smile to my lips. He couldn't resist, and had to steal a glance of what he used to know so well.

Waiting on the sofa in hopes of their return, I finish the bottle of wine while posing in provocative positions. The thought of him being under the same roof drives me crazy, and all sorts of sensual images float through my head.

If they come back down, I'll offer him the other flask of wine Paris bought today and we could all get tipsy, and naturally fall into a lovemaking session on the floor, warmed by the heat of the raging fire. Paris at least owes me that, one more time to enjoy the man she stole from me. She can't take him and expect to keep him all to herself now.

I flip and turn on the sofa, unknowingly dropping off to sleep after an hour. When I arise, it is the middle of the night, the fire has died, and unfortunately, Paris and Eric are still in the bedroom.

Creeping up the stairs, I stand outside their room, listening to the sound of slight snoring. My hand shakes as I ease the handle downward and open the door. Moving my body inside, I push it closed behind me, standing still as the sound of breathing continues.

I slip the straps of the negligee over my shoulders and allow it to fall to the floor in one fell swoop. Eric will find me thinner than usual, I think as I rub my palm over my bare ribs, but that's okay, he always did have a thing for petite women.

When my eyes adjust to the light and I find Eric's head in the middle of the bed, I walk to his side and slide beneath the comforter. Pressing my breasts against his smooth back, I wrap my arm around his chest and suck in the warmth of his body. The wonder of his skin is unreal, and I can hardly remember the last time I felt our naked bodies together.

"What the fuck?" he snorts, awaking suddenly.

"What?" Paris moans, turning over.

Eric reaches over me to turn on the light, squinting as brightness fills the room. "Get out!"

"Dana, what are you doing?" she asks, sitting up.

"You don't have to pretend," I say, holding his waist. "Paris doesn't care."

"Get off me," he yells, pushing me away. In my drunken confusion, I fall to the floor.

"This isn't fair!" I sit on the floor, naked and ashamed. "You all aren't fair!"

"Get out of here and put on some clothes," Eric says, turning over.

"No!" I scream, jumping up and running down the stairs and opening the sliding glass door.

"Dana wait!" Paris yells, clad in only a T-shirt as she runs to the top of the staircase.

I race through the door, over the patio and out to the beach, the cold wind whipping against my flesh. Running along the shore, the frigid water numbs my feet as they collect sand in clumps.

"Dana!" Paris screams a ways behind, and I run faster, stumbling through the surf.

As she gains distance on me, I dash into the incoming tide, hoping the chilly water will freeze away my shame and give me enough nerve to go into the ocean and never come back.

"Stop it!" she screams when she reaches me, tackling me and sending us both into the rushing waves.

Paris lifts me easily out of the water and takes me back to the edge of the beach, throwing a small wet blanket around my nude body.

"I just can't," I cry, while she walks me back to the house, where Eric is waiting on the deck. "It's not fair."

"I know," she says softly, stroking my soggy hair.

"It's not fair." I breakdown and sob in her arms as she takes me up the stairs and places me in bed.

📖

Nothing even matters, I sing to myself, repeating the title lyrics of a song Paris played over and over this morning from *The Miseducation of Lauryn Hill*. I had never heard the duet with D'Angelo before, didn't even know she had a new CD for that matter, but the song sticks in my head as I sit in the front pew of the church with Paris waiting for the choir to begin.

Nothing even matters, I think, and even though I know L-Boogie means nothing matters but her man, I relate to it literally. Nothing does matter to me, because I don't have my man.

The choir begins, led by a chunky Black woman with a heavenly voice. Her melody and conviction forces the other song from my head, and soon I can only relate to what she sings.

"…and now I'm standing here, in the midst of my tears," she croons, and tears begin to streak down my face.

I am embarrassed to cry in front of so many people, but at least these tears feel different than the ones I've cried the past few nights. These feel like tears of happiness, and when the choir finishes its repertoire, I sit entranced as a young jolly preacher takes the podium.

"Bless God. Today is a day that the Lord has made. Hallelujah!" he shouts, and the crowd shouts back. "This week is the last installment of our series on family mess."

Groans arise from the crowd, followed by laughter.

"Now I know most of you are ready to finally end this series, but neither I nor you knew there would be so much to preach on."

Ruffles of cackling erupt through the crowd.

"There are many types of mess that can be damaging to families. This week we'll concentrate on the types of situations that can hurt children, and cause them to grow up to be unhealthy adults.

"Children in dysfunctional homes may suffer sexual abuse, neglect or even vicarious abuse by witnessing someone else being abused. Also, a common form of neglect is practiced when parents abandon a child, either physically, mentally or emotionally."

As he speaks, occasionally glancing up, I feel he is looking and talking directly to me. It's a message for me, and I know at this very moment, every thing that has occurred in my life thus far has brought me to this church right now.

He preaches on, continuing with the types of evil that harm children until he reaches a fervent pitch.

"...it does not matter what your father has done to you, you have a heavenly Father that will always take care of you."

Members of the crowd erupt in jubilation. "If your father beat you, call on Jesus!"

"Yes!" screams a woman behind us.

"If your mother ignored you, call on Jesus! He will pull you through the storm. He is your savior, the Prince of Peace, your comforter."

"Alright," a man says to our left.

Paris and I rise to our feet, joining the other members of the crowd who are already standing.

"Lift your hands up to the Lord and embrace Him. Lift up your hands to Him seven times a day," he says, as both Paris and I lift our hands up.

I close my eyes and face my palms upward, and I am reminded of the few times my mother took me to the church around the corner from our house when she wasn't too hung over. By the time high school rolled around, I was always the one too sleepy from late-night partying to go, so I never returned to that church, and instead chose a different one later in life I thought was more suitable.

"Don't be afraid to call on God when you need Him," the preacher calms down. "Just know it in your heart that He will help you and it shall already be done. Know that with Him, all things are possible. Don't just say it without believing it. Know it. Surface Christianity equals carnality."

His parting words throw me for a loop, and I sit down on the pew, stunned, as Paris asks if I'm ready to go.

📖

"Let's take a walk," she says, soon after we arrive back at the beach house.

"Okay," I say, glancing at the packed suitcases by the front door.

We stroll along the beach until we reach the Harbor Island Lighthouse, its peppermint stripes of red and white circling its length. Pausing our conversation to walk up the narrow circular stairs, which shrink in circumference as we ascend, it feels like we are walking in circles as we get to the top. Going through the gift shop area, we walk outside.

"So," she begins, "we really have to go home now. I know you probably think it's a terrible place and that you don't want to go back there, but everything will be okay. It's not as bad as it may seem right now."

"I can't go home," I say, and Paris looks as if all the air has been let out of her face.

"Dana, don't do this–"

"No, listen. It's okay. I've got a proposal for you."

"What?"

"Okay, here it is. If you wouldn't mind helping me out a little, I want to move here."

Her eyes widen. "What? But you don't know anything about Hilton Head."

"No, I mean Charleston. This island's a little too rich for my blood."

"Oh. But still, you've never lived there either."

"That's the point. I've lived in Chicago all my life. I need a fresh start, and I think if I went back to Chicago with my mother, I'd fall into the same old traps."

"But you don't have any friends here."

"Well, it's not like I'll be hanging out with you and Eric in Chicago. I really don't have any other friends, and have to find a new job anyway."

Paris looks down. "You still have me."

"I know, and I appreciate everything you've done to make up with me. If I stay here, it'll be easier for me to have some distance from you and Eric, and it'll give me a chance to work on trying to forgive you all and get rid of my bitterness. We can never be friends like it was before."

"I know."

"If you helped me, though, I could get an apartment, look for a job down here and start a new life. I can even join that church in Charleston we went to today."

"That would be cool. I'll give you anything you need, money for therapy, whatever. I just want to make sure you'll be okay."

"Thank you. I'll try therapy but somehow I think that church will be my real healing. I prayed seriously last night for the first time in my life, not just for some man or to ask God for material things. I asked for strength, and now, I think I might really be okay. I think I just might be able to make it."

"With Him, all things are possible, right?" Paris says, hugging me.

I allow myself to hug her back, then we separate, both looking across the water at the gorgeous view of the ocean. We stay there for a while, motionless with the sun warming our faces.

Chapter 12

Maui, Hawaii

So they are no longer two, but one. Therefore what God has joined together, let man not separate.

Matthew 19:6

I want off this plane right now. The last hour of this final leg of the flight from LAX to OGG, Maui's airport, has been the worst. I'm so restless. I don't want to read, I don't want to sleep, I don't want to do anything but get off.

It's not that the nine-hour trip starting in Chicago has been that bad, in fact, it's been much better than I anticipated. It only got bad once we changed onto this huge Lockheed L-1011, the biggest jet I've been on, and all of us sat together in the five middle seats. I don't like the seating arrangements.

Anthony just had to sit his happy ass right next to Paris, even though that wasn't his assigned seat, claiming he wanted Stephanie to sit on the other side of him because she'd be up and down with the baby. How convenient for him.

Ever since I introduced him to Paris a couple of months ago, he's found every excuse in the book to be near her, acting like a giddy school-boy. Lately, he's even taken to stopping by the house unannounced, especially when I'm not home. I finally told her to not let anyone in when I'm not there, including family. She thought that was strange, but I had to put my foot down. I didn't exactly tell her why, but I'm sure she has a clue.

I mean, how can I come out and say that I'm afraid my brother will hit on her? That is, if he already hasn't. It's easy to keep her away from other men, but unfortunately she'll see Anthony all the time, especially now that Paris and I are getting married.

"Watch it back there," my mother says from in front of me, as my knees protrude into the back of her seat.

"Yeah, watch it Uncle Eric," my niece Kayla repeats.

"Hey, you hush up," I chastise, reaching between the seats to tickle her.

Sitting back, I glance at Paris, who's asleep with her head facing forward and her seat upright so as not to disturb the passengers behind. Next to her, Anthony's chair is reclined, and he naps facing Paris instead of his wife, his mouth much too close to hers for my comfort.

Why did Paris have to invite the whole family to Maui anyway? I'm glad they'll all share in our wedding, but she's acting like we're millionaires, footing the bill for our parents, siblings, their spouses and kids.

I appreciate that *Seducing God* is selling so well, but I keep telling her that we can't give it all away. We already spent half of the advance to buy the house, and the other half we need to live off of. I sold my car washes for a nice little profit, to devote more time to touring with Paris, but maybe I should have kept them.

But Paris tells me not to worry, that what goes around comes around, and the more we give the more we'll get, but I think she's getting a little carried away. Yet what can I say? Afterall, she wrote the books and made all the money.

I've never had a woman who made more money than me. It's unfamiliar. It's like they have all the control. Of all my ex-girlfriends, Dana had the highest salary, and that wasn't much at all compared to Paris now.

Speaking of karma, it's as if Dana has a hand in the problems I'm experiencing now with Paris. I can just see Dana now, smiling smugly at me worrying about my brother and fiancée getting together. Poetic justice for dogging her out so badly.

I love Paris so much, probably as much or more than Dana loved me, and it would kill me if she left me for another man. It would be just desserts for that man to be Anthony.

I wouldn't put it past him. Everything he has or does always has to be better than mine, and I know my new house and gorgeous rich fiancée is eating him away inside. Being the oldest, he has this odd notion that he should own the nicest house and car, and experience the best trips first like it's some kind of ritual of the first born. Now I've blown the pecking order and he can't stand it.

Anthony knows flirting with Paris gets my goat, and that's why he's doing it, hoping to get a response. If it came down to it, he probably would leave Stephanie and the kids at the drop off a hat to be with Paris, to prove he was still the best at everything. Thank God Paris would never go for it. Hopefully.

Touching her face, I awaken her and she turns to me and grins.

"I love you," she moans, twisting her body towards me under the constraint of her seatbelt.

I lift the armrest between us and pull her closer, sliding my hand down the length of her body to make sure no parts of her and Anthony are touching.

"I love you too."

We kiss, and I pull away, staring into her eyes, thinking that money better be the only thing she's so free with.

📖

Eventually mountainous islands protrude from the tedious miles of Pacific Ocean, and the pilot guides the plane into the valley between two immense volcanoes that make up Maui.

Leaving the rental car shop, we drive down a long road and observe clouds that linger over the high country while the rest of the sky is a pristine blue.

The open-air lobby of the Grand Wailea Resort and Spa is magnificent, complete with colorful artwork and statues of warriors and chubby people. The group checks in, and Paris and I traipse off to our room on the fourth floor, the same level as the lobby.

We are as excited as two-year-olds upon entering our corner suite, its bathroom complete with an oversized tub and dual showers. The balcony is an alcove of grass and tropical flowers, offering a slight view of the ocean between overflowing palm trees that rattle in the trade wind breeze.

Jet lagged, we quickly settle into the room and nap.

"I don't want to go to dinner," I moan, as our alarm wakes us up a few hours later.

"We have to," Paris says, sitting up. "Everybody's waiting for us."

"My body thinks it's midnight."

"Mine too, sleepyhead. Let's just go eat and then we'll come back and sleep."

I will myself to shower and dress, then Paris and I stroll the secluded grounds through torch-lit paths until we find the Humu Humu restaurant. Entering the eatery, a friendly hostess leads us past a salt-water aquarium filled with colorful fish and a diver plucking a fresh lobster from the water below, to our families waiting at a long table.

"We were about to send Kayla to come get you all," my dad says, sitting at the far end of the table next to my mother.

"Shoot, y'all were about to get no answer. Aren't you tired?" I ask.

"Mmnn," Paris' mother agrees. "That was too much flying for me."

"I didn't think it was that bad," my sister Renee says, sipping on a large margarita.

"Sit down," Anthony offers, pulling out the seat next to him.

"Why thank you," I say jokingly, sitting down.

"Thanks a lot," Paris says, still standing.

"Get used to it," Terra chuckles. "They'll start treating you any kind of way once you get married."

"Shut up and pass the butter," her husband Rodney says loudly, and everyone at the table laughs.

We order our dinners as the sun dips below the horizon, silhouetting a statue of a man spearing a fish in the pond on which the restaurant floats. Everyone's face is aglow in the golden light.

"Isn't it beautiful here?" Paris asks, to no one in particular.

"Oh, yeah," my mother agrees. "We got the chance to walk around a little bit earlier."

"It's nice. We saw an Asian couple getting married at that chapel over there," my dad whispers.

"Why don't you all get married there?" Stephanie asks.

"For one thing," I say, "it's $1,600."

"It's not like y'all can't afford it," Anthony sneers.

"I know, but we wanted to have something out in the open, in nature. Our location is real nice. Besides," Paris shrugs, "we don't have to have it in a church. God is everywhere."

"True. That reminds me," my brother says, reaching into Stephanie's purse and plunking a copy of Paris' book on the table. "You never did sign my copy."

"Jeez," I say, pushing the book back to him. "She's on vacation."

"I don't mind. Give it here."

Paris signs the book and hands it back to him, but unfortunately, he doesn't let the topic die.

"This book is a trip," he continues.

"As long as people buy it," Paris smiles, looking down.

"Hey, the valet told me that Michael Jordan just left here last week," I interject loudly, successfully turning the topic of conversation away from the book.

I've had a hard enough time trying to keep my parents from reading the damn thing, now Anthony waves it in their faces. He contin ues to get under my skin the rest of the evening, ogling Paris, then making it his duty to entertain us.

Finally, when the bill arrives, I've had all I can take.

"I'll get that," he says with flourish, reaching for his wallet and flapping his credit card on top of the $600-plus bill.

"No, let me," I say, reaching for the check. "It's our treat."

He slams his hand on top of the folder, so that I can't move it. "No, my treat. You all have done so much. Consider it a pre-wedding gift."

I attempt to hand my American Express card to the waiter, but Anthony stands and catches him before I can.

"Hey, if it's that serious," Paris' dad muffles, "I'll let one of you take me to dinner tomorrow night."

"For real," my sister Renee chuckles along with the rest of the table, but I don't laugh.

"Okay, let's get out of here," I yawn. "I'm about to pass out."

Paris and I walk back to the room, with me fuming over the way Anthony made such a fuss to pay the bill. When she asks what's wrong, I don't tell her, knowing she would interpret his need to show me up as nothing but a kind gesture. Instead, I remain silent, saying that I'm dead tired, which isn't far from the truth.

📖

Due to the time difference, we're up at dawn the next morning, listening to the chorus of exotic birds singing in the trees outside our window. After lounging around, making love, ordering breakfast and watching TV, it's finally time to meet the others at the hotel pool.

I stroll into the bathroom, watching Paris in front of the mirror applying suntan lotion to her golden skin. Wrapping my arms around her waist, I see her breasts bulge from the electric blue and gold swimming suit she wears.

"You're kind of overflowing there, aren't you?"

Her sexy smile turns to a frown as she pushes out of my embrace. "I thought you were going to say I looked nice."

"You always look pretty," I convince her, hugging her body close to mine again. "I just was commenting on the top being too small."

Paris slips out of my grasp again and walks out of the bathroom, with me trailing behind. "It's not too small, it's my size. What are you trying to say, I'm fat?"

"No, it looks like you were coming out of it to me."

"That's just the way I was standing. I bought this especially for our honeymoon," she says, becoming weepy.

"Come on, what are you crying for? I didn't mean anything by it. I just didn't want you walking around with your tits hanging all out."

"Please! My tits are not hanging out. This swimming suit is just fine. You always need to find something to complain about. You could at least be happy on our honeymoon."

"I am happy," I say, glancing toward the sports highlight on the TV.

"Yeah right. All you do is bitch. Our first night here you get all mad just because Anthony picked up the check at dinner."

"I wasn't mad at that. I just didn't like the way he brought out your book and how he made such a big deal out of paying for dinner, like it was a major event."

"So fine, he feels the need to be important. Who cares? Let him. You let your insecurity about him ruin everything."

"No I don't. I'm not insecure. I'm having a good time."

"You could have fooled me. We're in paradise and you still can't let yourself relax and have fun. Ralph Waldo Emerson said you can travel the world to find beauty, but carry it with you or you won't find it."

"Whatever. All I was doing was telling you about the damn suit."

Paris huffs. "No, it was more than that. You were once again trying to control a situation where you felt out of control."

"Here we go..."

"Yes, here we go. If you don't deal with a problem obviously it'll keep coming back. You never had closure with Dana so that still bothers you and you've never talked to Anthony about how you feel, so that animosity is still there."

"This has nothing to do with them. I just didn't see why you wanted to go down to the pool and show your stuff to all the men down there."

"Please! These women wear string bikinis and thongs down here. This is nothing. This suit is conservative. Since you forbade me from wearing a two-piece, not that I would wear one anyway, all I've done is wear one-pieces."

"I know, but–"

"And last night," she cuts me off, "when Renee and Terra were talking about finding me a male stripper for my bachelorette party, I nipped that in the bud right away."

"I know. I'm not having no strippers either."

"Right. I'm just saying, I've made compromises and tried to understand your feelings, but you take it too far. Everything doesn't have to be so guarded."

"I'm not. Go down to the pool like that if you want to. I don't care."

"Just fuck it Eric! I'll go buy a new suit that you approve of so we can swim."

"Forget it," I say, standing. "We can just go. I don't care."

"I don't want to. You've taken all the fun out of it."

"No, for real. Let's go. They're waiting for us."

Stomping through the lobby of the hotel and out to the pool, I try not to focus on Paris' attire of the questionable bathing suit and a sarong wrapped around her waist. When we reach the pool and Anthony's eyes nearly bulge out of their sockets, I hold my breath.

All the siblings frolic in the crystal blue pool at the top of the stairs, while Stephanie stays in the shallow end, teaching Kayla how to swim. One after the next, we each glide down the various water slides, plunging into the waiting pool below, then climb the stairs to do it all over again.

Taking a different path, Paris, Anthony and I perch atop a wide rubber slide with a flow of water so powerful, we can barely hold on. Anthony playfully slaps me on the back, pushing me down the ramp, and the waves carry me into a churning surge of rapids at the bottom.

I stroke hard to release myself from the whirl of water, then turn on my back to see Paris and Anthony letting go of the ramp's edge together. Screaming, Paris lands first against the soft wall, and Anthony is thrown mercilessly against her. They laugh as each struggles to get out of the rapids, finally swimming with me down the rest of the man-made river.

"Let's go in here," she says, wading into a cavern that leads to a hot tub.

"It'll be too cold when we get back out," I say, squatting on edge of the pool.

"Come on man," Anthony says, following her into the man-made grotto. "Don't be a wuss."

"I'm not," I say, wondering if Paris will come out as soon as she discovers I'm not coming inside.

As they disappear into the recesses of the steaming cave, their giggles echoing against the artificial rock, I feel as though I've been stabbed in the heart. This must be what Dana felt every time Paris and I snuck away to kiss or make love. Pure pain. I lean into the cave, spying the tops of their heads above the surface, quiet and relaxed, without a care in the world.

I linger to see how long she will actually stay there with him and leave me alone, but the waiting gets to be too long so I poke my head inside.

"You coming in now?" she asks, as if I am an afterthought.

"No. I'm ready to go. I'm tired of swimming," I say, treading through the water to the edge of the pool and exiting.

It is a small comfort when I turn around to see her get out to follow me, squealing at the coldness of the pool water, with my brother trailing behind like a puppy dog.

📖

"Come on Eric, let's dance," Paris says giddily, grabbing my arm.

She wiggles in her seat, watching Terra and Rodney dance beneath the pink and blue laser lights of the high-tech Tsunami nightclub on the lower level of the resort.

"I don't want to. They're just frantic because they don't have the kids tonight," I say, sipping my beer.

"Us too," Anthony says, downing his shot of Absolut Citron and standing. "Mommy and Daddy don't know they'll be keeping our kids for the rest of the trip."

When he grabs Stephanie's hand and they begin dancing, Paris moans. "See, now we're the only couple not dancing."

"My little baby will keep us company," I joke, reaching over to my sister Renee and tousling her hair.

"Stop it boy!" she screams, smoothing her long fine hair back into place. "I'll dance with you Paris."

"Uhn, that's gay." Raising one side of my mouth, I make a funny face as Paris bounds up from the table.

"No it's not," she says, following Renee onto the floor.

I suck down my beer and order another, determined not to let her goad me into dancing. I just don't like it, and Paris is always trying to force me out there.

As one song of the retro 80's songs switches to the next and the floor gets a little more crowded, our group is forced into the middle. Peering through the bodies, I see Anthony moving away from Stephanie to dance also with Renee and Paris.

"Go Anthony, go Anthony," Rodney chants, beginning a mantra of my brother's name being sung even from strangers, which urges Anthony to dance more wildly.

He grinds away like a fool in the middle of the floor, reveling in the attention, showing off his best dance moves. Paris cheers and claps with the rest of the group, and glancing over to me, beckons me to the floor.

"No," I mouth sternly, shaking my head. She frowns, returning to her seat.

"You're such a party pooper," she says, slurping down the rest of her drink.

"You didn't have to stop, but you better slow down with the drinking."

"Shoot, this is my bachelorette party night. I'm just getting started."

"You're gonna make yourself sick. You don't want to have a hangover on our wedding day."

Paris waves me off. "I'll be fine. It's not like we're going anywhere. We'll be right up in Terra's room acting silly. They'll probably give me a bunch of freaky shit we can use tomorrow night."

"Yeah, that's all they better do. I don't want no Chippendale's guys up in there."

"There won't be. I told my sister already. I'm surprised Anthony didn't get one for you."

"Naw, he didn't plan anything for me," I say, watching him gyrate close to Stephanie, making her laugh. "That boy don't think about nobody but himself."

"Well don't worry, I won't stay out long."

"Good, don't, 'cause you know I can't sleep without you."

"I know," she coos, planting a kiss on my forehead.

📖

An hour later, loud banging on our door awakens me, and I silently curse Paris all the way down the hall, knowing she probably lost her key card in a drunken stupor.

Peeking through the door, I see Anthony's huge face distorted in the fish-eyed lens.

"Hey, man," he says, holding up a bottle of champagne, as I open the door, "you didn't think I'd forget you, did you?"

I swing the door open for him to enter and walk into the room. "Man, it's too late. I was already asleep."

Suddenly, the feel of cold steel is on my wrist and look down to see him clamping a handcuff on me.

"What the fuck are you doing?" I ask, looking up to see Rodney entering the room with an attractive woman dressed like a hula girl.

"Hey partner," he grins, helping Anthony forcefully carry me to a chair at the writing desk, plunk me down, and attach my free wrist to the seat.

"No, y'all can't. I'm serious," I say, nodding at the woman.

Dressed in a fresh-flower lei, bikini and grass skirt, she sets a boom box on the desk and turns it on, spilling loud reggae music into the quiet room.

Rolling her hips rapidly to the drum beat, she unties the skirt and allows it to fall to the floor, revealing her thong bikini bottom.

"Anthony," I yell, "this is nice, but for real, I'm in my underwear man!"

"I know," he smiles, stretching the bow of her string bikini bottom to tuck a dollar bill beneath. "Just chill, it's alright. Paris is still over to her sister's room."

"Yeah," Rodney says, talking to me but looking at the stripper, "they should be a while."

I pause for a moment, enchanted by the exotic woman, her long wavy black hair falling softly around her browned torso. She reaches behind her and unties the straps to her top, dangling it in front of my face, as her pert breasts jiggle up and down beneath her lei.

"No, let me up," I say, wanting to watch, but also wanting to be released. "Unhook me, for real."

The dancer pauses and looks with confusion to Anthony, who urges her to continue. She winds her hips near me, gracefully turning around to give me a view of her round, smooth behind.

Reaching in her bag, she pulls out a chestnut-colored dildo, and fondles it with her hands before placing it on top of my crotch. Holding it at the base, she plunges the entire prosthetic in her mouth, then looks adoringly up at me as she sucks the plastic.

I laugh, thinking of what an effective trick it is. "No, honestly. Please let me up. I don't want to do this."

She continues, once again taking her cue from Anthony, who places another bill underneath the string of her thong.

To my horror, I suddenly hear a noise at the door, and I begin bucking my hips for the woman to get off me. "Get up, get up!"

Rodney and Anthony roar louder, thinking I'm moving because I'm getting off on her, when truly it's because, over the din of the music, I've heard Paris enter the honeymoon suite.

"Stop!" I yell, but it's too late.

By the time the trio realizes Paris is in the room they pause, but she has already seen the goings-on and stands there staring at me with her mouth dropped open.

"Baby, it's okay," I plead, but she turns on her heels and runs out the door. "Let me loose," I scream. "Get me out of this!"

This time, the stripper shuts off the music and Rodney unhooks me from the chair, freeing me. I throw on the T-shirt and shorts I wore earlier and run out the door. Anthony and Rodney follow, with the stripper behind them demanding her money.

I look down the hall, but Paris has disappeared.

"Come on man," Rodney says, patting my back. "She probably went back to our room."

I rush upstairs to the next level, running up to their door.

"Let me go in first." He holds his hand up to my chest as he knocks gently on the door then slips his key card in and opens it, disappearing inside.

I hear muted voices arguing behind the door and a few seconds later Rodney emerges with Terra, who glares at me with the stare of death as I duck into the room.

Paris sits on the floor with her knees drawn up to her chest, crying.

"Baby, please," I beg, walking to her with outstretched arms.

"Get away from me! Don't touch me!"

"I'm not."

"How could you do that to me? You let that whore suck your dick?"

"No!" I stand. "That was a fake. It was a dildo. She wasn't sucking me."

"Yeah, right."

"Seriously. I swear, she's right outside, I can go get it."

Paris bolts to her feet. "Don't go get shit. I don't care!"

"But it wasn't me; I wouldn't do that."

"It doesn't matter. She should have never been there in the first place. You fucking hypocrite."

"I didn't bring her there. Anthony brought her there. I thought it was just him and I let him in the room and he snuck her in there and they handcuffed me to the chair."

"Oh please, and you just couldn't get away."

"I couldn't! I kept screaming for them to let me up but they wouldn't."

Paris rolls her eyes and crosses her arms. "Yeah, you really looked like you were suffering when I came in there."

"I was. I didn't want this. Anthony did it."

"Give me a break," she huffs, turning away. "And all this shit you've been giving me this whole time about what to wear and not to have any strippers, and then you go and do this."

"Please, I haven't said nothing about you fawning all over my brother this whole time."

"What?" her head jerks up. "What the fuck are you talking about?"

"I've watched you all up in Anthony's face since you met him and I haven't said shit."

"Please! Don't even try and turn this around on me. You are not gonna make this my fault."

"I'm not, I said I was sorry."

"Oh, and that's just supposed to make everything okay? Fuck you!"

In one motion she slides her engagement ring off her finger and hurls it at me, bouncing it off my cheek. I bend down and take it off the floor, slipping it onto my finger.

"Get out! I'm tired of your shit! I don't want to marry a fucking hypocrite. Go find some other dumb-ass bitch to take your shit!"

I stand there, twirling the diamond around my finger, my anger about to explode. Her words sting straight to my heart, because I know she means them.

Turning around, I open the door to see Anthony, Terra and Rodney standing there, stunned expressions on their faces. I charge at Anthony, throwing him against the railing as I rip at his shirt.

"This is all your fault!" I scream, bending him over the edge.

"Man, what are you doing?" he laughs nervously, looking at the ground below.

"You never wanted us to get married anyway."

I hold him there for a few more seconds until Rodney pulls me off of him and holds me in a headlock.

"You're tripping," Anthony says, standing up and straightening his shirt.

"Let me go!" I scream. "I'm alright man, let me go."

Rodney releases me, as Terra and Anthony stand dumfounded, anticipating my next move. Instead of attacking him again, I bolt down the stairs into my room, letting the door slam shut behind me.

Tossing in the king-sized empty bed, I watch the starry sky brighten with the rising sun, reflecting its pink rays against the white satin of Paris' wedding gown. It is the first night we've spent apart since Charleston, and sleep only comes when I pass out at daylight from emotional exhaustion.

Waking at the blaring ring of the phone, I check the clock and see that it's well after noon and Paris still isn't back. Renee is on the line, wondering if there will still be a ceremony after Anthony filled her in on last night's melee. I don't know what to say, so I hang up and immediately dial Terra's room.

"Hello?"

"Terra, it's Eric."

"Oh," she sighs.

"Look, please, don't be mad at me too. I'm sorry."

"You don't have to apologize to me. I understand that things happen."

"Is Paris there?"

"No."

"Come on," I whine, "please let me talk to her."

"Honestly. She's not here. She left about two hours ago and didn't tell me where she was going. I thought she went back to you guy's room."

"No, she didn't come here."

"Well, I don't know then. I was just about to call to ask you all if we should still get dressed for the wedding."

"I don't know. I really don't know."

I hang up, unable to speak. For the first time in years, I cannot fight back the tears that well in my eyes. Letting them fall freely, I drop to my knees and pray.

God, please bring her back. Please. I know I messed up this time, but I can't lose her. Paris is definitely the woman for me, and I promise I won't do anything stupid like that again. I want to marry her today. I want to make her Mrs. Toomey. She's the only woman I want.

I'll do anything You want if she'd just come back. I love her so much. Please just let us–

The door opening stops me, and remaining on my knees, I tilt back to see Paris walking in.

"What are you doing?" she asks.

I wipe my face with my hands. "I was praying for you to come back."

"I guess it worked," she says stoically, plopping down on the bed.

I stay put, unsure of whether to touch her. "Honey, I'm so sorry. I didn't let that woman actually go down on me."

"I know, I believe you. I'm sorry too."

"What are you sorry for?"

"Well, today I did a lot of thinking and I guess you were right about Anthony. I've kind of been inappropriate with him and that was wrong. I liked the attention he showed me, and it made me feel desirable again."

"I knew it," I say, rising to sit on the bed with her.

"But, on the same token, that was probably the reason you didn't kick that stripper out right away. You probably liked the attention of a beautiful woman."

I shake my head. "No, I swear–"

Paris holds up her hand. "Don't swear, just listen. A marriage has to be based on honesty to work; the husband and wife have to be truthful with one another."

"I am being truthful."

"I know, on some levels, you think you are, but this is how we got into this mess in the first place. You don't have to hold back your feelings because you think it might hurt me. If you wanted a bachelor party, you could've told me."

"But I didn't want one."

"I think you just didn't want me to have one, so you told yourself you didn't want one. But it's okay, I'm glad you're not the type of man who goes flirting with every female in the room. On the other hand, you don't have to try and be Mr. Perfect."

"I'm not."

"You do try to. I mean, I don't need to know every single detail of your life with your ex-girlfriends and stuff, but you don't have to hide it if you find a woman on TV attractive. That's not going to kill me."

"I'm just being respectful," I say.

"I know, and I love that. But we need to tell each other our feelings; we can't be perfect and lovey-dovey all the time and neglect the bad stuff. I had been feeling a little neglected and resented for making so much money, and I should have shared those feelings with you."

"I don't resent you. I love you."

"I know you do. But having those feelings doesn't negate our love. Let's agree now to tell each other how we feel, honestly, or else things won't work."

"Okay," I say, hanging my head. "You're right about the money. It's kind of weird that for once I don't have all the control in a relationship. And I kind of figured about Anthony. I was afraid that you would find him more attractive than me and leave me."

"Oh honey," she says, reaching out and smoothing my head. "I could never leave you for anyone else. Your brother's a nice guy but there is no way he compares to you. You and I were meant to be together forever, and that's what's going to happen."

I grab her and hug her closely to my chest. We kiss, slowly and deeply, as if rediscovering a lost passion.

"I hate to break this up," she says, "but we only have an hour till the limo gets here and I need time to become a beautiful bride."

"You're already beautiful," I grin, taking the ring off my finger and sliding it onto hers. "Don't ever take that off again."

"I won't."

📖

"We were about to call out the armed guards," my father says, as we join the rest of the family in front of the hotel.

"We were busy," I say, walking over to Anthony, dressed neatly in his tuxedo.

"I'm sorry, man," I whisper. "Do I still have a best man?"

He looks at me guardedly, then grabs my hand and pulls me to his chest, thumping hard on my back. "No worries, man."

Paris and I dash into our stretch car as the rest of the family piles in theirs. During the hour drive to our private location, I hold her hand, overjoyed that we are actually getting married.

Once we reach our cliffside destination, the family takes its place in seats lined before a trellis decorated with flowers. Flaming tiki torches illuminate the aisle as Paris and I march slowly to the position in the front, stopping between two ice sculptures of cupids shooting their arrows at us.

"Love is patient and kind, love is not jealous or boastful; it is not arrogant or rude. Love does not insist on its own way," the minister begins, after singing a Hawaiian chant.

The descending sun paints the scenery of mountains and oceans an idyllic gold. The winds swath me in comfort, and I feel the spirit of the Lord there with us, surrounding our family, blessing the nuptials.

I smile a silent prayer of thanks, and in the moment that I take Paris for my bride, I feel a change within. A sense of well-being envelops me like a blanket, and I know it is God embracing me.

My life is renewed, given a second chance to know and understand God's mercy by bringing this love of mine back to me. I no longer will take His love or grace for granted, and will keep my promise to do whatever He wants of me, because He kept His promise to give me back my love.

Gazing at my wife, appearing angelic in her white gown, I feel His great love being poured on me, and after she has kissed me, the warm sun presses another kiss on my lips, and I know it is the kiss of God.

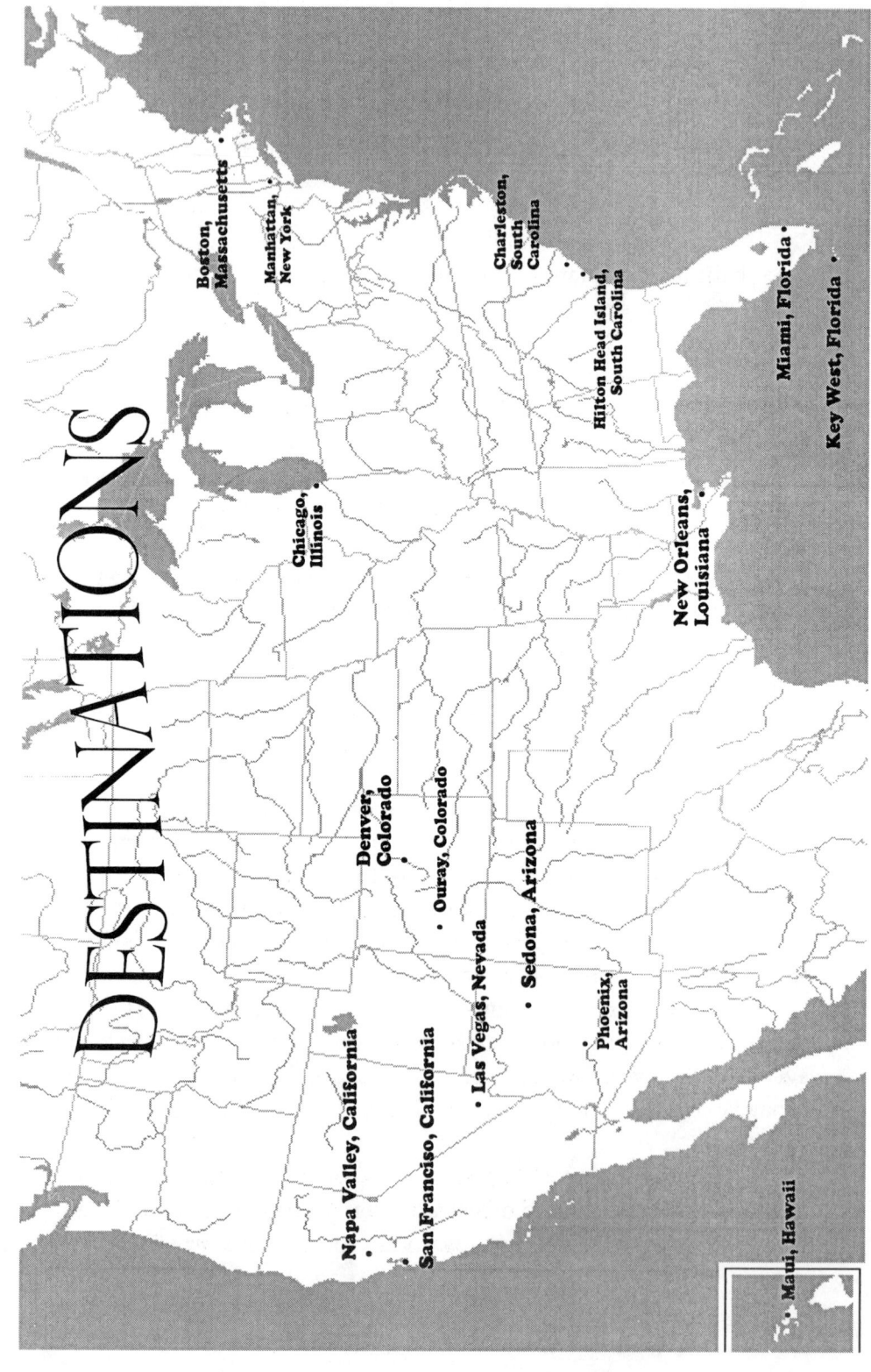

DESTINATIONS

Boston, Massachusetts

Manhattan, New York

Charleston, South Carolina

Hilton Head Island, South Carolina

Miami, Florida

Key West, Florida

Chicago, Illinois

New Orleans, Louisiana

Denver, Colorado

Ouray, Colorado

Sedona, Arizona

Las Vegas, Nevada

Phoenix, Arizona

Napa Valley, California

San Franciso, California

Maui, Hawaii